ANNIE HARLAND CREEK

EVERNIGHT PUBLISHING ®

www.evernightpublishing.com

Copyright© 2017

Annie Harland Creek

Editor: Katelyn Uplinger

Cover Artist: Jay Aheer

ISBN: 978-1-77339-353-7

ALL RIGHTS RESERVED

ANNIE HARLAND CREEK

DEDICATION

This book is dedicated to my mother who always believed I would become a published author. I miss you, Mum.

ACKNOWLEDGEMENTS

To my husband of 38 years. You are my inspiration, the love of my life, and my biggest supporter. Thank you for believing in me and encouraging me to keep trying. Thank you to my family who I adore. You gave me courage and understood when dinner was late because I lost track of time. Big kisses to my daughter Pamela who edited most of my drafts, set up my Facebook page and designed my website. More kisses to my daughter Brooke who helped me brainstorm and allowed us to use her face in my branding. Thanks to Annie Seaton for editing one of the first drafts, and a big thanks to Kerry, Efthalia and Lee Piper for your ongoing support and advice as my beta readers. I will be eternally grateful to Stacey and Evernight for having faith in me and my first book. A special thanks to my editor, Katelyn Uplinger for the helpful comments and advice and to Jay Aheer for the fantastic cover.

Thank you, dear reader for giving a newbie the chance to share her stories.

I hope you enjoy Kiss of Death as much as I loved writing it.

ANNIE HARLAND CREEK

KISS OF DEATH

Blood Brothers, 1

Annie Harland Creek

Copyright © 2017

Chapter One

Anna Derwent kept her eyes low as she scooped up the last of the floral tributes, ignoring the wave of nausea exacerbated by the heady fragrance of the oriental lilies. She drew in a deep breath, straightened her shoulders and kept her eyes trained straight ahead as she hurried towards the exit of the gymnasium where the wake had been held. Her heels clicked on the wooden floor as she hurried to avoid the last of the mourners who had come to pay their respects. Taking a deep breath, she stepped into the hall and paused.

The door to her father's office was closed and she hesitated before crossing the dark hallway and turning the handle. The familiar smell of leather and liniment suddenly became suffocating and as the door closed behind her, she closed her eyes to steady herself as the room began to spin. Gripping the oak desk for support, she re-opened them and distanced herself from the pain that had attached itself to the room. Although, thankfully, she did not experience the actual sensation of pain, her hand instinctively flew to her chest. She gulped down a wave of nausea as her knees buckled beneath her. Before her eyelids fluttered closed, a shadow filled her vision and she sank to the floor with a soft moan.

"Anna!"

Firm hands caught her before she hit the floor and lifted her gently. The owner of the unfamiliar voice placed her on the leather chesterfield that had been in the corner for as long as she could remember. She opened her eyes as the strange voice permeated the fog.

"I'll get you some water."

The room swam around her and she frowned; everything had changed since she had last visited Dad. Only the couch she was lying on was familiar. It was as though Jake Derwent had never existed.

"I'm fine." She said to the man hovering over her. Her fingers gripped the cold leather. She tried to push herself up but the weight of his hand on her shoulders prevented her from moving. His touch was firm, but gentle and her already palpitating heart skipped a beat when she looked up into his eyes.

"Who are you and why are you in my father's office?"

"I'm Derrick Corel," he answered in a voice oozing raw sensuality.

She gazed into the face of the stranger and her breath hitched. His tailored suit accentuated his muscular form and the stitches strained against the bulge of his biceps. But she had met plenty of buff men in her day and it was not his muscles that forced a gasp to her lips, it was his eyes. The bluest eyes she had ever seen. Unbelievably blue eyes that held her gaze and robbed her of rational thought. She absently ran her fingers through her shoulder-length copper curls as she admired his perfectly coifed hair.

"Have we met Mr. Corel?" She asked with a

shiver, suddenly aware of his icy hands on her shoulders. She doubted whether she would have forgotten meeting such a striking looking man as Derek Corel. Even with his square jaw set in a concerned grimace, his movie star features shone through and his eyes … a woman could get lost in those eyes. "Where you at the funeral?"

"No, we haven't met, Anna. I was … unavoidably detained so I was unable to attend your father's funeral. I can't tell you how sorry I am for your loss. Jake will be sorely missed in both the fitness community and the town. He was a great man."

He lifted his cold hands from her bare shoulders and stood gazing down at her with his penetrating eyes.

"Yes he will." She swung her legs down off the couch and rose, strangely missing the skin to skin contact of the handsome stranger. She moved towards the door. "Now if you'll excuse me. I'll like to be alone."

Derrick picked up the flowers that Anna had dropped by the entrance and passed them to her.

"Of course. Please allow me to walk you to your car."

Anna held her palm to her throbbing forehead and closed her eyes. "You misunderstand me. I was asking *you* to leave."

"Oh, then that makes it rather awkward," Derrick answered, his eyes intent on hers. "You see, Anna. This is *my* office."

Anna's eyes flew open and she took a step away from the door as she stared up at him. Her mouth opened but words didn't come. She turned around and stumbled back to the desk. She shook her head as she surveyed the room. There was nothing in this room that was remotely familiar, nothing—apart from the old leather couch—that reminded her of her father, nothing but the emptiness of his passing. She turned to face him, leaning heavily on the desk in an effort to support her weight as he approached. With each step he took closer to her, the pain in her head increased. By the time he had reached her, her thoughts were swirling in confusion and excruciating pain.

"I'm sorry, Anna. I thought Jake's attorney contacted you this morning to explain the situation."

Anna slowly shook her head and the pain intensified. "I let the call go to voicemail. I thought he was calling about a will and I had enough on my mind with the funeral."

"Understandable." Derrick nodded. "And you've had a long drive getting here so you must be exhausted. I'll give you some space to rest for a while." He walked to the door and opened it. "This conversation can wait."

A rush of adrenaline propelled her towards the open door. Pushing herself between Derrick and the door, she slammed it shut and thrust her hands to her hips. "You can't just drop a bombshell on me like that and then walk away. We'll discuss this now."

"Are you sure you are up to it? You *did* just have a fainting spell." He pointed out with a hint of concern in his voice.

Heat burned her cheeks. "I am not in the habit of fainting, Mr. Corel. As you said, it has been a long day and the shock of seeing this office…" She took a deep breath and forced the sob from her throat.

"You don't like the office?"

"Of course I like the office, it's beautiful but … don't change the subject, I want to know what claim you have on my father's business. When did this become *your* office?"

He cupped her elbow and motioned for them to return to the couch with his other hand. Anna pulled away and strode ahead of him. She flopped onto the couch and crossed her arms as he sat beside her. Darkness crept over the room and she shuddered. A familiar feeling of dread wormed its way into her consciousness. Not a good sign.

"Were you aware that your father was having financial difficulties?" His words cut straight to the point.

Anna bit her bottom lip and nodded.

Of course she was aware. She was the reason for them.

"I was in the market for a Dojo and this business had a lot of potential, so, I offered to buy into it. We signed a partnership agreement and became co-owners, sixty-forty."

"So, you own forty percent of dad's business now?"

"No, Anna. I own sixty."

Anna squared her shoulders and frowned. "And I'm expected to just take your word for that?"

"No. Of course not." He reached into the inside pocket of his jacket and handed her a business card. "The papers are filed with this office. You should give them a call."

She snatched the card from his hand. "You bet I will." Staring down at the small white card she pondered out loud. "So, where does that leave me?"

Anna cringed. Her words sounded too desperate; too flustered. This place had been her sanctuary; her father had been her anchor. Now they were both gone and she was alone.

Derrick sighed and ran his fingers through his dark hair. "This would have been less painful for you if the lawyer had spoken with you first. I really think we should—"

"I asked you a question. Where does this leave me?"

"It is entirely up to you. Either you sell me your share of the business—"

"Not gunna happen. Next option."

"Or we work together."

Interlocking her fingers to still her shaking hands, Anna sighed. How could this ever work? He oozed self-assurance while her confidence had hit rock bottom. There were too many memories in this town, bad memories, but what choice did she have? She had quit her other job as they had refused to give her time off for the funeral. She was trapped.

"I don't play well with others," she said slowly. "I am a very private person and I don't like sharing. How would this work?"

Derrick smiled. Dimples creased his cheeks as he told her, "There is a way we could make this work."

Anna furrowed her eyebrows. "I'm listening."

"My classes are at night and I run another company so I'm not here in the day. You can have the office from six a.m. and I'll take over at six p.m. Does that suit you?"

"Don't you want to ask me if I am qualified to run a gym? You know nothing about me."

"I know enough, Anna. Your father spoke of you often and he told me that you are a certified gym instructor with a diploma in business management. I think you'll fit in fine."

He offered his hand which she reluctantly shook. The chill sent another shiver down her arms and she controlled her voice. "I guess I'll see you bright and early tomorrow morning then."

"No, you won't." He reminded her with a look that prickled the hairs on the back of her neck as he turned and walked away.

Chapter Two

The doors to the elevator opened and once again, Anna came face to face with Derrick Corel. She hadn't expected to see him at the solicitor's office as he had already signed off on his part of the agreement. The lawyer had explained all the legal details and given her the death certificate and deeds to the house along with a personal letter from her father. She was anxious to return home to read it and the appearance of her new partner meant an annoying delay.

"Hello, Anna."

"Mr. Corel."

He frowned and his eyebrows knit. "Look, if we are going to work together, don't you think you could call me Derrick?"

"Fine ... Derrick. What are you doing here anyway?"

"I thought you might need a lift home. I expect this has not been an easy morning for you."

Anna reached to lift the sunglasses down from the top of her head and lowered them back over her eyes. Of course the morning hadn't been easy, especially since she had broken down in tears in front of the solicitor. Her eyes were still stinging so they were likely to also be puffy and bloodshot. *Just great.*

"Thank you, but I'm quite capable of getting home."

The elevator ride down to the carpark was painfully silent except for the irritating piped music and Anna hurried out when they reached their floor, anxious to be alone with her letter, and pleased to leave the confined space of the elevator. There was something about Derrick that made her uncomfortable. A dark shadow seemed to surround him. Her throat felt dry and swallowing became difficult. Invisible fingers tightened around her neck as though the oxygen was being sucked from her lungs. *Got to get home.*

"Goodbye, Mr. ... I mean Derrick," she called over her shoulder as she hurried through the darkened carpark and into the comforting rays of the morning sun, leaving him standing beside the elevator. Surprisingly despite him making her uncomfortable, distancing herself from Derrick left her feeling empty and somehow... lost. For a moment she stood by the boom gates, contemplating returning to the elevator to apologize for her rude behavior but as she turned, the boom gates lifted and a black Porsche with heavily tinted windows drove slowly past. She expected the driver's window to lower but the car left the car park and sped up the street without stopping.

Anna watched the away, pondering the sinking feeling in her stomach, then turned and bumped into a tall, well-dressed—and unfortunately—very familiar figure.

"Anna?"

She took a deep breath as she attempted to step around him. "Hello, Patrick."

He grabbed her arm and she spun around defiantly, pulling away from his grasp as she glared up into his face.

"Is that all you can say? Hello?" He reached towards her with his arms extended for an embrace. She pushed him away.

"Oh, I'm so sorry." Anna's pulse raced. Heat flooded her cheeks and ran down her neck. "Was I being rude? It must be my small-town mentality because I'm not sure of the correct etiquette for addressing one's former fiancé. Someone who leaves her standing at the altar reading a note to inform her that she isn't quite up to his standards. Perhaps you could suggest a more appropriate response?"

"I guess I deserved that."

"You think?"

"We were young, Anna. I know that's a pretty lame excuse but I realized that I wanted more out of life than to be saddled with one woman for the rest of my life."

Anna gazed into the face of the man she'd once loved. True, there was a hint of sincerity in his expression despite his insensitive remark. His eyes were bright with excitement and his smile spread from ear to ear. He looked genuinely pleased to see her. Wrinkles creased his forehead and the corners of his green eyes. He looked older. It had been seven years since she had seen him. The eve of their ill-fated wedding.

"Saddled? I'm not a horse, Patrick. And if memory serves, *you* were the one who proposed." She turned abruptly to leave, needing to put distance between them.

"Wait. Please, Anna."

He reached out and touched her hand and Anna sank her teeth into her quivering bottom lip before rage could consume her. *How dare he?*

"I have to go."

This time she didn't give him the chance to stop her. Too much pain for one day. Salty tears burned behind her eyes as she left him in her wake. None of this was fair. There was no way she would allow herself to break down in front of Patrick Miller. She wouldn't give him the satisfaction of crushing her twice. Sure, he hadn't witnessed her heartbreak after reading how he left on their honeymoon with some bimbo he picked up in a bar the night of his buck's party.

He hadn't been around to observe the looks of pity she received for weeks after the cancelled wedding and he certainly wasn't there with an offer to help compensate her dad for money wasted on a reception that didn't take place. If it wasn't for Patrick Miller, she wouldn't have moved away from her dad for seven years. Seven years she would never get back. She picked up the pace of her steps until she had run all the way home. Her heart pumped heavily against her chest wall and her breathing was labored as she opened the front door. Once inside, she slumped onto the couch and took a large swallow from a bottle of water that she had left on the table, although, she considered opening the cask of wine in the fridge.

The sound of the landline ringing startled her. She had forgotten that her dad refused to use the mobile phone that she had given him. He complained that carrying a phone was a yuppie habit. Instinctively she reached for the phone but then decided to let the answering machine take the message.

Beep: "Anna. Are you there? Please pick up. Oh, whatever. We really need to talk. I know you're still upset with me and with good reason but I have a business proposal for you. If we could just—"

Anna snatched up the receiver and answered curtly. "What do you want, Patrick?"

"Oh, you *are* there … good. I was wondering if you would like to have dinner with me tonight. We could—"

"You said something about a business proposal."

"Yes. I'd prefer to discuss it over dinner."

"I'd prefer not to discuss it at all but if we must, we'll do it now, over the phone."

"Oh, come on, Anna. You have to eat. Let me buy you a really nice dinner at Stefano's."

"If you think one dinner in an expensive restaurant will make up for what you did to me, you've—"

"Give me credit for some sense. Let's just call it a peace offering. Come on, you have to eat."

Anna pictured Patrick's face as he pleaded his case. He had a way of pouting his lips when he begged, an expression that always melted her resolve to stay angry. He knew that she was a sucker for a sob story. She was glad he couldn't see the effect he still had on her, even after all these years.

"All right. What time will I meet you there?"

"I'll pick you up at 7 p.m. Thank you, Anna. You won't be sorry."

You won't be sorry. Anna shook her head as she put down the phone. She was already sorry. Sorry that, because of him, she had moved far from the beach to the city where a day at the beach meant a four-hour return journey. Sorry that the only way she could communicate with her father was by phone. And sorry that despite being glad to be home, it took the death of her father to bring her back. Patrick had ruined her life and made it impossible for her to form another romantic relationship. Hell, she could barely form a friendship. He had left her feeling worthless and inferior and, since that fateful day, she had never trusted another man. She balled up her hands and pounded her knuckles against her forehead.

Why did I accept his dinner proposal? Hadn't she promised herself she would never have anything to do with that cockroach again?

She leaned back in her seat and considered her options. She could ring and cancel the date but that might make him suspect that she still had feelings for him and there was no way she wanted him to believe he still had the power to hurt her. The other option was to allow him to pay for a big expensive meal and then make it clear that she had moved on. At least that way she could keep her dignity. She smiled to herself but the smile soon faded when she realized that she had nothing suitable to wear to a fancy restaurant like Stefano's and little money to purchase a new outfit. *Decide, Anna. Which is more important? Food for the rest of the week, or make Patrick squirm?* Grabbing her handbag, she headed out the door.

****

The search for the ideal dress proved harder than she had anticipated but finally, in the fifth boutique, Anna found the perfect outfit for revenge.

"That dress suits you to a tee." The initially snobby shop assistant exclaimed as Anna watched her mentally calculate the commission. "Your man will be mesmerized."

Anna studied her reflection in the mirror, surprised how good she looked, even with her current pallor. The back of the dress dipped low, almost to her waist, showing off the lats that she had worked hard to shape and the deep sapphire blue color contrasted nicely with the paleness of her eyes. Although quite large for her petite frame, her breasts held their shape beneath the folds of the silky fabric without the support of a bra. She ran her hands down her waist, checked the split that rose to her right thigh then turned, inspecting her bottom in the mirror. Not too bad, although she would need to wear a G-string in order to lose those panty lines. *Maybe I should really drive him wild and go pantie-less altogether?* She shook her head and rolled her eyes, dismissing the idea outright. With her luck, a sudden breeze would probably steal the last smidgen of self-respect she had left. She grimaced as she read the price tag. The dress was perfect but the price would cripple her budget. Even reduced to half price, the dress was well out of her price range. Was torturing Patrick really worth $300?

"So? Should I wrap it up?" the hopeful saleswoman enquired.

"What the hell."

Anna handed over her MasterCard and stepped back into the dressing room. Silently she prayed the card wouldn't be declined. It must have been very close to maxed out by now. As luck would have it, Anna left the store with her new purchase in an ostentatious carry bag and thanked her lucky stars that she already had a pair of shoes in a color that would coordinate with the dress. If all went well, Patrick would be cursing his own bad judgement at deciding to jilt her and the evening would be topped off with, hopefully, a huge delicious meal. With what would probably be a week of toast and vegemite as her staple diet, she hoped that tonight's dinner was going to be worth the sacrifice.

****

"Wow."

Anna inwardly smiled as she stepped into Patrick's Silver BMW. His eyes glazed a little and he blew out a breath. She knew she had achieved the 'look' she was after.

"Wow." He repeated. His lips parted slightly as he licked his lower lip.

"You already said that."

"I'll say it again. Wow, Anna, you look gorgeous."

"I'd be tempted to thank you if you hadn't sounded so surprised."

"Not surprised, just impressed." He fastened his seatbelt and pulled away from the curb. "You never wore dresses like that when we were together."

"You'd be surprised what things I do now." She

flinched at the double-entendre, knowing that Patrick would use it against her. She was correct.

"You *could* bring me up to speed." Patrick looked Anna up and down. His hungry expression turned her stomach and when he stroked her leg, she knocked his hand away.

"You gave up that right seven years ago."

"I'm sorry. Force of habit," he mumbled. "By the way, I was sorry to hear about your old man."

Anna nodded but remained silent. *Not sorry enough to attend the funeral.*

"I heard you inherited his business."

So that's what this was about. Patrick wants something to do with the gym.

"I inherited less than half of the business."

Anna waited for a response that didn't come. Patrick remained silent for the rest of the trip and she too, had no inclination to make idle conversation. She could sense his disappointment at discovering that she had not inherited a gold mine and despite her resolution to forget him, the revelation still stung. When the car pulled into the driveway of the fancy Italian restaurant, Patrick suddenly reanimated, as if motivated to make an impression. A broad smile spread across his face and his eyes widened with enthusiasm.

"Here we are."

He bolted from the car to open the passenger door and offered Anna his arm before throwing his keys to a parking attendant. She declined his assistance, preferring to walk unescorted up the stairs to the restaurant. Hungry and impatient to find out what Patrick was planning, she took the stairs faster than a woman in six-inch-high heels should attempt and when she reached the top step, she caught her heel in the hem of her dress and stumbled forward, bracing herself for a humiliating face plant into the marble tiles.

"Careful there."

A large hand shot out to support her elbow, catching her effortlessly as she fell, saving her from injury to both her face ... and her dignity. The diamond cufflinks were a dead giveaway. Derrick Corel was making a habit of catching her.

"It would be a shame to ruin such an exquisite dress," Derrick supported her arm with one hand while unhooking her trapped heel with the other. "And yet, as beautiful as it is, I fear it still doesn't do you justice."

Unaccustomed to compliments and unprepared for the rush of blood to every cell in her body, Anna lowered her head. Words eluded her.

"Anna, are you all right?" Patrick came dashing up the stairs as Derrick brushed dirt of the hem of the dress, his hand resting for a moment on her thigh.

"Patrick Miller, I'd like to introduce Derrick Corel ... my *business* partner."

"I know Mr. Miller," Derrick informed her as he turned his back on Patrick and reached for her hand.

She shivered at his touch as he lifted her hand to his lips. His lips were as cold as his hand. "If you'll excuse me, Anna, I'm late for an appointment. Enjoy your meal."

Anna stared as Derrick walked past them into the restaurant. She could see the maitre'd escort him to a private booth where another elegantly dressed man was already waiting. Although he had saved her from humiliation, Derrick Corel had completely snubbed Patrick. She could hardly believe his attitude. He didn't seem like the type to look down his nose at others. She sensed hostility between them. Her interest piqued. *Did they have a history? Was Derrick aware that Patrick had jilted her? Why was this man getting under her skin?*

"Shall we?" Patrick once again offered his arm and this time Anna chose to accept his support. She had no intention of repeating the fall, especially while the waiter led them past Derrick's table. Both Derrick and his guest watched with obvious interest as she walked by and she could feel their eyes on her as she deliberately sashayed her hips.

"That's his brother."

"What?"

"The man sitting with your partner ... that's his brother, David."

"Oh. I didn't know he had a brother." She glanced back. Both men were watching her with intensity. The brother raised his glass and smiled at her. A blush warmed her cheeks. Something in their gazes suggested more than admiration of her dress. *What are you up to, Derrick Corel?*

"I bet there's a lot you don't know about Derrick Corel."

The irritated tone in Patrick's voice reminded her that she was staring back at the brothers. She turned her attention back to her date. His frown spoke volumes.

The waiter drew out a chair for Anna and she waited until he had handed out the menus and taken the wine order from Patrick, almost afraid to ask the question that was burning in her mind.

"I'm assuming there's something in particular you want to tell me about, Derrick?"

She took a roll from the basket on the table, broke it in two and was about to spread butter on one half when Patrick reached over and laid his hand over hers. Instinctively, she pulled away almost knocking over the basket of bread. His eyes lowered. He slowly withdrew his own hand and began to tap his fingers on the table.

"Let's have dinner first. I have a feeling that the

conversation may upset our appetites."

Anna nodded. As desperately as she wanted to know more about Derrick Corel she couldn't ignore the rumbling in her stomach. After maxing out her MasterCard on the dress, she wasn't about to waste a free feed. The waiter brought the wine, and held it out for inspection.

"Ceretto 2003 Brunate Barolo Nebbiolo, sir."

Patrick checked the label of the bottle and nodded. The waiter poured a small quantity into a glass which Patrick swirled, making a grand gesture of sniffing before tasting. Screwing up his nose in a gesture of distaste, he addressed the waiter.

"I expected better for $79."

"Put the bottle on my tab, Mario…"

Anna shivered as cold hands rested on her shoulders. Derrick's touch was intimate, hinting at a relationship. She was tempted to brush them away, until she noticed Patrick's expression. His nostrils flared and the vein in his temple throbbed. She bit her bottom lip to hide the threatening smile and allowed Derrick's hands to stay where they were as he addressed the waiter.

"And please be so kind as to bring a decanter."

Mario smiled and made a short huffing sound at Patrick as he left the table leaving Derrick to inform him, "I believe the flavor of the wine will improve if you allow it to breathe, Mr. Miller."

"Oh, yes. How careless of me to forget. I must have been distracted by my beautiful companion."

Anna suspected that Patrick had no idea of how to treat a good wine. He was no more a connoisseur than she was. The contempt on his face as he stared at Derrick's hands provided a measure of satisfaction. His gaze still fixed on the hands that hadn't moved from her shoulders.

Derrick's thumbs traced lazy circles on her skin

yet despite the chill that spread across her skin and the electricity that prickled every nerve-ending in her body, she made no attempt to shake him off. Closing her eyes, she concentrated on the energy emanating from him.

Yes, there was definitely something dark about Derrick but nothing threatening. She couldn't imagine him hurting her. Despite his cold touch, she sensed warmth in his soul, kindness. She trembled as a strange feeling ran through her. It was almost a tug at her thoughts, as though someone was trying to read her mind. Anna instinctively blocked the invasion with the protective barrier she had been forced to use many times before. She opened her eyes and the coldness of Derrick's skin forced her thoughts back to the morgue where her father lay lifeless and waiting for identification. She had been warned that his skin would feel cold but nothing could have prepared her for the icy sensation or the solid smoothness of the husk that had once been her father. Jake Derwent's soul was gone. She had tried to take comfort in that while she made funeral arrangements, convincing herself that she was not cremating her father, but the body he had once inhabited. Now, faced with the same bitter sensation, she wondered about Derrick's soul and the darkness that surrounded him.

"I can understand your loss of concentration, Miller." Derrick ran his fingertips up and down the outside of Anna's arms, sending wave after wave of goose bumps through her body as he continued his conversation with Patrick. "Anna does indeed interfere with a man's capacity to think clearly."

Anna's eyelids fluttered and her body warmed to his touch.

"Thank you for the wine, Mr. Corel. I don't want to keep you from your guest." Patrick hissed. His eyes remained focused on Derrick's hands.

"Yes, I suppose I shouldn't keep my brother waiting."

To Anna's surprise, he bent down and kissed her cheek, his lips lingering tenderly on her face, his cool breath ticking her skin. "I'll see you tomorrow, Anna," he whispered in her ear.

As Derrick returned to his table, Patrick stared daggers at the back of her partner's head.

"You should stay away from that man, Anna. For your own good."

"That sounds remarkably like a threat, Patrick."

"No. Oh god, no. Of course not." Patrick stuttered over the words of his apology. "You know I would never hurt you, Angel."

"Once upon a time I would have believed you, but we both know that isn't true, don't we?" She raised her hand to silence Patrick before he could argue. "No excuses, Patrick. You hurt me. You really, really, hurt me. Because of you, I felt obligated to move away from everything and everyone I loved…"

There were many things she wanted to tell this man. Words she had practiced over and over until she knew them verbatim. But, she didn't want to make a scene in the restaurant and if she finished with the often rehearsed "storming away" scene, she would miss out on her only decent meal of the week. As the waiter returned with the decanter, she waited until he had poured the contents of the bottle into the crystal receptacle and left them alone before she finished her speech.

"This isn't the time or the place to finish this conversation, Patrick, so I will wait until a time when we are alone." She accepted a glass of wine from him and continued. "But don't you ever call me Angel again. You gave up any right to endearments years ago."

"Okay, Anna." He picked up the menu and read

silently.

Anna did the same, disappointed to find the list in Italian, a language she had never learned. Never having travelled and with no real desire to venture abroad, there wasn't much point in learning a language she would never need, until tonight. Tonight, she wished desperately that she had some idea what she could order. Something tasty and hopefully very expensive would serve Patrick right.

"Would you like me to order for you, Ang … Anna?"

"Thank you, that would be nice." Under the table she crossed her fingers, hoping that he wouldn't order something with tentacles or smothered in garlic sauce.

****

"So that's the infamous Anna Derwent? Cute."

"Are you blind, David? She's breathtaking."

David laughed and raised his glass. "Yes, Derrick, she's definitely a keeper." He took a sip and gestured back at Anna's table. "What do you think *that* is about?"

"They have a history. Maybe he's offering his condolences."

"Or maybe he's offering something else?"

Derrick glared at his brother. "He'd better not try."

"Calm down. I'm only pointing out the obvious." He kept his eyes locked on the couple. "We both know what that rogue wants and I'm sure he won't give up until he gets it. He obviously believes he can entice Anna into helping him convince us to agree to his proposal."

"Anna has more sense than to get involved with him again." Derrick told his brother while he kept a watchful eye on Anna's companion. "Jake told me that the bastard crushed her spirit when he left her at the altar. It was his fault that Anna felt compelled to leave town. It almost broke Jake, both financially and emotionally."

"They look pretty chummy to me," David observed.

"Looks can be deceiving, brother. We both know that very well."

"I *do* know. And we *both* know that a woman in love does not always act in her own best interests."

Derrick nodded and drained his glass of wine, staring at the empty glass as his thoughts drifted back to a time long ago. He understood the implications of his brother's comment only too well. Their sister had died at the hands of the man she loved. A man she had trusted.

"I'm sorry, Derrick, I shouldn't have said that but you should stop beating yourself up about it. There was nothing we could have done to foresee what happened and you aren't the only one who feels guilty. As the eldest, I should never have left you and Isabelle to follow my dreams in Paris but what's done is done. We can't bring our darling sister back. You should be focusing on what's happening over there." He motioned over to Anna's table where Patrick appeared to be going out of his way to impress his date. "That Miller is a persistent little bugger with a reputation for always getting what he wants."

Derrick slammed his glass down on the table. "Well he can't have Anna."

"Calm down." David patted his shoulder. "When it comes to charisma and persistence, no-one can out-charm a Corel."

****

Anna's stomach protested the large quantity of wine she had consumed in order to drown out the taste of the greasy, sauce covered *whatever the hell that was* that Patrick had ordered for her. As she brushed her teeth and swilled water in her mouth to remove the horrid taste, she remembered her father's term for fancy food. Mucks and messes he used to say. Give me a good old mixed grill any day. She could almost hear his voice reminding her that she had brought this on herself. *No good can come from revenge.* Despite how much heartache Patrick had caused; she had been foolish to believe that she could convince him that she had moved on. This so wasn't worth eating toast and vegemite for a week, Anna despaired as she leaned over the bathroom sink.

Chapter Three

Anna was halfway up the stairs when Derrick's voice startled her.

"I heard that you called in sick this morning."

She grimaced up at him from behind her dark glasses. He stood in the doorway to the Dojo looking more handsome than she could stand in her condition. She swallowed another wave of nausea and wished the stairs would devour her whole. "Yes, I think it might have been food poisoning."

"Sorry to hear that," he told her as he stepped into the hall. "You certainly don't look very well." As he walked towards her, he suggested, "You might want to step back."

A chorus of voices yelled OOS and her head throbbed in response. As the students bowed at the door and left the Dojo, she looked up at him over the rim of her glasses and realized that despite his martial arts attire, he looked and smelled fantastic.

"I guess you're one of those teachers who bark orders but do little work, you're not even flushed."

He shrugged and smiled, offering no explanation. She leaned back against the wall to allow the stream of students to pass her on the stairs and mentally prepared herself for the avalanche of emotions that inevitably hit her when confronted with a crowd.

"Thanks for a great class, Sensei." One of the male students interrupted. "Maybe one day you can explain to me how you are able to outlast all of us without any noticeable signs of fatigue. Is there a secret to your strength?"

"Ah, yes grasshopper. But then if I told you, I would have to kill you," he said with a wink and a curl of his lips.

"He's such a crack up." One of the female students elbowed Anna in the ribs. "I don't know how he does it but I keep coming back hoping that I can get to his fitness level."

"And you will, Lizzie. *If* you put in the hard work." His forehead creased slightly and his lips tightened but just as quickly they curled into a smile. "Go home and practice what I told you."

"Oos. Sensei." The woman bowed and waved as she limped down the stairs behind a trail of other students, all smiling and congratulating each other on a hard training session. Anna counted at least thirty students of various ages and colored belts leaving the dojo.

"Business is good?" She asked after the last of the students hobbled down the stairs.

"That surprises you?"

"Honestly, yes. The last time I was here there were only a handful of gym junkies working out and a staff of two. Your class appeared to have around thirty students."

Derrick nodded. "Actually this is a slow night. There was a tournament on the weekend so some of the students stayed out to celebrate and weren't feeling too well this evening. Judging by your appearance, I'm sure you can relate."

"I wasn't celebrating," Anna protested. "I know that my being here at night isn't part of our agreement but I needed some fresh air and somehow ended up here." She continued up the stairs and stood by the door of the Dojo to peek in. "Impressive."

The room was well equipped with weapons and protective equipment. She slipped off her shoes and bowed before entering. The ground beneath her feet gave a little. "Sprung floor?"

"Yes, I prefer the feel of wood under my feet and the tradition of having the lower grades sweep the floor before class builds character."

"And cuts down on the cleaning bill," she teased.

"Yes, there is that," he agreed with a big grin.

Anna wandered around the large Dojo, taking note of all the equipment. She noticed something amiss. "I'm surprised there are no mirrors in here. I thought that, like in the gym, mirrors make it easier to check if the stance is correct. Any reason why you don't use them?"

"Vanity. I found that some of the students became distracted by their appearance. Besides, it's the job of the higher belts to correct the stances."

"Fair enough. I don't know anything about Martial Arts but that makes sense."

After collecting her shoes, she walked gingerly down the stairs, holding onto the railing for support. Her head pounded from the blinding headache and she headed straight to the office to search for aspirin. As her hand touched the doorknob, she realized her mistake. She turned back towards Derrick. "Sorry, force of habit. It's your office now isn't it?"

"I thought we had worked this out. Just because you are here in the evening doesn't mean we can't share the room." He opened the door and ushered her in.

Anna allowed Derrick to offer her a chair. Arguing was useless. How could she explain to him why she preferred to work alone? Being an empath was hard enough in an ordinary environment but here, where her father worked, surrounded by people who loved him … the sorrow was unbearable. Somehow she had managed to avoid most of the staff tonight, sparing her from the avalanche of emotions that would bombard her senses and make her both physically and emotionally ill. Sharing an office with Derrick would be uncomfortable, possibly unbearable, especially knowing that he was part of the reason for her recent headaches. Since the day of the funeral, every meeting with Derrick had been clouded with pain. Every time she even thought about him she could feel her senses go into overdrive but something or someone, always blocked her.

"Look, I'm sorry if I sounded ungrateful. This was a wonderful and gracious gesture, it's just that…"

"It's just that you would rather not have anything to do with me."

"No. That's not it." She sighed and closed her eyes as her left hand shot to her chest. The gripping sensation that had caused her to faint after her father's funeral was back … with a vengeance. It was time to go home.

"All right, I'm listening." Derrick's voice startled her. She opened her eyes in time to see him fold his thread-bare black belt and begin to untie his Gi jacket. "Will you excuse me while I change?"

Despite the pain and overwhelming desire to escape, her interest kept her bottom planted firmly on the seat. *What does Mr. Armani look like under the suit?*

"Oh, sure. Go ahead."

Although etiquette ruled that she should turn away while Derrick removed the heavy canvas jacket, Anna found that she could not take her eyes off him, especially after getting her initial glimpse of his perfectly toned physique. Beneath his clothes, he concealed taut, pale skin and if there was an ounce of fat, she couldn't see it and she *was* looking … hard. Her fingers twitched in her lap. She imagined tracing the outline of his body from his solid pectorals, down his six pack abdominals to his narrow waist and beyond. As he turned around to grab a fresh shirt, she admired the solid muscle of his shoulders and back. No wonder he felt so cold, he appeared to be carved from marble.

"Well? What do you think?"

"Huh?"

Derrick stood facing her, his hands resting on his waist and his pants hung low around his hips. The white t-shirt he now wore only served to make him appear larger. His biceps strained against the cuffs on his sleeves.

"Do you think that we can make this arrangement work?"

Anna shakily rose to her feet and extended her hand. It would be a real hardship being forced to endure working alongside this perfectly chiseled specimen of a man, but someone had to do it. "Fine. I'll try, but no promises."

She noticed that Derrick was hesitant to accept her offer of a handshake. When he did consent, she shivered. Despite what was obviously a very vigorous work out, his hand was still like ice. Derrick watched her reaction and a concerned expression crinkled his forehead.

"You know what they say, 'cold hands, warm heart'."

"I thought it was cold feet?" she flopped back in her chair.

Derrick shrugged and took a seat opposite her at the desk. "Whatever."

"You should really see someone about that. It could be a circulation problem."

"Thanks for your concern; I'll keep that in mind."

"Okay then," Anna slapped her hands on her knees. "Well, I guess we should discuss my place in this partnership. What position in the gym should I take?"

Derrick scratched the back of his head and

grimaced. "At the risk of having my head chewed off. There's not really a lot for you to do."

"Let's get one thing clear—" Anna stood her ground, literally. She rose from her seat and stared down into Derrick's eyes. For a moment, she was sure she saw the color of his eyes flash from royal blue to violet. She tried to concentrate, to block out the searing pain but there was something in his eyes that suddenly terrified her. Everything about him oozed charm, sophistication, and composure except there was more to Derrick than meets the eye. Something blocked her empathetic push into his psyche. She felt danger, remorse, and aggression but there was something more. Something she couldn't read. Startled, and dizzy with pain, she lost her train of thought, giving him the opportunity to interrupt.

"I know what you're thinking, Anna, and let me assure you, I'm not keeping you out of the loop. We have an excellent staff including an experienced manager and an accountant. You are welcome to go over the books but there's nothing for you to do besides enjoy the fruits your father's labor." As soon as the words left his mouth, Derrick's hand shot to his temple. "That's not what I—"

"I think that is exactly what you meant." Her hands balled into fists and she scowled as she accused him, "You think I'm here for money."

"Not at all." Derrick sighed. "I'm merely pointing out that there is no rush for you to begin work. You should take some time to deal with your father's sudden passing."

"And how much time are you suggesting? A week, a month, maybe a year?"

"Whatever you need."

"Why don't you just say what you are thinking? You don't want me here. I can feel it." There was an element of truth in her words. She could sense a shield around his emotions, keeping her from getting a good read on his true feelings. He was an enigma and one way or another, she planned on working him out.

"Look, Anna. I don't know why you would think so little of me. I've gone out of my way to make you feel comfortable but my presence seems to irritate you. You're grieving and you're obviously feeling under the weather tonight, so perhaps we could discuss this some other time."

"So..." *He was dismissing her?* Her head pulsed with pain but she pushed through it as her anger rose. "It doesn't suit you to talk with me so I should leave? What about the other day when I asked you to give *me* some space? Just because I have a knack of making people feel uncomfortable doesn't mean I don't have feelings and opinions you know. I can't help the things that happen to me."

Derrick's eyebrows furrowed. "Who said you make me feel uncomfortable? What sort of things happen around you?"

She took a deep breath. How would he react if she answered his questions? Would he run a mile if he knew about her ability to predict the future or quake in his boots at the thought of being in a room with someone who could sense his darkest secrets? Well, usually. Somehow her ability was useless with him. "It doesn't matter." Anna waved her hands in the air and shook her head. "Sooner or later you will see for yourself."

"You're making too much out of this, Anna. Calm down..." Derrick's expression remained relaxed. "You look as though you might burst a blood vessel."

"Don't you dare tell me to calm down." *How could he possibly know what she was going through? Look at him, standing there with his air of confidence, presuming he had the right to tell me what to do. He* was the one hiding something, not her. "You can't fool me, Derrick Corel. I know you harbor secrets." She held her head between her palms, trying to shut out the pain. "What are you hiding from me?"

"Nothing." He let out an audible sigh. "I've been completely up front with you."

Anna wrung her hands as she paced the room. *What is happening to me?* She shook her head. "No, there's something you're not telling me. Something about my…" *Mother*? No. That didn't make sense.

"Something about your what?" He grabbed her by the shoulders. His eyes widened. "Anna, you're soaked in sweat and burning up. Why are you so upset?"

Pain shot through her chest and spread across her shoulders. Her jaw ached. She stared up into his eyes and held back a sob as she confided. "I don't know what's happening to me."

He pulled her against his chest and rested his chin on her head. "What can I do to help you?" He said in a voice barely above a whisper.

His gentleness offered comfort. Comfort she desperately needed but she shook her head.

"I have to go."

****

Anna had stumbled almost the entire distance home before she remembered that she had *driven* to the gym. She stopped cold and, for a moment considered going back for the car then changed her mind. She didn't have the strength to face Derrick again tonight. She touched her hand to her forehead. Strange how his cold skin had the opposite effect on hers. Heat radiated through her as she remembered the intimate gesture. Stranger still, despite her accusations, she somehow knew that she was safe with Derrick. But what was the connection with her mother? She was only a child when her mother died and—although she didn't know much about her partner—surely he wasn't in the same age bracket as her parents? *No.* She shook her head and laughed. What was she thinking? There was barely a wrinkle on his perfect face and *that* was most definitely not the body of a man in his early fifties. She bit her bottom lip and smiled, breathing easier since the pain in her head and chest had dissipated.

She drew in another deep breath, gagged, and covered her nose as a putrid odor assaulted her sense. *Eeeww.* Rotting garbage spilled from overturned rubbish bins and a few of the street lights had been broken. *When did this neighborhood become a dump?* The street came to a dead end. Nothing about this place looked familiar. *Okay, where the hell am I?* She looked back in the direction that she had come. *How did I get so turned around?* A chill ran down her spine and she rubbed her arms against the cold while she hurried back to the main street.

"Hey, lady. Could you help me out?"

Anna spun to see a young man, around sixteen years old, standing at the entrance to a side alley. He had a battered skateboard tucked under his arm and wore a cap hung low over his eyes. Wisps of greasy blond hair poked out at the sides. Although his face was half concealed in shadow, she could see his skin tone was blotchy and his face acne scarred. His clothes were dirty and his jeans slung around his hips in the fashion of teenage males.

"Help you, how?" Anna remained where she was, reluctant to move closer to the young man. The throbbing in her temples suddenly returned with a vengeance.

"I had a spill on me skateboard." He pointed to the tear in the knee of his jeans. "And I wanted to call me mum to come get me but I ain't got a phone. Can I borrow your mobile?"

"Sorry kid. I left it in my car." *Idiot. Now look what you've gotten yourself into*. She looked back towards the street, hoping to see another adult. *Anyone*.

The boy held out his hand, palm up. "Well, can ya spare some change for the bus?"

"I guess I could do that." *Stay calm, Anna. Don't make any sudden movements.*

"Thanks lady. My knee really hurts."

Anna's hands shook as she took out her wallet and upturned the coins into the palm of her hand. "I think this should be enough." She wasn't surprised when he showed no interest in the coins.

"Thanks. Do ya think you could help me over to the bus rank? I can't put much weight on it."

Anna looked down the street to where the boy was pointing. The bus stop was only a short distance down the road. A distance the boy could have easily travelled despite his grazed knee. His gaze darted from her handbag to her face while he stepped slowly towards her.

"I've got to go." She told him as she threw the coins in his direction. She turned to run. He charged at her, faster than she had anticipated, grabbing for her handbag.

"Give me your bag bitch."

Anna held him at arm's length, struggling against his assault. "No. I don't have any money. Just take the coins and go." She managed to push him a short distance, enough to attempt a retreat. The pimply skinned punk grabbed her hair from behind, and dragged her, kicking and screaming into the darkest section of the alley. He produced a switch knife from his pocket and held the point against her throat.

"No!" Anna struggled against the teenager's grip.

Her thrashing drove the tip of the blade into her neck. She screamed as the knife pierced her skin.

"Shut up!"

Her attacker threw her to the ground. She landed heavily on her side, where she instinctively curled into the fetal position. When he raised his leg, she held her hands up to protect her face as she braced herself for the impact. Instead, a rush of air chilled her. The boy flew through the air and landed back in the alley, screaming in pain. Her attacker struggled to his feet and ran away from the alley, still clutching her purse.

"Are you all right, Anna?"

She recognized the voice instantly. "Derrick, he got my handbag."

"Go home. I'll get your handbag and catch up with you. Go *straight* home, Anna." He gently lifted her to her feet but with such speed that she almost toppled.

"But—"

"Don't argue with me. Just go."

Tears burned in her eyes as she told him, "I don't know where I am."

Derrick shook his head but smiled. "Come on." He lifted her into his arms, cradling her close to his chest. "Close your eyes, I'll have you home in a flash."

Anna closed her eyes for what seemed like only a few minutes before he spoke again.

"Do you have a spare key?"

She blinked then blinked again. *Not possible.* "How did we get here so fast?"

"It was only a block away from where I found you."

"You carried me for an entire block?"

Derrick laughed. "You're not that heavy."

Anna frowned. "But it has barely been—"

"You're in shock, Anna. It's been longer than you

realize. Now, you need to go inside and I need to go after that punk. Do you have a spare key?"

She walked up to the front door, pausing to point to a small rock in the garden. Derrick bent down and moved the stone. He picked up the key and unlocked the door.

"Go inside and stay there until I get back." He planted a kiss on her forehead and then smiled. "Please. I'll be back as soon as I can."

She grabbed his wrist. "Don't go, Derrick. I'm afraid you'll be hurt."

He shook his head. "You should be worried about the other guy."

****

"Derrick. Is that you?"

"Yes, I'm here."

Opening the door, she ran her gaze over his face and body, relieved to see that he appeared unharmed. He held out her handbag and shrugged. "I'm afraid he cleaned you out. There wasn't any cash left."

She accepted the bag with a shrug, "There wasn't any money in the wallet to begin with." She walked back to the lounge room and turned to wonder why Derrick wasn't following. "Are you coming in?"

"Is that an invitation?" His wide smile sent a pleasant shiver down her back. She absently returned it.

"Will you just come inside before all the neighbors start gossiping?"

"Anna. Stop worrying about what other people think of you. Either invite me in because you want my company, or ask me to leave."

"Come in, for crying out loud." She shook her head as she examined the contents of her bag. "Are you always so formal?"

"I guess I am." He shut the front door behind him.

"You know, you sounded so much like your father when you said that."

"What? For saying crying out loud? Yeah, I guess I did." She giggled, although the realization stabbed at her heart. "He wasn't much for swearing, so that was as close to cussing as he got." She flopped down onto the couch.

"Anna. Could I ask you something?" Derrick sat beside Anna. His voice soothing and full of what seemed to be genuine concern.

She nodded her answer.

"Why did you risk your life for an empty bag?"

Anna shrugged. "I guess I was silly, wasn't I?"

"You value your life so little?"

"No. Nothing, like that. It's just that ... I don't like people trying to control me. If I gave him my wallet, I would be giving him authority to change my life and I can't allow that to happen, not anymore. Besides, if I had lost my wallet I would need to replace my license, my library membership, my Medicare card, my car registration, everything. My world has been turned upside down lately and I don't need any more changes."

"Finding out that you had a business partner didn't help either, did it?"

"Oh well, you made yourself useful tonight. I don't think I've even thanked you."

"You have now." He flashed his dimples and Anna noticed for the first time since he had sat beside her there was a rosy glow to his usually pale cheeks. "How badly were you hurt?"

"Cuts and bruises." Lifting up the corner of her shorts, Anna showed him the patch of purple radiating from mid-way up her thigh to her right hip, and then held out her grazed elbow.

"Your neck is bleeding." Derrick's eyes grew

wide as he motioned to her throat. "He cut you?"

"Damn, I thought I'd stopped the bleeding." She swiped at it with a tissue. "It's nothing, really." She smiled but the bile rose in her throat and her hand clutched at her neck. It could have been much worse. The punk had intended to cut her throat.

"Let me see." Derrick supported her head between his palms and tilted her neck into a position where the lounge room light would illuminate the area. "This could have killed you if he had pierced the carotid artery."

"But it didn't."

The heat radiating from his palms as he cradled her face surprised her. Only hours earlier, his hands had been ice cold. Now, his touch made the temperature of *her* skin rise. She closed her eyes when he leaned closer, his mouth inches away from hers and closing in but he paused. Instead of the expected kiss, he inhaled as if to draw in her fragrance and he nuzzled her neck with his face. When his tongue slid seductively over the skin on her throat, casually licking a bead of blood from her wound, her body went limp with desire. A tiny mewing noise slipped from between her lips as she cupped the back of his head, holding his face to her neck.

Derrick stilled. He withdrew his lips.

"You should be more careful." His eyes widened, then he looked away. He kept his chin down as he rose from the sofa. "I ... I should be leaving."

"Why? Because you licked my neck?" she stood up and followed him to the door.

"What I did was unforgivable." He kept his back to her as he spoke.

"Do you hear me complaining?"

When he turned around, she could see the strain on his face. Wrinkles worried his brow.

"Good night, Anna." He opened the door and

before she could blink, he had disappeared, the door closing behind him.

****

Derrick drove home to the mansion at break neck speed, anxious to discuss the incident with his brother. He found David in the kitchen, dumped the package he'd brought home on the Italian tiles, and confessed his transgression. Big mistake.

"You *tasted* her?"

"I know. I should have been more careful. It's just … she was so warm and soft and so … vulnerable. I wanted to give her comfort but her scent overpowered me. When I saw the drop of blood on her neck … I lost control."

"Don't beat yourself up, brother. You've been torturing yourself over this woman since you first laid eyes on her photo. Now that she's here in the flesh, it stands to reason you would want to ravish her."

"Who said anything about ravishing her?" Derrick leaned back against the support beam in the center of the large kitchen and accepted the wine glass that his brother offered.

David smiled a wolfish grin. "Come on little brother. I've seen the way you devour her with your eyes. It's only a matter of time before you sink your teeth into that pretty neck."

"No. I *can't*." Derrick downed the thick dark liquid with a gulp. "She's just lost her father. She's not ready."

"She is obviously in need of comfort."

"It wouldn't be right: she hasn't had time to grieve. It would be taking advantage."

"You don't have to *marry* the woman." David patted his brother's shoulder. "Love 'em and leave 'em, has worked well for me for many, many years."

"I'm well aware of your creed." Topping up his glass, he filled David's as well. "Someday you will find *the* woman and you'll realize how important it is to go slowly and give her a chance to settle into her new life before complicating it with our lifestyle."

"Touching speech." David reached over and removed the catheter from the arm of the pimply youth lying on the floor against the fridge. "I think this fellow is getting a bit low. Maybe it's time to drop him off to the ER before we drain him completely."

Derrick crouched down in front of the semi-conscious teenager and stared into his vacant, bloodshot eyes. While they were in the alley, he had been tempted to rip the boy apart, tear him limb from limb for trying to hurt Anna.

"You're going to move back to your parents' home. Attend school and fall in love. Living on the streets is no way to live. It would be bad for your health if you persist in living this life of crime. Do you understand me boy?"

The youth nodded absently. He would not remember his vicious attack on Anna or the beating he took from Derrick. He would awaken feeling sore and tired but happy to be home. Tomorrow, the incident in the alley would be a distant memory. A nightmare in vivid color … predominantly red.

Chapter Four

The accounts did appear to be in good order, at least as far as Anna could tell. The gym was in the black and actually making a lot of money for the first time in its history. Even the higher prices weren't keeping people away, despite what her father had always predicted. During their weekly telephone conversations, Jake Derwent had always insisted that the day the gym raised its prices to meet the cost of other club memberships they would lose all their loyal clients. *All twenty of them.*

According to these bank statements, he was wrong. There were more than three hundred memberships on the computer and she wondered if it was less to do with the running of the gym and more to do with the instructors. It hadn't escaped her notice that the fitness trainers were all extremely good looking males and females in their mid to late twenties. Superbly toned physiques and tanned skin. They oozed health and vitality.

Not for the first time, she wondered what she was doing there: out-of-place and possibly even in the way. Over the last couple of weeks, she had let herself go as far as toning her body but at least her tan was real thanks to the recent days spent convalescing and mourning at the beach. The beach always cheered her up and her best memories of her dad were their regular swims. Going back there helped her grieve. Nevertheless, she cringed when she caught a glimpse of her reflection in the large mirror at the front of the weights room.

"Aagh." Turning left and right, she examined her butt with disapproval. She may have a tan but the body left a bit to be desired.

Hopefully, the share of the profits that Derrick

had promised would ensure a few vegetables and some real protein in her diet and she could get back into condition. Her body had been toned at her fitness peak but she had let herself go. Being broke had been her excuse for a poor diet. Toast and vegemite had lost its appeal after a couple of weeks. At least gravity hadn't affected her C cup breasts yet. Pinching the loose skin on her thighs, she cringed. *Okay legs, you're up first.*

"Need a little help with shaping?"

Anna forced a smile. "No thank you. I can manage it myself." she told the twenty-something blonde before walking away.

She was in no mood to take advice from a—probably silicone enhanced—gym bunny with a perky little nose and 100-watt smile, despite the enthusiasm that radiated from her. Anna hated being rude but she was in no mood to be overwhelmed by the optimistic chirpings of this stranger. She often found joyful people as emotionally draining as encountering pessimists and her senses hadn't recovered from the physical assault from the previous night. She hurried her steps, hoping to leave the young woman in her wake but the perky blonde followed along behind, cheerfully offering more assistance.

"Sometimes it's easier to get results if you have a training partner." She offered her hand. "My name's Susie Lister by the way."

"Anna Derwent." Anna shook the extended hand, hoping her new shadow would give up and go away if she kept the conversation brief.

"You're the new boss aren't you?"

"Yes, I am." Anna took another step away but couldn't shake her: the blonde followed her, offering training tips.

It was more than Anna could stand. She wanted to

be left alone and Susie almost buzzed with enthusiasm. It was a nice change from the negative energy that she had been experiencing lately but too much for her already shaky nerves. Anna turned on her heels.

"Look, I really appreciate your enthusiasm and your offer to help me, but, this isn't a good time for me." She quickened her step to escape.

Susie rushed ahead, stopped directly in her path and stared her down. "Look, Ms. Derwent. I loved your Dad, everyone here did, so I realize you're grieving and maybe you think you need time alone, but, that's not the answer."

"I—"

"Please let me finish. People often misinterpret my friendly nature and assume me to be a dumb blonde. Most of the time I don't care because I know better but if there's one thing I do know, it's that grief loves company."

Anna smiled. Susie's warmth wrapped around her like a comforting blanket.

"Nice speech."

"Thank you. It has been useful at times." Susie giggled and held out her hand once again. "Can we try this again?"

There was warmth in the young woman's handshake. She had a pure heart. Anna could feel the kindness radiating from her.

"That would be nice." Anna agreed. She made a gesture of sweeping the imaginary chip off her shoulder. "Okay, chips gone. So, what can you tell me about this place, Susie?"

Motioning towards the office, Anna led Susie in and shut the door behind them. She offered the fitness trainer a coffee from the newly installed cappuccino machine—one of many presents from Derrick— and they sat down at the desk. The moment she sat, Anna groaned and clutched at her chest. The pain returned, as it had done every time she sat behind the desk. She screwed up her face as she held her hand to her chest and tried to breathe away the familiar crushing feeling.

"Oh my god, Anna. Are you okay?"

Anna opened her eyes and saw the look of terror on Susie's face. Her tanned skin had paled a shade and her eyes were as wide as saucers.

"Yeah, sorry to frighten you, Susie. I don't know what it is but every time I sit in this chair, my chest objects. Don't worry, the pain usually only lasts about twenty minutes then it disappears."

"You frightened me." Susie took a deep breath and let it out slowly. "I don't think I could go through that again."

"Go through what again?" Anna sat forward at her desk and leaned her forearms on the top. The shiver going down her spine was a precursor for upsetting news. It had been for as long as she could remember.

"Oh, Anna. I'm sorry … I thought that you knew…"

The penny dropped. "My father died at this desk?"

Susie nodded. Tears welled in her eyes as she explained, "I was having coffee with him, as we usually did before my night shift. He was telling me a joke and laughing so hard that tears were streaming down his face. Suddenly he clutched his chest and his forehead beaded with sweat. He said he had indigestion but I could see his complexion turning gray so I called for an ambulance. Derrick rushed in just as your father lost consciousness and we started CPR. Derrick tried so hard to bring him back. He broke a couple of your dad's ribs trying to restart his heart but it was too late. The paramedics later said that there was nothing more that we could have done." She reached forward and cupped Anna's hands between her own.

The pain dissipated faster than usual and somehow Anna knew that it would not return.

"Thanks for telling me, Susie. You know, Dad and I once discussed death and he said that he wanted to die laughing. I guess if it was his time, at least he went on his own terms." She swiped at the tears forming behind her eyes. "Now, enough about death. Tell me about the gym."

"Okay, here's the skinny. There are six fitness instructors, including me. We are all aerobics and Pilates trained so we share the classes and it works out pretty well that way. There are three martial arts instructors—all black belts—including Derrick. Two receptionists, a day manager, a night manager, a masseuse, and the accountant. You have two cleaning people who come before opening in the morning and a laundress who picks up the soiled towels at night and brings them back first thing. Twice a week a woman delivers fresh flowers for the foyer and … I guess that's it."

"How long has Mr. Corel been here?"

"Derrick? Oh, around seven years I've been told."

"So he took over almost as soon as I left?"

"If you left seven years ago … yes, he did." She took a gulp of her coffee. "I've only been here for four."

"And the martial arts classes? They're popular?"

"Packed to the rafters, six days a week."

"Derrick—he only teaches Karate?"

"No. He works out in the private gym for hours before and after his classes. Sometimes he lets a few of us work-out with him but never in the main gym. For some reason he doesn't like the mirrors. He trains like a man possessed. I've never seen a man with such a perfect body." She waved her hand in front of her face while she pursed her lips for a whistle. "Mind you, he works hard at it. He has a degree in Exercise and in Sports Science and a diploma in Remedial Massage, plus … I was told he got Fifth Dan in Shotokan Karate while training in Japan."

"Does he ever work out during the day?" Anna wondered if they were likely to bump into each other this morning. After his frosty and sudden departure last night, she wasn't sure she felt up to more humiliation.

"Never." Glancing at her watch, Susie stood up and took Anna's empty coffee cup to the sink. "I have a new client coming for a training session, so I'd better get back outside. Thanks for the coffee and chat."

"Thank *you,* Susie. Sorry again for the bad manners, it's been a trying week. I'm glad you put me in my place."

Susie was almost out the door when she turned back. "By the way, I go for a run along the beach every morning at six and pass your house around ten minutes' past. Maybe you'd like to join me sometime?"

Anna sighed. Lately she wasn't a morning person as she had begun to have trouble sleeping but if she was going to take this position seriously, she needed to get into shape—fast. "It's a date."

"The story of my life." Susie sighed, but a broad smile lit her face. "My first date in ages and it's getting sweaty with a female. Not exactly what I had in mind."

"I hear you, sister!" Anna called back to her. "But at least being dateless is better than spending the night with your head in the toilet."

Susie looked like she was at a loss for words. She stood in the doorway, mouth open until Anna waved her off. "Long story, I'll tell you over coffee some other time."

****

Despite repeatedly telling herself that she didn't want to run into Derrick Corel, Anna found reasons to remain at the gym until the night staff began to arrive. During the day she had even managed to get in some weight training with Susie and an hour in one of the Pilates classes. The class left her with little doubt as to why the memberships were high ... it was fantastic. If the other classes were of the same standard, she might be able to save enough money to have a real holiday someday.

After her shower, she changed into the clothes she had brought from home in her backpack, applied fresh makeup and dried her hair using one of the gym-supplied hairdryers. No wonder the gym was so popular; the ladies room looked like something out of a fashion magazine, even supplying shampoo and conditioner. Heading back to her office to collect her things, loud voices greeted her. She stopped to listen to the two men arguing inside. One she recognized as Derrick, the other sounded like ... Patrick? Hesitant to intrude, she waited impatiently outside the closed door, trying to pick up parts of the conversation without being forced to actually lean her ear against the door. Whatever the topic of conversation, it was heated.

"This is the last time I'm going to tell you. Someone has filled your head with lies."

"We both know that's not true Mr. High and mighty Corel. You just can't stand to see me as your equal. I don't understand why you won't help me."

"It will never happen, Miller. Please do us both a favor and give up asking."

"No. I don't see why this is a problem to you. I will do anything—*anything*."

"There is nothing you could offer that would interest me."

"Are you sure about that?"

The sound of shuffling feet became louder, closer. Suddenly the door was flung open. Patrick fell through. She scurried to get out of the way before he knocked her over.

"Patrick! Derrick! What the hell is going on here?" The room almost buzzed with negative energy. The hatred emanating from both men was palpable. Derrick's clenched knuckles white.

"Anna?" Derrick appeared shocked to see her. "I thought you were only coming in during the day."

"We made an arrangement to share the office. I didn't know I was actually barred from entering the gym after dark."

"Of course not. I just … didn't expect to see you tonight."

"I hate to interrupt." Patrick stepped beside Anna and slipped his arm around her shoulders. "But it looks like I've outlasted my welcome. Could I give you a lift home, Anna?"

"*I'll* escort Anna home." Derrick took her free arm and held it.

She pulled clear of both of them. "I can get myself home thank you both very much."

Turning her back she headed for the foyer.

"Damn," she muttered. Her handbag was still in the office. She reluctantly turned and walked past them into the room, grabbed her things and left.

She crossed the street to the carpark and pressed the unlock button on her car key. *I wonder what that was about?* She glanced into her rear vision mirror and noticed Derrick roughly escorting Patrick out of the building. Their discussion appeared to have started anew and her curiosity got the better of her. She adjusted the mirror for a better look. Patrick waved his fists in a threatening manner while Derrick remained motionless, seemingly in control and unaffected by the aggressive gestures. Suddenly he lunged forward, shoving Patrick ... hard. He seemed to fly across the bonnet of his car, setting off the car alarm. When he recovered, Patrick slid off the hood and scrambled into his car. The tires squealed as the car peeled away from the curb and disappeared down the street in a haze of smoke.

"It isn't polite to watch other people's disagreements."

"What the—"

How the hell did he do that? Somehow Derrick had managed to get from the front of the building to the car park in what seemed like only seconds.

"I wasn't watching. I was just ... okay, I was watching. So sue me."

He opened the car door and offered his hand.

"Your hands are cold again." She squirmed in her seat before stepping out. "You really should see a doctor about your circulation problem. Seriously, I've never known anyone with a body temperature as cold as you."

He smiled and shrugged, then tilted her chin with his fingers and examined her neck. "Looks like that cut is healing nicely. It shouldn't scar."

"The bruises are already going yellowish too."

When Derrick lifted her skirt slightly to inspect her thigh, she slapped his hand.

"Just wanted to be sure." He flashed his dimples and she felt a flutter in her stomach.

He moved closer. She leaned back against the door frame. He nuzzled her neck with his cheek. His cool breath tickled her skin sending ripples of warmth through her body. *Not this time.* Reluctantly she pushed him away and slipped back into the driver's seat, starting the engine. It was his turn to suffer. "I'll see you later."

As she drove away, Anna glanced at the rear vision mirror but Derrick was already gone.

****

"She insists I see a physician," Derrick told his brother.

"Whatever for?"

"She believes I have a circulation problem resulting in my low body temperature."

"Oh." David laughed as he helped pack away the training equipment. "Why don't you tell her it's a family problem? Something in the genes. I could demonstrate with a laying-on of the hands if that would make things easier to explain?"

"You keep your hands to yourself."

"I'm only trying to help. I got another glimpse of her as I pulled into the car park tonight. She really is a cute little firecracker isn't she?"

"Did you also happen to notice Patrick Miller leaving the gym?"

"What does *he* want? As if I didn't know."

"He's beginning to act desperate, even threatening to go public about us. I'm afraid if I don't agree he'll find another way."

"So, where's the problem in that? It will keep him out of your hair."

"There is something unstable about him. If he continues along this path … someone might get hurt."

"Someone like Anna?"

"He's hurt her before."

"I know the story."

"I'm not sure if he would follow through on his threats. He's greedy but I don't believe he's entirely ruthless. Jake once told me that, although he hated the pain it caused Anna, he was glad that the wedding didn't go ahead. He said that Patrick was immature and impulsive due to his fatherless upbringing. Money was hard to come by in his youth and he was always looking for a way to make a quick buck."

"We've met his kind before." David threw a medicine ball at Derrick who caught it effortlessly and tossed it back. "He won't give up easily. You'd better watch your back."

"Thank you for your concern." Derrick locked the weapons cabinet and turned off the lights to the Dojo as they left. "I have every intention of watching my back. You do the same."

"So"—David slapped his brother's back—"are we heading out for a night of debauchery?"

"I have other plans."

"Plans that include your little firecracker?"

A wide smile spread across Derrick's face. "You never know."

Despite the sermon he had given his brother on his intention to give Anna time to grieve, he found himself unable to function every time they parted company. It was as though she took a part of him with her and his body grieved for its loss. Without her, he was incomplete … defective. And it was not a condition he enjoyed. Never, in all his years as a vampire or the previous years as a human, had he ever felt such a strong connection. Not even with his beloved Isabelle, his little sister who had been left in his care after the sudden deaths of their parents.

David rested a hand on his shoulder and Derrick knew by the expression on his brother's face that their psychic connection had revealed his thoughts.

"I wasn't your fault," David told him. "There was nothing you could have done."

"I should have been more perceptive." Derrick maintained. "She was my responsibility. I should have protected her."

"She was a married woman, Derrick. She was no longer in our charge."

"She was still our sister!"

David shook his head. "We've gone over this more times than I care to remember." He picked up his jacket and headed for the door. "It's been over one hundred years. When are you going to forgive yourself?"

****

After David left, Derrick sat cross-legged on the Dojo floor and contemplated his brother's words. He had dedicated his entire second life to the protection of women and instructing them in the art of self-defense, and he had trained his body to become a deadly weapon, but none of these things would bring his sister back. If he lived a million lifetimes, he would never forget the vulnerable look on Isabelle's badly beaten face as she took her last painful breath. If it had not been for David's unexpected return from Paris, he too would be dead. Many times he wished he were, and blamed his brother for not allowing him to join their sister in the afterlife. He had felt as though he did not deserve to live and, until he met Jake and eventually Anna, he never wanted to part of this world, but now … now he had a reason to wake up each night and a plan for the future.

****

"How long have you been waiting here?" Anna asked. She unlocked the door and waited for an answer.

"I came straight over from the gym."

"Why?"

"I thought I owed you an explanation."

"For the way you acted at the gym? Or do you mean for humiliating me in front of the whole town?"

"You aren't ever going to let that go, are you Anna?"

"No, Patrick. Some memories stay with you forever." She stepped inside and started to close the door.

"Please, Anna. Just let me come in for a while and try to explain. You promised at the restaurant that we could finish this discussion in private. I'm only asking for an hour. Surely you can't deny me one hour of your time? I know that deep down inside you're still the sweet, thoughtful Anna I fell in love with. *That* Anna would give me a chance."

"That's not fair." If she had indeed buried the sweet Anna down deep, it was to protect herself from having her heart torn out and handed to her on a silver platter. It was all Patrick's fault she had become the cynical person she was today. "Don't you blame your problems on me."

"*Please,* Anna. Half an hour? Twenty minutes? I'm begging you."

"Oh, come inside before I change my mind." She threw open the door and allowed him to enter.

"Do you have any wine?"

"Don't push your luck Patrick. I said we could talk, not socialize."

"I thought it might ease the tension, that's all."

She crossed her arms over her chest and frowned. *I should tell him no. Hell, I could use a drink myself.*

"All right then. Just one." She walked into the kitchen and opened the fridge door. "Is red okay?"

"My god, Anna … red wine in the fridge? And in a cask no less?"

"I like my wine that way. What's wrong with that?"

"No, no. I'm sorry. The wine is fine. It's great." He hurried to the kitchen cabinet for glasses and poured them each a drink. "Let's talk."

"Whatever." Anna sat on the sofa and as she did,

her hand accidently knocked over a small silver frame, containing a photo taken seven years earlier, when she was around nineteen. It had been taken after an especially enjoyable day at the beach with her father. Her nose was spotted with freckles and her skin flushed with color from the race up the sand dunes to the car to get the camera. Her wind-tousled hair was slightly shorter then but it was the same coppery blonde. Void of makeup and still laughing from one of her father's lame jokes—her face positively glowed with joy. It was one of the happiest times in her life. A life that Patrick had torn apart.

Patrick sat beside her and took a sip from his glass. His nose crinkled as he swallowed the cold Dolce Rosso.

Anna watched him warily. "There was a time when you would have enjoyed that."

Patrick shook his head. "That was the *real* problem with our relationship. I tried to enjoy the things you enjoyed but it wasn't for me—not really."

The remark hit her like a slap to her face. "Was my way of life so bad?"

"Of course not."

He tried to touch her hands but she pulled them back into her lap. "You loved the simple pleasures, walks on the beach ... going to the cinema, watching old movies on television. Those things are ... nice. I needed excitement, travel, night life. I love nightclubs and gambling. Fast cars and—"

"Fast women?" Anna took a large gulp of her wine.

"Maybe."

"So what you're saying in a nut shell is that I was too simple for you?" She swallowed more wine, half emptying the glass.

"You know that's not true. Things *happen* around

you. Strange and bizarre things. I don't think anyone at school will ever forget when you lay down in front of the school bus and refused to budge until they had a doctor check the driver."

She let out a deep sigh. Yes, she remembered the day. How could she forget? It was the day she became an outcast. "He was about to have a stroke. I couldn't let him get behind the wheel. He could have died. We all could have died."

His expression softened. "Yes, you were right about that, and all the other things you predicted. Even when it cost you all your friends. Life with you was never simple, Angel."

"I told you not to call me that." She finished her drink and poured another. "And while we're talking about the strange things in my life, how much worse do you think it got after you walked out on our wedding? Everywhere I went, people stared and whispered. It was bad enough being the town weirdo without being the *dumped* weirdo. It forced me to leave town."

Patrick leaned forward, she leaned back.

"Leaving you was the biggest mistake of my life. I know now that your abilities only make you more desirable. I want a second chance. I'm begging you to forgive me. You may not believe it, but I have changed."

"You're right. I don't believe it."

"Anna. Why won't you give me another chance? I've seen the error of my ways. Since we broke up, I've never been happy with any of the women I've dated."

Anna knew where he was going with this. When they first started dating, Patrick always had a way of crawling back after every faux pas and she'd always taken him back. Even when she knew he wasn't sincere. But she had truly believed he'd changed when he proposed marriage. He had promised he could accept the weirdness that was her life, and then he had left her.

"It took you seven years to discover that?"

"I never stopped caring about you."

"I don't believe you even gave me a second thought."

"That's not true. I wrote you many letters over the years."

"Funny. I never received a single word from you."

"Well, I didn't post any but I did write them and tear them up."

"You left me standing at the altar, Patrick. My father spent a fortune on a wedding that never happened. Did you ever consider compensating him? He almost lost his business over the debt. And for that matter, I don't remember seeing you at the funeral."

"I—I meant to attend. I wasn't sure if I would be welcome."

"Sure you did." With a wave of her arm she dismissed him. "Just go, Patrick. It's been a long day and I've had enough."

"There's something I need to discuss with you first."

"We've already been through this."

"No," he kept his eyes down as he took a deep breath. "It's a business matter."

"What business?"

"Your business. The health club."

"What about it?"

"I want in."

The uncharacteristic way Patrick got straight to the point sparked Anna's attention. She realized the significance. Normally, he would have done his usual hinting and bargaining, and then eased it into the conversation.

"Why?"

"It's a real money-maker, Anna. Derrick Corel isn't building it the way he could and it's not like he doesn't have the money."

"I've seen the books. He's doing a good job. The place looks great and it's full to the brim with clients. What more could he do?"

"I have lots of ideas." Patrick sat forward on the edge of his seat, he positively buzzed with enthusiasm. "More advertising, sexier staff in more alluring outfits. We could approach local celebrities for television commercials."

"I gather Derrick isn't interested in your ideas?" Now she understood the earlier confrontation. Patrick could be like a dog with a bone when he wanted something. Derrick would have good reason to lose his temper.

"He's narrow-minded. Says he doesn't need more money and he doesn't want his staff paraded around in their underwear."

"Understandable." She sipped her wine. "I don't know why you're coming to me with this?"

"You are half owner."

"Less than half Patrick. I only own forty percent."

"That would be enough to force him to listen to you. Make me your manager and I will make you a fortune. If I was the manager, we could spend more time together. I could prove to you how much I've changed. Please, Anna. Think it over?"

Anna crossed her arms, lifted one hand to her face and tapped on her chin. "Okay, I've thought about it. The answer is no."

He made a grab for her, managing to snag her right hand. "If you'd just—"

Anna pulled free of his grasp and stood up. "It's time for you to leave."

She escorted him to the front door, opened it and her followed her out.

As they stepped out onto the porch, there was a distinct drop in temperature. Anna hugged her shoulders and wished she had worn a cardigan over her bare arms. Her sleeveless cotton shirt provided no protection from the chill that peaked her nipples, and Patrick made no attempt to avert his eyes. There was a time when his hungry expression would have excited her, now it left her feeling exposed, vulnerable. The hem of her short skirt danced in the soft cool breeze, lifting slightly, sending a chill down her legs. She tried to hold the skirt down as the wind picked up and Patrick's eyes dropped to her bare legs.

"Patrick. I told you it's been a long night. Please go."

"I'd almost forgotten how beautiful you are." He moved closer. His hot breath against her neck. She moved away until her back connected with the wooden frame of the door, trapping her. As he leaned in for a kiss, she turned her head to the side.

"Patrick. I told you it's been a long night. Please go."

"The lady asked you to leave."

"How the hell—"

Derrick shoved Patrick aside as he stepped between them. His smooth voice was edged with annoyance as he addressed Patrick.

"Must I forcibly remove you?" His biceps rippled as he clenched and unclenched his fists. *Oh, my god. He's going to hit him.* She reached up to grip his bicep and gave a small squeeze.

"There's no need to get physical. Patrick was leaving."

"Okay, but only because *you* asked." Patrick

smiled but Anna could see the fear in his eyes. He nodded to Anna. "Promise me you'll think about my request?"

Reluctantly, she nodded. It was the only way she could think of to calm the situation. Patrick gave Derrick one final defiant scowl and then turned on his heels and left. The moment he was out of ear-shot Anna challenged Derrick.

"What gives you the right to order people from my home?"

Derrick lifted his hands, palms up, in the air. "He was making moves on you. I was trying to help."

"What if I had *wanted* him to make moves on me?" Anna argued as she leaned against the doorframe. A tremor ran through her body. Patrick was not one to take no for an answer. *What if Derrick hadn't arrived when he did?*

"No—you didn't. You asked him to leave. I heard you. I also saw the way you covered yourself in his presence. That is not the act of someone wanting to be kissed."

"You were spying on me?"

"I was on my way up the drive. You were busy arguing and didn't notice me. I heard the conversation and noticed the way that Miller was leering at you. I saw the way that Patrick was reacting to your body when the wind lifted your skirt."

Anna strained to look down the dimly lit path. It was possible he was telling the truth but she doubted it. There was something in his eyes that told her there was more to it than that.

"What do you want anyway?"

"I think we should go inside before you catch your death." Cradling her elbow, he maneuvered her into the house.

"What? This time you walk straight in? Last time

you were here you asked permission to enter."

"That was then. I had never been in your home before so it was polite to ask."

"Not even when Dad was alive?"

"Of course I was here when Jake was alive, many times."

"Did you ask him permission to enter?"

"Yes. On the first occasion I did."

"You're a strange man, Derrick Corel. A really, really, strange man."

"And if I'm not mistaken, you Miss Derwent, have been drinking."

Anna shrugged. "Do you want one?"

She stopped at the fridge, expecting him to react. His left eyebrow rose as she poured a glass but he didn't comment, besides answering, "Sure, why not?"

"Aren't you going to belittle me for drinking from a cask?"

"I'm not even going to comment on the wine being stored in the refrigerator."

"But you just did."

Another flash of the dimples, followed by a deep, throaty laugh. Anna's heart somersaulted in her chest. She handed him a glass and sat beside him on the couch.

"Let's change the subject. What was Patrick Miller doing here?"

Despite her reluctance to share information with her new partner, Anna felt a compulsion to tell him anything he asked. She wondered if it was the cheap wine loosening her tongue or if it was the way those blue violet eyes broke down her resistance. Whatever the case, she told him the whole story.

"What are you going to do?" He placed his glass on the table beside hers.

"It's not up to me. You own the majority share.

You built the business to where it is today."

"Let's get something straight, Anna," he reached for her shoulders, holding her gently. She placed her hands on his chest to keep him at a safe distance but left her arms limp enough that she could feel his breath on her face. "You are just as much a part of the gym as I am."

Anna nodded. "I guess the place is in my blood. Dad loved it and I loved being there with him. To be honest, Derrick, being there makes me feel closer to him. In a way, it's my sanctuary."

He leaned closer, nuzzling his cheek against her neck, his soft hair tickling her skin while his masculine scent assaulted her senses. He released her arms to run his fingers through her hair.

"Nice," she murmured, closing her eyes as she eased her head back into his palms. "That's really nice."

"What about your mother? Jake never discussed her. Was she involved in the fitness industry?"

Anna opened her eyes as the familiar pang hit her. "My mother died as a result of a car accident when I was only a child."

Derrick cupped her cheek in his large palm. She nuzzled against it.

"I'm sorry."

"Me too. I was so young when she died that I feel I know hardly anything about her."

"Your father didn't speak of her?"

"Rarely." She swallowed the lump caught in her throat. "I don't believe he ever fully recovered from her death. He would tear up every time I asked him about her so I gave up trying. I couldn't bear to hurt him."

Derrick's arm crept behind her and he drew her into his chest. "David and I had a younger sister. Her name was Isabelle. When she died, she took a part of me with her."

"Was she ill?"

Derrick's bicep flexed, his grip tightened around her shoulders. "No, she was killed by her two-timing husband."

"Oh. How horrible." She lifted her head from his chest and looked up into his eyes.

His eyes lowered to her lips which she parted, expecting, no hoping for a kiss. He hesitated.

"Anna." He said quietly, his voice barely above a whisper. "Do you still have feelings for Patrick?"

"I don't think so but, maybe he really has changed."

"I don't believe that for a moment." Derrick snapped his face away from hers. "His type will never change. He will only bring you heartache. Stay away from him Anna."

"Strange, he said the same thing about you."

"What else did he say about me?" He leaned back against the lounge. His shoulders stiffened and his eyebrows knit but he kept his arm around her.

"Nothing besides warning me away from you." She mirrored his expression, frowning as she asked him, "Are you hiding a dark secret? What does Patrick know that I don't?"

"Patrick Miller is looking for an easy way to make money. He believes that my associates can offer him an affluent lifestyle. Possibly they can, but the price is high and if he succeeds I worry…" He shook his head and looked down at the floor.

"What worries you?" she pinched his chin between her finger and thumb, lifting it so their faces were only inches away.

"I worry that he will not be the only one to pay the cost." He reached out with his free arm. She allowed him to draw her closer, their bodies pressed together, his lips inches away from her mouth as he gazed into her eyes. His eyes blazed with desire.

"Anna." He sighed as he took possession of her mouth. His lips pressed against her with moist heat, overwhelming her senses with cravings for more kisses.

She wanted him. Needed him. Ached for his touch on her skin.

When he eased the cotton shirt up from her waist, she lay back, raising her arms over her head. He tenderly kissed the junction of her breasts, her cleavage strained against the lacy fabric of her bra as she leaned against his mouth, his moist lips sending a flood of warmth through her breasts. She lay back while he pulled the elastic-waist skirt down her hips, pausing to kiss the yellowing bruises on her thighs. She squirmed on the lounge, lifting her legs out of the skirt and wrapping them around his waist while she fumbled with the buttons on his silk shirt. As she leaned forward to peel the shirt from his torso, he unfastened the clasp on her bra spilling her breasts into his cupped hands. She gasped as he lowered his head to suck a nipple into his open mouth and arched her back, digging her nails into the flesh of his bare skin. When she could stand no more, she traced her hands back to his waist and began to unfasten his belt.

"I feel so safe around you," she whispered into his ear. "Despite the shadow that hovers over your aura."

"What?" Derrick pinched her chin between his fingers and stared into her eyes. "Why would you say that?"

Words tumbled unrestrained from her mouth. *I can trust him.* "I know how it feels to keep secrets."

Derrick's expression hardened but his tone remained gentle, intoxicating. "What's *your* secret?"

She ran her fingers lightly over his chest causing

his skin to ripple in response. "I don't know what my father told you about me but … here goes. I can't be around large groups of people. Actually, I don't like being around more than one person at a time. You see … I am what they call an empath. I feel the emotions of others. I feel their pain, their anger, and their desperation. It's horrible. Sometimes alcohol helps numb the emotions but the relief is usually only temporary."

"That must be terribly difficult for you." He kissed her neck, her shoulder while she continued to stroke his skin on his back.

"All my life, people have been uncomfortable around me and I feel miserable around them. It's like I have multiple personalities." Tears burned behind her eyes as she confessed "I just want to be like any other *normal* person, Derrick. The only feelings I want to experience are my own. I'm never sure if my emotions are my own or someone else's."

"Is that all you want?"

Anna forced her shoulders back and gazed into his eyes. *I could spend the rest of my life staring into his handsome face.* "No. That's not all I want." She cupped his head in her hand and kissed him. His mouth scorched her lips. He returned the kiss, his tongue stoking the flames of her desire. She told him in between kisses, "I need someone strong enough to cope with my idiosyncrasies…"

"What else?" He asked as he fondled her bare breasts. His lips kissed a trail down to her nipple and he drew the hardened peak into his mouth, moving his tongue around the tip in agonizingly slow circles.

She gasped and let out a tiny groan as she held his head to her chest. "I want the whole shebang. Walks on the beach, making love on the sand while the sun warms our skin, and eventually children." She slipped her fingers inside the waistband of his trousers and fumbled with the zipper.

His mouth stilled on her breast. His hand closed over hers.

"You should have those things. You deserve those things. But, I can't give them to you."

"I don't understand. I thought you—"

"I *do*, more than you know."

"Then why?" she attempted to pull his head towards her, lower his mouth to her lips but he refused to budge.

He retrieved his shirt from the floor and passed her the cotton shirt he had earlier removed, turning away as she covered herself. "Your gift of empathy, your description of the simple pleasures that you enjoy, I just—"

"Just what? No, let me finish that sentence for you. You just need excitement, travel, night life. You love nightclubs and gambling, fast cars and fast women." *Like I haven't heard that before.*

"No. No, nothing like that." He reached for her but she raised her arm to stop him as he offered an apology. "I don't want to see you get hurt."

"Spare me the platitudes." Humiliation washed over her. She had opened her heart to him and had it ripped from her chest. Worse still, her body still felt the impression of his hands, and her lips tasted the sweetness of his kiss. She tried to draw on her gift to ascertain his mood but she could sense nothing but the erratic beating of her own heart. "You think I'm not good enough for you."

"No. That's not what I said, not what I meant."

"I few minutes ago you were more than ready to take me ... here on the lounge," She motioned to the bulge in his pants, "but, I scared you away by revealing my secret."

Derrick scratched his head. "It's true. Although I appreciate your honesty and the courage it took to tell me, you've made me realize that I can't give you what you desire. There is no hope of living a *normal* life with me. It just isn't possible."

Anna shook her hands in frustration. Tears ached in her throat and she was desperate to hide her pain from this man. She had opened her heart to him, revealed intimate secrets and he had crushed her. "How would you know that? You didn't even give me a chance to demonstrate my feelings for you. You know nothing about me."

"Maybe so, but I know *me*." He turned towards the door. "Making love with you could never be a one-night stand. To me, it would be a commitment—a demonstration of love."

"Then why—?"

"Because it would never work out."

"I see." Anna rose to her feet and led him towards the door. "I think you should leave."

Derrick left without another word, closing the door behind him as he disappeared into the night leaving Anna mortified. She threw herself onto the couch and cried, realizing that once again she had allowed a man to crush her spirit and make her feel worthless.

****

Anna came to a decision during the night as she paced the lounge room, wringing her hands. She had always considered her abilities a curse, making her an oddity that separated her from the normal world and prevented her from living a normal life. Judging by the visions and premonitions that had recently developed, her "otherness" would only drive a bigger wedge between her and the world. *Damn the world and damn Derrick.* She would transform herself into the type of woman both Derrick and Patrick doubted she could be—then, she would play them against each other and when she had them both completely under her spell, she would sell her share of the business and leave town … for good.

Chapter Five

"Good morning, Susie."

"Well, what a surprise," Susie said between puffs as Anna ran out the front door to join her on her morning jog. "I really didn't expect to see you today."

"I wasn't sure I would be here either," Anna confessed. In her attempt to block out her emotional evening, she had almost emptied the wine cask on her own. "But I need to burn off some emotional baggage."

"Sounds like man troubles. Anyone I know?"

Anna ignored her new friend's question and picked up her pace. Running along the road to the beach gave her a chance to tune out the world and concentrate only on the sound of her shoes as they slapped against the bitumen. When they reached the beach, they stopped and drank deeply from their water bottles, Susie the first to break the silence.

"Tell me boss, who's the guy that has you steamed?"

"Actually, there are two men who are driving me mad." Anna took another swallow from her bottle while Susie tried to encourage her with a quizzical look. "It's a bit complicated."

"I would be happy to take one of your problems off your hands," Susie told her, "especially if they are both good looking."

Anna nodded and smiled but the smile only reached one corner of her mouth. Two handsome men professing to care for her yet neither willing to share her strange way of life.

"I'll race you to the gym," she called over her shoulder as she bolted in the direction of the gym, grateful in the knowledge that Derrick would not be around when she arrived.

"That was a great workout." Susie gasped as they entered the gym. "Luckily I have a change of clothes in my locker or else my clients would be complaining about my personal hygiene."

Anna lifted her arm above her head and sniffed. "I guess I'll need to run back home and have a shower." In her haste to join Susie, she had forgotten to grab her backpack with her change of clothes.

"Not necessary." Susie grabbed her elbow and led her to the supply room. "One of the perks of being the boss is that you can take what you want." She motioned to the shelves full of gym clothing, and then began to sort through the rows of bike pants and t-shirts checking for sizes. "Here, these ought to fit." She threw the items to Anna who had already located a sports bra and undies in her size. She was amazed by the range of clothing the club appeared to sell. The women walked into the staff-only ladies room with the new clothes in tow.

"Do you have your lanyard?"

Anna nodded and removed the lanyard that held her identification card and keys from her short's pocket.

"If you check inside your locker—Susie pointed to the row of lockers in the change area—"you'll find the locker key on your lanyard next to the office keys. Derrick called me last night. He must have realized that he hadn't told you about your locker. He was pretty insistent that I show you today. You'll find a bag of toiletries and a couple of towels."

"You're kidding? The gym supplies us with toiletries?"

"Yep. This is the best place I've ever worked. Derrick treats us staff like we're gold. I've never had such a great boss." She turned back to Anna tilted her head and winked. "Until you of course."

"Suck up." Anna smiled as she opened the locker marked with her name using the key that Derrick had supplied on an earlier tour of the building. Her mouth dropped open in surprise. "Wow."

"Hey, no fair." Susie flung open the locker door. "I didn't get anything like this. This sucks."

"I thought Derrick was the best boss in the whole wide world?"

"Yeah, so did I, until now. Geez, Anna … Chanel." She took the large bottle of perfume from the top shelf to examine the packaging. "All I got was a can of perfumed deodorant." Rifling through the other packages she continued her inventory. "Shower gel, body lotion, talc, salon quality shampoo, and conditioner … Anna, there's even a cosmetic case."

Anna opened the case with Susie breathing down her neck squealing with enthusiasm and delight.

"Oh that's it. I'm putting in a complaint." Susie almost snatched the case from Anna's hands. "I couldn't afford all this if I saved for a month. You lucky duck, there's even a couple of Nike tracksuits in here." She rifled through the contents of the locker. "And what's this…."

Lifting a hanger from the rod, Susie held out a dress covered in clear plastic with a note attached.

Anna ignored the slinky black frock to read the note. "My sincere apologies for last night's behavior. Please join me for dinner tonight."

"Shoes too!" Susie was still sorting through the treasures in the locker. "Asics gels and a pair of black stilettos. Damn girl, what do I have to do to get all this? Or should I ask, what did you do?"

"I didn't do anything." Anna hung the dress back in the locker. "Derrick made it perfectly clear that I'm not good enough for him."

"Ah, so he's the one who got your knickers in a knot this morning. By the looks of all this, I think he's trying to make amends."

"I can't be bought."

"Anna," Susie shook her by the shoulders. "In all the years I've worked here, I've never seen Derrick give a woman *anything* like this. Sure, he's generous and kind but there is no way he would try to buy someone's affection. There is no need. Women throw themselves at him every day but he never gives them any encouragement. Since you arrived in town, I've noticed a change in him. He lights up when you walk into the room. Seriously … he has it bad."

"That doesn't change the fact that he told me that it would never work out."

"He told you that?"

"Verbatim."

"I'm shocked. Well, I guess still waters run deep. What are you going to do about it?"

"Last night I made up my mind to become the type of woman he and Patrick want. When I have them in the palm of my hand, I'll crush them and leave them in my wake."

"You go girl. Wait a minute … who's Patrick?"

"That's another story."

"Your stories sound a bit nasty. Does this one have anything to do with spending the night throwing up?"

Anna nodded and laughed.

"Well, I still need to freshen up so you can tell me while we shower." Susie took her own toiletry bag from her locker and retrieved a towel and a change of clothes. She turned to see Anna staring blankly at the contents of her locker.

"You know, Anna. If you're truly serious about

becoming the woman of their dreams, you have all the weapons right in front of you."

****

The day flew by quickly and by the evening, Anna had decided to take her new friend's advice and take Derrick up on his dinner invitation. She spent an hour readying herself for the date using the armory of weapons he had supplied and when she'd finished, she felt prepared for battle. She made her way to the foyer to wait for her prey.

"I see you've been in your locker."

Anna spun around to face Derrick, expecting to see him in his usual attire of white canvas training Gi. Her heart skipped a beat. Dressed in a navy blue evening suit and cream-colored silk shirt, his dark hair combed back and a twinkle in his eye, he looked the epitome of masculinity. Handsome didn't come close to describing him. He was perfect. The sight of him, standing before her in with his youthful good looks and smelling so agreeable, made it difficult to remember why she had been so angry in the first place.

"Not teaching tonight?" she asked casually, hoping he wouldn't notice the catch in her breath.

"I called in a favor. Are you ready to go?"

"Don't I look ready?"

As Anna did a little swirl, her new black dress floated in soft waves around her knees. Derrick caught a whiff of her perfume—Chanel. She was wearing the fragrance he had bought for her and as he had suspected, the combination of her body chemistry blending with the designer fragrance made for an exquisite scent. He breathed in her fragrance, closing his eyes as he savored the moment before returning his focus to her beautiful face. He noticed that she had drawn some of her coppery curls back to produce a half up style and the effect drew attention to her eyes, making them sparkle with life. Her makeup was understated despite the fact he had purchased enough product to cover every season and color according to the sales assistant, but he liked it that way. Anna's features didn't need artificial enhancement. She was a natural beauty. Staring at her pouty bowed lips, he fought the urge to kiss the glossy pink color from her mouth.

"Well, do I?"

"Oh, sorry." Derrick realized he had been caught up in the moment and was still staring. "You look beautiful, Anna, absolutely stunning."

"Where are we going anyway?"

"It's a surprise," he answered, offering his arm but no information about the evening.

As Derrick led Anna down the flight of stairs to the car park she tried not to let her emotions get the better of her. She had wanted to tell him that he looked pretty damn stunning himself but that would put the ball back in his court and she wanted to play it cool tonight.

Susie passed by, giving her a thumbs up signal and Anna smiled in reply despite the thumping of her heart.

Maybe this wasn't such a good idea after all? If they were going somewhere high class, she would surely do something to embarrass herself. The last time she'd tried to act upper class; she had spent the night feeling desperately ill and this time she was in the company of someone who was actually accustomed to living in high society. Patrick, by contrast, had been putting on airs and graces, he probably knew as much about the elite as she did. But there was something else that gnawed at her insides, something that warned her she would be in danger if she got into Derrick's car. By the time they reached his Porsche, she was hyperventilating.

"Maybe this isn't such a good idea." She told him as he opened the door.

"Why not?"

"I'm not feeling very well. I think I'd like to go home."

"Anna." Derrick stroked her cheek tenderly with his finger. "There's no need to be afraid. It's only dinner."

"I just don't feel like being around a lot of people, that's all." Her gut instinct warned her that there was danger waiting for her—a sinister presence watching, waiting.

"Well, luckily, there will be no one besides us." He helped her into the passenger seat before she had time to protest, then ran around to the driver's side.

"Where did you say we were going?" she asked once he started the engine.

"I didn't." he drove slowly out of the underground car park, passing a few people Anna recognized as gym patrons at the exit. Momentarily, she was distracted as a couple of women tried to see inside the car but the dark windows blocked their view. She was tempted to pull a face at the rude women who stared blatantly into the car

"They can't see us?" she asked.

"No."

"Why the tinted windows? Do you fancy yourself a rock star?"

"No. I just like my privacy."

"So you became a teacher and you work in the fitness industry. That doesn't make sense."

"Why not?"

"Wherever you go, people recognize you as their Sensei. I've seen the way students react to you, especially the females. You can't tell me you don't enjoy that."

"I enjoy teaching. The rest of it—well let's just

say that's a cross I have to bear." The corners of his mouth curved in a sly smile, as if he was remembering a joke.

"Then why do it?"

"Part of being a Martial Artist is sharing what you've learned with others. I have been fortunate enough to train with many masters over the years so I feel it is my duty to pass on my knowledge."

"That sounds noble." Her voice barely concealed her surprise. It didn't sound like the actions of a man who flaunted his wealth.

"It may *sound* noble but I haven't always acted that way. It may surprise you to know that there was a time when I went looking for fights. I was a bit of a brawler in my day. For many years I kept my experiences to myself and concentrated solely on making myself a stronger and faster fighter. Like you, I preferred to be alone."

His words touched a nerve. *Alone? No Derrick. That's far from the truth.* She wanted to tell him as much but the words caught in her throat. Instead she made light of the subject.

"You talk like an old man." Anna giggled. "In my day … we hung out at the local tavern…" she teased, in a voice mimicking his.

Derrick smiled. "It's nice to hear you laughing. I do believe that this is the first time I have heard you laugh since we met."

Anna's cheeks reacted with a slow burn. She turned her head to look out the window. She hadn't found many reasons to laugh since returning to her old home. "I haven't felt much like laughing lately."

She felt the slight pressure of his hand on her thigh as he gave her leg a squeeze.

"Well, the smile becomes you, you should do it

more often. I think that I'll make a point of trying to make you smile every day."

"And how will you do that?"

His laugh was immediate and intoxicating. He grinned wickedly as he said. "I have my ways."

After around thirty minutes of awkward silence with intermittent casual conversation concerning the freaky weather or the running of the gym, Derrick turned the car into a driveway and pressed a button on his dashboard to open the large metal gates that blocked their path. As they passed through the entrance, Anna gazed in wonder at the huge estate. They travelled for another half a kilometer before she noticed the huge house, high on a hill top surrounded by palm trees and lush gardens full of tropical flowers. She had lived on the Central Coast of N.S.W for most of her life and never knew this place existed. When she turned to Derrick with her mouth agape, he shrugged.

"What can I tell you? I always wanted to live in Hawaii."

"So why don't you? It looks like you can afford the move."

"The climate doesn't suit my … *condition*. I have allergies to the sunlight and as you probably know, Hawaii is sunny most of the time."

"I wouldn't know." The subject of Hawaii was a touchy one because she had made plans to go there with Patrick for their honeymoon. Worse still, he had taken some bimbo he hooked up with at his buck's party. She was still thinking about her wedding fiasco when Derrick pulled up in front of his house.

An elderly butler hurried over to open the door for Anna. "Good evening, ma'am. Master Derrick." He nodded to Derrick who was on his way around to her side of the car.

"Is everything ready, Evan?"

"Everything is as you instructed, sir." Evan shuffled up the stairs to the main door.

Anna noticed he had a slight limp and arthritis gnarled his hands. He struggled with the door knob. She thanked him as she stepped into the foyer and after excusing himself, he left for the kitchen.

"A little old to be still working isn't he?" She suspected he should be resting at this time of night, curled up on a couch in front of a television with a hot casserole and a cold beer.

"He's been with us for many years and refuses to retire." Derrick motioned for Anna to head down the hallway. "We only have him do a minimum of work now. It makes him feel useful and we can keep an eye on him."

"We?"

"My brother, David and I."

"Oh, that's right. Patrick told me you have a brother. He was with you at the restaurant."

Derrick nodded. He led Anna through the house and opened a large sliding door at the end of the hall. They stepped out onto the balcony. Anna stood transfixed. The scene was something from a fairy tale. The sound of violins floated through the night moments before the musicians stepped into sight. There was a small round table set for two. A fragrant candle burned in the center of the white lace tablecloth surrounded by fresh yellow and white frangipanis and pink hibiscus. Illuminating the surrounding area, a multitude of fairy lights twinkled and as the warm summer breeze caressed the flame of the candle, causing it to flicker, and the fragrance of tropical flowers filled the air. A crystal decanter of red wine sat beckoning to them beside its matching bohemian crystal goblets. Anna suspected that she had stepped into a dream.

"You've gone to a lot of trouble." Anna noticed as she accepted the seat Derrick had offered her. He tucked her in before taking the seat opposite.

"Do you like it?"

"Yes. It's very nice." The beauty of the setting was overwhelming but despite the enchanting atmosphere that Derrick had created, unease had settled in her chest. Her senses were on high alert. There was a foreboding in the wind, a hint of something rotten that even the fragrant candles and flowers could not mask. Something or someone posed a threat to her. Someone close by. *Stay cool*, she reminded herself.

Derrick reached out and touched her hand, his contact drawing her back to the conversation.

"I'm glad you like it." His beaming smile freed a kaleidoscope of butterflies in her stomach and lifted her spirits. "I wanted to make up for my behavior last night."

Almost as quickly as it arrived, his smile disappeared and his expression changed to annoyance as he glanced over Anna's shoulder. "Looks like we have a guest."

A tall, handsome man popped his head around the corner and made his way over to the table to stand beside Derrick. Anna recognized him as the brother, David. She would have known they were related had she not been told. He had the same dark hair and violet blue eyes but there was something different about this one besides his rounder chin and higher cheekbones … something wild and unreserved about him. He looked like the kind of man accustomed to getting his own way, especially with women.

Derrick crossed his arms over his chest and growled. "I thought you were out for the night?"

"On my way out, brother dear." He slapped Derrick across his back. "Aren't you going to introduce me to your little friend first?"

"Anna Derwent… this is my brother, David."

"A pleasure." David took the hand Anna extended and kissed the back of her palm, before turning it, lingering for a moment at the wrist. "Chanel?"

"How did you know?"

"I spend a lot of time in Paris." David's bottom rested on the arm of Derrick's chair, his attention focused on Anna. "That dress is from their spring collection."

"Is it?" She looked to Derrick for confirmation. Derrick nodded.

"So, do you spend a lot of time at French fashion parades?"

"Not unless I'm dragged there kicking and screaming by a beautiful woman." He grinned wolfishly. "But, I promise I won't protest if you want me to go to one with *you*."

The smile escaped Anna's lips before she had time to stop herself but when she saw the effect it had on Derrick, she was glad she did. He stared daggers at his brother.

"I've never been outside the country, David," she told him, eager to encourage the brother as she suspected it might get a rise out of Derrick.

"Then the world is a sorrier place for not ever meeting you." David's smile was disarming. Not as beautiful as Derrick's, but very cheeky and even contagious. She watched with delight as Derrick's face flushed with color.

Derrick rose from his seat with such force he almost upset the table. "Didn't you say you were leaving?"

"Aren't you going to offer me a glass of wine first?" he winked at Anna.

"Bugger off!" Derrick gripped the edge of the

small table. His knuckles turned white and Anna wondered if he would take a swing at his brother.

David ignored the curse. He lowered his gaze to Anna's chest and as he reached out his hand, she opened her mouth to protest. He lifted the cord supporting the stone on her pendant. The gesture appeared to infuriate Derrick even more but he returned to his seat as David remarked.

"Tiger eye. It's a lovely stone, always a favorite of mine."

"I saw it in a shop window the other day and felt compelled to buy it." Anna was surprised she had disclosed the information.

"It is supposed to protect the wearer from the evil eye." David turned to his brother. "As a matter of fact, there are many types of protective amulets and tiger eye is one of the most common."

The word common hit Anna with the intensity of a physical blow. *Common.* Is that what she was? Was that a message he was trying to convey to his brother? She noticed Derrick glare at David and wondered if he had come to the same conclusion. David seemed oblivious to her reaction as he continued to admire the pendant.

"But this one, this is a really lovely piece, Anna. The setting is very unusual, very rare. Do you know much about its designer?"

Self-recrimination flooded through her. Once again she had jumped to conclusions and taken offence at a casual remark that was not meant to slight her. She had been doing that more frequently and if she kept it up, she doubted she would have any friends. Her self-esteem had hit rock bottom and her nerves were frayed. She smiled at David and shook her head. "I found it in an Op shop. I have no idea of its history."

David allowed the cord to slip from his hand. "I

have a friend who would probably be able to tell you a lot more about it if you would like to know its origin. She has a knack of knowing things, if you know what I mean. She owns a crystal shop around the corner from the gym."

David snatched Anna's hand off the table to kiss it once more before saluting Derrick on his way out.

"Remember little Copper top. If you ever change your mind about Paris, I'll take you to places you'll never forget." He disappeared inside the house before either she or Derrick could respond.

"Please excuse my brother." Derrick apologized as he poured the wine. "Everything he says or does is for effect."

"Why should I be offended? At least he seems honest."

"You think me dishonest?"

"I don't think of you at all," she lied. She thought of little else since their first meeting. Mostly she thought about how much she wanted to see him naked in her bed.

"Anna, mon amour, my behavior last night was unforgiveable. Would you please allow me to try and make amends?"

"I may not have travelled but I do know that mon amour means 'my love' in French. I am not your love so don't call me that." She took a sip from her glass.

"It was merely a nickname."

"I don't like nicknames."

"You didn't seem to mind when David called you copper top?"

"Well, that's different."

In truth, she hadn't noticed his term of endearment but it didn't bother her now she knew how much it upset Derrick.

"How is that different?"

"I don't know. Listen, if you plan on interrogating me all night… I'd rather go home." She put down her glass and rose from the table ready to leave. The wind blew a leaf into her hair and in it she smelled the stench of decay. She picked it from her hair and looked anxiously around the patio for the source of the smell.

"No. Please stay." Reaching for her hand, he gently guided her back to the table. "We'll change the subject."

Anna nodded and sat back down. Her eyes quickly doing another scan of the area. The danger was closer. A chill spread its icy tentacles over her skin. She shivered.

"What would you like to talk about?" Derrick topped up her half empty glass and refilled his own. "I know. Let's talk about the health club," he took a sip from his glass "I'd like your opinion on the changes."

"Everything looks great although I can't understand how we could be making money with the free products you give away."

"Such as?"

Anna gestured to her dress. "If all the women's lockers are stocked with the goodies I received, I doubt we'll stay in business very long."

Derrick shook his head and rolled his eyes. "Ah. It seems I have unintentionally offended you once again."

"I won't be bought or paid off, Derrick. Material things mean nothing to me."

"It was my way of an apology. I should have known better than to accept the advice of my brother. He suggested that the gifts would smooth the waters between us. I realize now that it was a mistake."

Anna shrugged. "I guess you both *meant* well."

"So, you like the gifts?"

"Of course I do. I would have liked them more if I

had bought them for myself that's all."

"Well, if it makes you feel any better, in a way you did."

Anna raised an eyebrow. "Explain yourself."

"You plan to continue working in the gym, right?"

She nodded. "Go on."

"The gym clothes, shoes, toiletries etc. are a tax deduction. You need to look the part to work there."

"Okay. I'll accept those items but how do you explain the perfume and the evening wear?"

"Schmoozing the clients. Everyone does it. It's expected, especially in the fitness industry where customers need a role model to live up too."

"You're smooth, Corel. I'll give you that." She tried unsuccessfully to hide a smile.

"You *definitely* should do that more often."

"What?"

"Smile. You have a beautiful smile, Anna."

Anna lowered her chin and bit her bottom lip. Finishing the last drop of wine in her glass, she licked her lips appreciatively as she tried to change the subject.

"Mmm. This is really nice Derrick. I like even better than the one you paid for at the restaurant, which was very kind of you by the way. I might buy a few bottles." She allowed Derrick to top up her glass as she contemplated how bottled wine may improve her image. "Is it more expensive?" She noticed that Derrick was trying, unsuccessfully, to prevent his mouth curling at the sides. He cleared his voice before telling her.

"Around seven hundred dollars a bottle more."

Anna choked on the mouthful of wine, coughing and spluttering until Derrick patted her on the back. *Eight hundred dollars for a bottle of wine?* She could purchase six weeks' worth of groceries for that amount of money.

Stay cool, she ordered herself. *Act as though money wasn't an issue. Don't show him how unsophisticated you are. Change the subject.*

"So"—she coughed and excused herself—"David. He lives here with you?"

"Yes he does," Derrick's voice sounded serious. "Usually we get along quite well but he can also be a shameless flirt. Don't take anything he says seriously."

"I don't take *any* man seriously."

"I got that impression." Derrick waited until Evan served the entree and hobbled away. Before he had a chance to ask Anna about her statement, she fired out a question of her own.

"Why are you so dead set against giving Patrick a position at the club?"

"You can't hop from telling me you can't trust men, to asking me to employ the man who disillusioned you in the first place."

"What do you know about that?" The familiar sting of humiliation returned.

"Your father told me. Although he understood why you couldn't stay in town after the incident at the church, he never got over the disappointment of having you live so far away."

"I don't want to discuss this." She swallowed a mouthful of chicken and crab soup, trying to concentrate on the delicious flavor, anything to distract herself from the thoughts of her father. She missed him, so much.

"You brought it up." Derrick held his spoon up to his mouth but barely touched the soup.

"I'm still waiting for an answer to my question. What do *you* have against Patrick?"

"Patrick Miller has a reputation that could bring ill repute to our business. Your father worked long and hard to develop the character of the gym and I won't have that slimy little worm sullying your father's good name. Does that answer your question?"

"Not quite." Anna finished her soup and placed the spoon in her empty bowl for Evan to remove. "What has Patrick done to you to deserve being called—what was it you said? Slimy little worm wasn't it?"

"Isn't it enough that he hurt you?"

"No. You can't punish someone for not wanting to be with you. Besides, people can change." *Isn't that what she was trying to do?*

"A leopard can't change his spots."

"That's a bit judgmental isn't it?"

"Not in this case."

"But—"

"Look, Anna. I'm sorry to pull rank but it isn't going to happen. Not while I'm the major stock holder anyway."

As tempting as it was to argue, she could see Evan shuffling over with the second course wobbling precariously in his arthritic hands. She was about to take the tray from him. Derrick subtly shook his head. After the meal was served and Evan departed, she was given an explanation.

"I know you meant well but he would have been embarrassed. It isn't often I entertain, especially female guests and he has been looking forward to making everything perfect for you."

"How sweet." She licked her lips when Derrick uncovered the meal of Chinese fare. All were her favorites. Chicken Chow Mein, Beef in Black Bean sauce and San Choy Bow, served with a steaming plate of special fried rice. "These are my favorite dishes."

"I know. When I had meals with your father, he told me that you both loved Chinese food, especially these dishes."

"Thank you." She rewarded him with another smile. "I mean it, Derrick. Thank you for the meal, and also for being a friend to my dad when I wasn't around."

"My pleasure."

They ate their meal in relative silence, savoring the delicious offering while making small talk. Derrick was about to offer dessert when his words were interrupted.

"Master Derrick?"

Evan's voice sounded strained. Derrick excused himself and rushed inside, leaving Anna alone on the balcony. She rose from the table and did a lap of the terrace. The musicians had discretely moved inside but she could still hear the soft cords of a beautiful sonata as she descended the stairs adjacent to the terrace to inspect the grounds. The estate was massive, larger than anything she had seen in magazines and although dark outside, the garden was bathed in soft light from the numerous imitation bamboo torches lining the paths.

As she neared a clearing in the thick tropical setting, a familiar, gut wrenching sensation took hold of her. Danger awaited her at the next turn. She stopped abruptly and surveyed her surroundings. Even the moon had taken refuge behind a heavy cover of clouds. The crickets ceased their chatter as if they too were waiting for something to happen. Anna held her breath. For most of her life she had suppressed the visions that her doctors had tried to explain away as ocular migraines but now, there was no disputing the seriousness of the auras that colored her sight.

Recently, since the death of her father, she had begun to experience memories of earlier years spent with her parents. These memories—which often appeared in her dreams—revealed an aspect of her mother that she had somehow repressed since her mother's death. An aspect which seem to explain why Anna was sometimes able to predict the future or sense danger. She now understood that what she had was what some people call a gift and that the ability was hereditary. Now, at this very moment, the gift was screaming at her … run!

Chapter Six

"What are you doing out here?"

She turned and drew a sharp breath placing her hand to her chest.

Derrick looked agitated and appeared to be looking for something before he grabbed Anna's elbow and began to steer her back towards the house.

"Yes, little Anna." Agreed the dark stranger who stepped from behind a large alocasia to their left. "It isn't safe to wander around this particular estate at night. You never know what might be lurking in the bushes."

Anna stood rooted to the spot. This tall, twisted, skinny man with sunken cheeks and long yellow fingernails acted as if he knew her and worse still, somehow he did seem familiar to her. Although she couldn't remember his face, it was as though he played an important part in her life. Derek's nostrils flared and he frowned as he addressed the stranger.

"I heard that you were back in town. What are you doing here, Torke? You know you're not welcome in my home."

"And so, I wait in your garden." The mysterious stranger smiled menacingly at the couple as Derrick shifted Anna behind him. "Besides, Derrick, the view from the garden is prettier," he winked at Anna "much prettier."

Anna's throat began to throb, her neck pained her and she fought the impulse to cover the healing wound near her carotid artery. Torke's dark eyes bore into her. Her stomach churned at the sight of him. His facial skin appeared to be rotting, like a type of leprosy and the smell … it was the vilest stench she had ever experienced. He looked as though he had clawed his way out of a grave and, although she had never before entertained any real belief that such a creature existed outside of the movies, she suddenly knew exactly what he was. A vampire.

"Leave." Derrick squared his shoulders at the intruder who shrugged off the territorial stance. "Before I physically remove you from my property."

"Tsk, tsk, Derrick. Don't be so rude. Before you and your brother arrived, I was the leader of this area. My visit is purely a courtesy call to inform you that I have returned and I intend to take back control." He turned his gaze back to Anna and added. "I have unfinished business here."

Hate laced his words. Hate aimed at her, although she couldn't understand what she could have done to incite those feelings in someone she had never met. Footsteps pounded behind her and turned in time to see David hurrying towards them with long, focused strides. His playful demeanor gone, replaced by a solemn expression and a look of determination as he stared down the vampire.

"So, the rumors of your return were not unfounded."

"I suddenly found myself drawn back."

"You have no jurisdiction here anymore." Derrick told him. "David is the leader now."

"Funny," Torke pointed out in a gleeful tone, "I was told you and your brother were joint leaders."

"That's true." David agreed, casting Derrick a warning look that he reacted to with a forced sigh.

Their eyebrows shifted in silent correspondence. Anna gasped. It was almost as though they were communicating telepathically.

"If you can't even agree on who is in charge, how can you expect to protect those in your care?"

Derrick drew back his shoulders, his jaw tightened. He clenched his fists, his knuckles turning white as he edged towards Torke. She expected him to take a swing at the intruder, but, before he could act, they were joined by another couple who had silently come up from behind them.

"You called?" said the huge man in a deep monotone voice.

Anna guessed by the way he towered over her five feet four-inch frame; and stood at least six inches above Derrick, he must be over seven feet tall. The stranger's female companion gave him a backhanded slap across his broad chest.

"Don't mind Stan, Derrick," said the petite dark haired woman with a roll of her eyes. "He's been watching re-runs of the Addams family on television," she turned back to her companion "and it's 'you rang' you idiot."

"You watched them too, Celeste," Stan protested, his voice now musical and animated.

"What's the skinny?"

Anna spun around. Another guest had appeared from nowhere. He looked young. Anna guessed around twenty. He turned his attention on her. "Oolala. Who's the babe?" he sniffed the air "Dinner guest?"

Derrick looked agitated as more and more "guests" materialized from the darkness. "Why did you call a meeting, David?" He slipped an arm around Anna's shoulders and squeezed protectively. She leaned into his embrace, somehow aware of the increasing danger and grateful for Derrick's protective stance.

"I'm sorry, Derrick. I wouldn't have upset your dinner plans without a good reason." She noticed that David kept a close eye on the group.

When Derrick grabbed Anna's hand and led her

away from the growing crowd of strangers who seemed to be choosing positions either behind David or Torke, Anna made no attempt to resist. Neither did she look back for fear of what she might see. As frightened as she was of leaving with Derrick at this minute, she knew the real threat was a number of people in the group they left behind. The air rippled with electricity and Anna sensed a power in the group that she had never experienced before. It was clear that these people had never suppressed their abilities and the closer she came to them, the harder it was to hold her own at bay. It was almost as though she was somehow connected to them, that a psychic door had been opened to her.

Evan had parked the car directly outside the front doors in readiness for their swift departure and Derrick almost pushed Anna into her seat before running to the driver's side and turning the ignition.

"Is David in some sort of trouble? Will those people hurt him?" she finally found the courage to ask as they sped away from the house.

"What do you mean, Anna?"

"I have been slow on the uptake, Derrick, but I've finally figured it out."

"Figured what out?"

"The cold skin, only coming out at night, tinted car windows, pretending to eat … shall I go on?"

"All right, so you guessed it." He stared straight ahead at the road "I have allergies to the sun. I thought I already told you? It's an embarrassing condition and I don't like to discuss it."

"The other night … you *licked* blood of my neck. How do you explain that?"

"It was an impulse. I have no idea why I did it."

"How long have you been a vampire?"

"You've been watching too many horror movies,

Anna. There are no such things as vampires."

"Fine then, why don't you meet me at the gym tomorrow morning at 8 a.m.? We can discuss this after you join me in a morning swim at the beach."

"Sorry, I'm busy in the morning," He turned his head slightly to reveal a wicked smile. "I'll take you for that swim after 7 p.m."

"Ah, huh." Anna pointed her index finger accusingly. "I knew it."

"You knew I was busy? I guess I do lead a hectic life."

Anna shook her head. Derrick knew exactly what she meant. He was endeavoring to put her off the scent with humor. It wasn't going to work. There was a visible change in his demeanor. Despite his jovial words and sarcasm, his expression had darkened. There was no hiding the concern etched on his perfect face.

"I knew you wouldn't be able to come out in the daylight."

"Nonsense, Anna." This time his tone sounded more agitated. "Leave this silly witch hunt alone."

"Fine." Anna sat silently, her arms crossed over her chest the rest of the drive to her home, hoping to think of a way to trap him into a confession. By the time they pulled up outside her house, she had formulated a plan.

David stepped out of the car and walked around to the passenger side door. As he opened it, he offered his hand and helped Anna out. They stood motionless for a moment until Derrick suddenly leaned forward and kissed her cheek.

"Good night, Anna. I'm sorry we were forced to finish the evening early. I had hoped to make this evening memorable."

And you think this wasn't? Anna found it difficult

to keep the words to herself. Instead, she asked, "Why does it have to finish early? Wouldn't you like to come in for a while?" *You can't leave yet! Not until I get to the bottom of this.*

Derrick leaned back against the door of the car and folded his arms across his chest as his eyebrows drew into a frown. "You hardly talked to me all the way here. Why the sudden mood swing?"

Anna gazed down at her feet, buying time while she tried to think of an excuse. "I'm sorry if I seemed distracted. I was … disappointed that our dinner was interrupted. It was going so well."

"It was beginning feel that way. Especially after you acknowledged my friendship with your father."

Anna grinned. Derrick had gifted her with an excuse to draw out the evening. "Exactly!" she said, a little too enthusiastically. "I mean, it would mean a lot to me if you came inside and told me a bit more about your conversations with my father."

Derrick shook his head and grimaced. "As much as I would like to come inside, I think I should find out why we have unexpected guests at the manor."

She grabbed his arm and edged closer to him as she lowered her chin and pouted. "Please, Derrick. I'm feeling a bit rattled by all those unexpected guests, especially that Torke guy." She involuntarily shuddered as she recalled his features. "I'd feel much safer if you came in for a while."

Derrick's shoulders drooped. He sighed and nodded. "For a while."

She held tight to his arm with both hands as they walked up the path to the house, worried that he might change his mind. He had every right to wonder about the house guests. They were the strangest group of people that she had ever met. She worried about David. They had left him outnumbered and despite Derrick's insistence to the contrary, she knew he was in the company of dangerous creatures who may or may not have his best interests at heart.

"Do you think David will mind being left alone to entertain your guests?" *That was a reasonable question, right? Something quite normal to ask?*

"David is in charge of that particular group of people. I guess you'd call him the director. A spiritual guide perhaps. It was David who called the meeting. That's the reason Evan called me inside … to warn me they were coming."

"Warn?"

"Evan thought their presence would disturb our meal, which it did. He was giving us the opportunity to sneak away before you were bothered by their … peculiar ways."

"Why did David call a meeting anyway? Wasn't he out on a date?" Anna unlocked the front door and stepped inside. Derrick remained on the porch.

"A matter of great importance came up. Evan informed me that while he was out on his date David was made aware of a serious matter that needed urgent attention."

"What was that?"

"I wouldn't know, Anna. Maybe you should ask David?"

"Maybe I will." And while she was at it, she'd pump Evan for information too. Hopefully, the elderly servant would be the talkative type.

"Wine?" she asked as she headed towards the kitchen.

"Ah, give me a minute." He disappeared and returned with a bottle of the red she had enjoyed at dinner. "Why don't we drink this?" he offered as he took the wine glasses from her hands and poured them each a glass.

With hands on hips she said. "You expected to be asked inside?"

"Not expected … hoped. I asked Evan to put a bottle in the car."

"I can live with that." Anna tapped her glass against Derrick's in a toast. "What should we drink to?"

"To Jake. A fine man and a good friend."

Anna raised both her glass and her eyes to the ceiling. "To Dad."

A flood of emotions bubbled to the surface. She had been raised to be better than this. Better than the person Patrick had forced her to become. For the last couple of days, she had pushed her grief down deep, focusing solely on her efforts to discover as much as possible about her new partner. She lowered her head, hoping to hide the tears that threatened behind her eyes.

"I'm sorry if I've stirred up painful memories."

Anna raised her head as Derrick took the glass from her hand and gently eased her onto the sofa. He positioned himself beside her, their knees touching as he took her hands in his. His compassion soothed her, comforted her, and informed her that she was safe in his company. If he was indeed a blood sucking fiend, he wished her no harm. Not at this moment anyway.

"Anna. Are you all right? You glazed over there for a moment."

"Oh, sorry." Anna blinked away the tears. "It's been a strange night."

"Would you like me to leave?"

"No! I mean, no. Please stay a while longer. I was just thinking about my Dad, that's all. I was wondering … how did you meet him?"

"Let me think?" His fingers lightly brushed her

hands as he spoke. The sensation so intimate, so arousing she could barely concentrate on his story. "It was around seven years ago. I had been out for a stroll one evening and found myself outside your father's gym. There was a commotion out the back and I followed the sound of the voices around to the back alley. Your father was trying to evict a couple of hooligans from the building and they had no intention of leaving until they'd caused significant damage. I offered my services."

"So in other words, you beat the hell out of them?"

Derrick's laugh came out of the blue. So did Anna's reaction to the delicious tones in his warm chuckle. Her skin prickled from the top of her head to the tip of her toes.

"Not as serious as that my little firecracker, but let's just say … your father never had trouble from those particular people again."

"So, he invited you to become a partner in order to protect his business from thugs?"

"Not straight away." He held up the wine bottle and Anna accepted a top up. "We became friends first. It was around six months later on before we decided it was in both our interests to join forces, so to speak."

"I wonder why Dad never mentioned you." She gasped and lowered her eyes. "Sorry, that sounded a bit rude didn't it?'

"Not at all. It's a perfectly reasonable question."

He leaned back on the sofa but kept their skin to skin contact. She shivered as his shirt gaped open, exposing his chest. Heat flooded her cheeks. She was grateful for the distraction when Derrick continued his story.

"Your father once told me that he worried about you in the 'big city' and didn't want to add to your concerns with his own problems. According to him, you have control issues."

"Is that what he told you?" She shook her head in disbelief. How could her father think she had control issues? Just because she wasn't comfortable being told what to do? Or was it the need to keep to a routine in order to cope? *Maybe ... maybe he knew her better than she knew herself?* "What else did he tell you about me?"

"He told me how much he missed you. How he detested Patrick Miller for hurting you and driving you away, although, he never thought the man was good enough for you in the first place."

"Is that so?" Anna kicked off her shoes and tucked her feet up under her as her body relaxed. *It must be the wine.* Warmth spread over her. She yawned and stretched out her arms behind her as sleep threatened to take her. She imagined how it would feel to curl up and sleep in his arms. "Tell me more?"

"Such as?"

"Why would you want to invest in a run-down gym when you could just as easily start a better one in competition?"

"I had no real interest in owning a gym. I only suggested the partnership in order to help your father. Until I met Jake, I was a bit self-absorbed."

"So, you're not perfect after all." Her hand shot to her mouth and her eyes widened. *Did I say that out loud?*

"I don't ever remember saying I was." He leaned closer, his cool breath icy against her cheek. "Did you form that opinion yourself?"

"You're changing the subject."

"I thought I *was* the subject?" he flashed his dimples. "Fine. Ask away."

"It's my fault Dad had to take on a partner isn't it? I crippled him financially with the failed wedding reception."

"No. No, I don't believe that." He slipped his arm around her shoulders and drew her into his body. "The fitness industry is a fickle business. It was a slow year."

Anna knew she should object to the physical contact but her body betrayed her, warming to his touch. She leaned her head against his cool chest and took comfort in his arms. "So you don't think it was my fault?"

He kissed her forehead. A small gesture, but filled with intimacy. "Just a twist of fate."

"Derrick. Do you think … did he ever say anything to imply that he was disappointed in me?"

"Never! Your father loved you more than anything else in the world. He told me so daily in words and actions. Did you know he kissed your photograph every time he entered this room?"

"I had no idea."

"I have a confession to make, Anna."

Anna lifted her chin and became lost in his eyes. "Yes, Derrick."

"I was jealous."

"Jealous? Of me or my father?"

"Both, I guess." He lowered his eyes and his eyelashes fluttered a little. The butterflies in her stomach took flight as she listened to his confession. "My own father died when I was only in my early twenties and he had never shown me the sort of affection that Jake had for you."

Anna took a deep breath before asking, "And why were you jealous of him?"

"Because he had you in his life. And because— even though it was only a pale imitation of the real thing—the photo was a reminder of your love."

An overwhelming sense of guilt washed over her.

She reached up to cup his cheek, gaze into his perfect eyes. "I owe you an apology. I don't know what's gotten into me lately. I have been so rude when all you have shown me is understanding and kindness."

"You have nothing to apologize for. You've lost a parent," he reminded her.

"Along with my manners." She added with a shy smile. "But that is about to change. Things will be different from now on."

"For instance?" he leaned back against the sofa, his grip around her shoulders tightening as he twisted a few strands of her hair around his fingers. Her heart missed a beat in reaction to the intimate gesture. She lightly brushed his chest with her fingertips as he kissed the top of her head. She felt safe in his arms. Safe enough to forget her suspicions.

"For instance..." Her fingers traced a path from his square jaw to cup his head in her palm, pulling his mouth down to meet hers, "...this."

For the briefest moment, he melted into the kiss but almost as fast, he pulled away.

"I wish with all my heart that we could be together Anna but I would only end up hurting you."

"I'm a big girl, Derrick." She slid her hand inside his shirt and traced his chest with her fingertips, savoring the feeling as his skin reacted with goose flesh. There was no hiding his attraction. His body told her what his words could not. There was no doubt in her mind that he wanted her just as much as she wanted him. "I can look after myself." She found his nipple and gave it a squeeze between her fingers, watching with delight as he closed his eyes and moaned.

"No ... you can't." he pushed her away and held her at arm's length. "I am a dangerous man, Anna. I deal with treacherous people every day. You would never be safe."

"Treacherous people. You mean vampires?"

"You're like a dog with a bone aren't you? You won't give up on this ridiculous notion?"

Anna shook her head. "I have a sixth sense that is screaming at me. You're a liar, Derrick Corel. The only way you could convince me is if you stay until dawn."

"I can't do that, Anna."

"Ah-hah. I knew it."

"It's not because I fear turning to dust or spontaneously combusting if that's what you think."

"Well, prove me wrong. Stay."

"No." Derrick rose from the lounge and walked towards the door with Anna close at his heels.

"You liar. You're a vampire and you can't stay because you fear you'll burst into flames."

The speed with which Derrick turned almost knocked Anna off her feet. He caught her before she fell—holding her firmly by the shoulders. "I fear *you,* Anna. I fear the effect you have on me, on my body. I can't think when I'm in your presence. I can't sleep without dreaming of you." He kissed her. Hard. Taking his time as he explored her mouth with his tongue. Anna pressed her body into his, wrapping her arms around his neck. He reached behind his head and grabbed her hands, drawing them together in a prayer position in front of her chest. "But we can't be together. I can only bring you more suffering." With that, he flung open the door and disappeared into the night. With a roar of his car's engine, he was gone.

****

Derrick's dark mood preceded him into the kitchen where he found David clearing away empty wine glasses that contained a familiar sticky residue. He looked around before asking.

"Have they gone?"

"They only stayed about an hour—" David barely had time to react when Derrick picked him up by the collar and forced him against the kitchen cabinet. Glass from the door shattered against his head sending shards sailing in all directions. "Hey, bro. That's a bit of an overreaction isn't it?"

"How could you put Anna in danger like that? What were you thinking?"

"I wasn't thinking. I'm sorry." David shook the fragments of broken cabinet from his hair. "It was an emergency."

"Nothing is so important it is worth putting Anna's life in danger. Do you understand? Nothing."

"I beg to differ, little brother." He touched his hand to a tender spot on his scalp and licked the blood off his fingers. After scowling at Derrick, he began to sweep up the mess.

"Well, what is it?" Derrick's mood grew darker as he considered what could have happened to Anna, alone in the garden with Torke. "What did Torke have to say?"

"You heard him. He wants control."

"I hope you made it perfectly clear that he isn't welcome here."

"It would have been easier to convince him if you hadn't given him ammunition to use against us." He shot David an 'I told you so' look. "I tried to caution you against objecting to our co-leadership."

"Okay." Derrick took a dustpan from the cupboard and held it as David swept the glass. "That may have been stupid on my part, but hindsight is twenty-twenty. So, is he leaving?"

"Not yet. He says he has unfinished business here."

"What sort of business?"

David shrugged. "He told me in no uncertain terms to butt out."

"Why didn't you insist?"

"As you know, he was previously in control of the district and does not readily accept authority. He promised to resolve his problem quickly. There was little else I could do except to remind him that his presence is unwelcome."

"So, it's been taken care of?"

"Not exactly."

Derrick held out the small plastic waste bin so his brother could empty the dustpan but David hesitated. Wrinkles formed on his brow.

"There's something I think you should know Derrick."

"About?"

"About, Torke. And Anna."

Derrick dropped the bin. "What about Anna? What did he say?"

"It wasn't so much what he said, but *how* he said it. After you left he asked about her." Before Derrick had a chance to interrupt, David added. "No, I didn't tell him anything."

"What did he want to know?"

"What was your interest in her? How long has she lived here? But what stood out in my mind was that I get the impression he knows her or at least *of* her."

"Come to think of it, he *was* showing a lot of interest in her before you showed up and the way he looked at her…" He shook his head. "Something doesn't feel right. She wasn't just a potential meal to him. He seemed angry at her."

"Exactly," David agreed. "Warning bells starting ringing in my ears the moment I joined you in the garden. He seemed both excited and furious. The hate in the air was palpable."

"I sensed it too but I thought that the hate was directed at me." Derrick remembered a crack of electricity he had become aware of shortly after Torke's appearance. "And you're sure you didn't give him any information about Anna?"

David held up two fingers to his temple in a scout salute. "Scout's honor."

"You've never been a boy scout." Derrick shook his head and sighed.

"No." David grinned. "But I've bitten a few. They taste like girl scout cookies."

****

Anna awoke to pounding on her front door. After rubbing the sleep from her eyes, she checked the time on the clock, groaned and struggled into her dressing gown. She was exhausted, both physically and emotionally. The dreams were coming more frequently and the danger seemed more real. She woke many times during the night with a feeling of apprehension, especially after what she had learned from the information she had found on the internet. Information about vampires.

"Patrick." She complained after she had opened the door. "What are you doing here at 6 a.m. It's Saturday morning for Pete's sake?"

"I was worried about you." He barged his way past, uninvited. "I heard you went out with Derrick Corel last night."

Anna noticed the way he tried to spy past her into her bedroom, and then strutted into the kitchen to poke around.

"He isn't here, Patrick."

"I knew you wouldn't sleep with him." Patrick announced, almost too confidently. "I just wanted to be sure."

"What do you mean by that?"

"You're not the type to sleep around, that's all."

"I may surprise you."

"Come on, Anna, be serious." Patrick flopped down on the sofa as if he owned the place, a gesture that infuriated Anna almost as much as his confidence in her fidelity. "It took me years to get you into bed and *we* were engaged."

"I've changed, Patrick, in more ways than one."

"A leopard doesn't change its spots." He smiled a saccharin grin. "Let's face it babe, you're not wild about sex."

"That's it." Anna stormed over to the front door and opened it wide. "Get the hell out of my house."

"Oh, come on babe. You know I was only pulling your leg." He slowly rose from the sofa and stood near the door. "You have to admit though. You weren't chomping at the bit to get into bed with me." Casually, he loosened the front of her gown exposing her flimsy nightgown. "You could *show* me how much you've changed? Maybe teach me some of your new moves?"

A leopard can't change his spots? Anna remembered Derrick saying the same thing about Patrick when she insisted that he genuinely loved her and wanted her back. She hated to admit that Derrick was right but Patrick was displaying the same characteristics as when they were together. No wonder she hadn't been thrilled at the prospect of lovemaking with him. He was crude and vulgar and his idea of foreplay was telling her that he *felt like a bit*. He was the same self-centered, egotistical creep and she knew now that he would never change. She leaned forward and wrapped her arms around Patrick's neck, widening his stance with a nudge of her knee. "You want to see my new moves?" she asked in a low, sultry voice. "How's this one?" With one swift action, she drew her knee up to connect with his groin, then pushed him out the door where he lay curled on the ground in the fetal position, clutching his privates.

As she slammed the door, Anna called out "And don't call me babe."

Chapter Seven

"You knee'd him in the family jewels?" Susie almost tripped over her own feet as Anna related her story during their morning jog to the beach. "You go girl."

"I know I should be ashamed but if felt great bringing him down a peg or two. I can't believe he said I was frigid."

Susie motioned for Anna to stop jogging. She bent over and stretched her hamstring, pulling on her toes for a deeper stretch. "Cramp … in my … leg."

"I guess I have been driving us hard this morning." Anna surveyed her surroundings and realized they had covered at least six kilometers. "Do you want to have a breather?"

"Oh, thank god." Susie slumped to the sand and lay on her back. "I didn't want to be a wuss but I ran out of steam about a kilometer ago."

Flopping down beside her, Anna admitted to her own exhaustion. With less than two hours' sleep, it was only the adrenaline and anger driving her on. Now that she'd finally calmed down, every muscle in her body screamed for attention. She threw herself backwards onto the sand. "I think I'm dying."

"No, I think dying would be less painful than this." Susie reached into her pocket for her mobile phone and punched in a number.

"Hey, Carol. Does Frank have any appointments open today? I'm booking for Anna and myself."

She held her hand over the receiver as she explained the call to Anna.

"Frank is our resident masseuse. His skilled fingers will do wonders with your aching muscles—" She pointed her finger to the sky and answered the phone. "Oh, can you hold on a sec?" she turned back to Anna. "He can see one of us this afternoon and the other this evening around eight. I have a yoga class tonight. Do you think I could have the afternoon appointment ... pretty please?"

"Sure. Eight is fine." Anna lay on the sand and contemplated her evening. Baked beans on toast while watching the Saturday night movie on television. Frigid Anna, alone again.

****

Anna arrived for her massage at ten to eight, anxious to relieve the pain of her tortured muscles.

"Go straight in and strip down to your undies," Carol informed Anna the moment she walked into the gym. The tall dark-haired woman grabbed her handbag from behind the counter and rushed past to lock the back door, before returning with the keys jingling in her hand.

"Hello to you too, Carol." Anna could sense Carol's rush to leave. The short dress and expertly applied makeup implied a night out. The air was heavy with perfume. "Hot date?"

"Yeah, sorry to be rude, Anna. Derrick asked me to lock up and I'm kind of anxious to leave, if you know what I mean?" She tugged at the hem of her snug dress.

"No, probs." Anna held the front door open as Carol rushed out. "Have a great time."

"You too." Carol didn't bother to turn around as she raced to her car. "Don't do anything I wouldn't do."

"As if." Anna muttered to herself as she locked the door. The way Carol was dressed, her appointment suggested pleasure and lots of sex. Anna's, in comparison, promised pain and the only release she could expect would be from her physical tension. She slowly made her way to the therapy room feeling miserable and lonely.

The door to the room was open so she walked in and dropped her bag on a chair near the closest wall, taking mental note of the "torture chamber" sign as she stepped behind the screen to disrobe. There was a bottle of Moscato on the bench with instructions to "help yourself" so she obeyed, and downed a whole glass full. It was her first massage and she was a little anxious as to what to expect. Not long after she had positioned herself face down on the table, the towel draped over her bottom to cover the parts left exposed by her G-string, and then a CD player clicked on. Soft music filtered into the room while the fragrance of white musk and vanilla began wafting from a newly lit candle. The lights in the room dimmed moments before quiet footsteps stopped directly to her left. Through the face hole in the table, Anna spotted a pair of ASICS-shod feet. Wrapped in barely more than a towel, she felt vulnerable and awkward when she felt her only covering being rolled down almost to her hips and tucked into the top of her panties. She tried to break the ice.

"Hi. I'm Anna."

"I know," Derrick answered.

Anna covered her breasts with her arms as she turned to face him.

"What are you doing here, Derrick? Where's Frank?"

"Frank had to leave early so I offered to do your massage."

"Are you qualified?"

"I have the same qualifications as Frank but if I make you uncomfortable … we can reschedule."

Anna thought for a moment. The old Anna would have rescheduled in a heartbeat. Derrick's signals were all over the place and it confused her. She didn't want to give him the advantage of touching her while he maintained that there was no chance of a relationship but, the thought of his hands on her body…

"No. It's okay." She placed her face back down in the hollowed part of the table and was grateful that during the massage, Derrick wouldn't be able to see her expressions.

She sighed as she waited for her massage to commence. It seemed like an eternity of waiting and concentrating on the sounds in the room, while she assumed he was massaging oil into his palms but she wasn't prepared for the attack on her senses when the large hands made contact with her bare skin.

"Oooh." She gasped as the heat from his hands warmed her aching flesh. "Your hands are warm. I wasn't expecting that."

"Shhh. Just relax" mumbled her masseuse.

Fine … be that way. Anna thought to herself as she closed her eyes and tried to ignore the sullen man whose warm fingers kneaded her back. She sighed with approval as her muscles relaxed beneath the magician's hands, deeper and deeper he delved into every fiber of her tense and knotted ligaments. His magic fingers massaged away at the stress in her neck and shoulders. He began kneading in small circular motions at the muscles and ligaments in her arms and then her lower back, his thumbs locating all the tension triggers and releasing them one by one. Try as she might, she couldn't prevent the groans of relief escaping as all the drama and tribulations of the last month melted away. Tempting as it was to praise him for his skill, she didn't want to admit to him how wonderful his hands felt on her bare skin. Experience had taught her that every time she let her guard down with him, he took off and if he stopped now, she feared she would die from the disappointment.

When another mewing sound stole quietly away, Derrick paused. He seemed to lose concentration. His hands froze on her lower back.

"Don't stop. Please don't stop." She pleaded. "I really need this … ouch, ouch, ouch." Anna twisted her arm around to rub her right thigh.

"Cramps?"

"Yes." She groaned again. "I overdid my run today."

"Relax. I'll see what I can do to help." He eased her back down on the table, this time with a smooth caress of his palms against her skin as he started work on her legs. To Anna's surprise, he began with the toes.

"That's not where it—"

"Relax." He repeated, rubbing scented oil into the soles of her feet. Gently he bent her knees and drew her feet up, placing them to rest against his belly, soles up so he could massage both feet at once. The sensation was almost more than Anna could bear. There was something sensual about having her feet rubbed, her ankles manipulated, and when he worked his magic on her calves … whoa baby. She had read about the big "O" in women's magazines but never expected to feel anything like this from her calves. As his warm hands worked their way up her thighs and under the towel to cup her buttocks, she instinctively thought to shoo them away but she was past the point of no return now. All her frustration rose to the surface, building to a crescendo. She didn't want this to stop. She needed this and she was going to see this massage through to the end, even if it cost her last shred of self-respect.

He massaged every inch of her skin, from her toes to her the tip of her spine. His firm but gentle touch stretching her skin, manipulating her senses and sending waves of pleasure through her core. The terry cloth of the massage table scraped her sensitized nipples as she wiggled and squirmed against the fabric. This was the closest thing to sex she had experienced in seven years—and what she had once considered "the norm" with Patrick didn't hold a candle to this—so she lay there, completely under Derrick's control while she allowed him to rock her world. And rock her world he did. Wave after wave of pleasure rippled through her body taking her to dizzying heights until she felt she would die from satisfaction. When her body stopped shuddering from the most mind blowing release she had ever experienced, Anna realized she had wailed with enthusiasm. She waited for him to make another move fully expecting him to roll her over and make love to her. Surely this had been his intention all along? The wine, the music, and the candles. Hadn't he set the scene for romance? She waited, wondering what she should do next. Should she roll over and reach for him? Was he waiting for her to make the next move? She felt confused. What *was* he waiting for?

While she was trying to regain composure, she heard the door open and recognized the sound of hurried footsteps as he fled from the room leaving her feeling confused, physically drained and still, sexually aroused on the massage table.

What did I do wrong? She wondered as she dressed quickly, suddenly ashamed of her nudity. Leaving her shoes off—which she carried for a stealthy escape—Anna stole out of the "torture chamber" after first checking around the corner to see if the coast was clear. She tiptoed towards the door, passing the men's shower as she tried to make her exit. The sound of running water attracted her attention and knowing that Derrick was the only one left in the gym, curiosity got the better of her. After all, moments ago he had his hands all over her near-naked body. It was only fair that she could at least take a peek at his. Leaning against the wall for support, she peered into the stall and spotted a very firm bare behind. *Nice.*

His long lean legs were paler than the tanned type she usually preferred but heavily muscled with a generous sprinkling of fine dark hair. His buttocks were firm and rounded but not big. Her masseuse had broad shoulders that tapered down to a narrow waist, and the biceps in his muscular arms flexed as he vigorously shampooed his hair. When he shook his head to rinse out the bubbles the beads of water glistened in his dark hair like diamonds.

He was as perfect beneath his Armani clad body as she had suspected and the reality only made her feel worse. She wanted him so badly that she physically ached for him and his body language seemed to indicate that he felt the same but he constantly pushed her away. She wiped away a tear as she wondered about his strange behavior. *Why don't you want me?*

As if hearing her thoughts, Derrick suddenly turned to face her. He remained motionless for a moment as if trying to think of the right words. Finally, he spoke.

"I'm sorry, Anna. When I read your name on the client list, I talked Frank into allowing me to take over. I didn't know it would go this far."

Anna fisted her hands and pounded the air. She stopped abruptly when she noticed Derrick's very impressive erection as he stood stark naked facing her. "I can't think while you're pointing that thing at me."

"I never meant to hurt you," Derrick told her as he reached for a towel and wrapped it around his waist. "My behavior was inexcusable and I promise it will never happen again."

"You keep saying that you don't want a

relationship but then you try and seduce me," she reminded him. "You're a tease Derrick Corel. A low-down, no-good, manipulative bastard!"

As she ran from the building, she heard Derrick call for her to wait but she hurried her steps not wanting to discuss the matter. Not tonight. Not while her body still throbbed and tingled from the effects of his massage. Not while her mind raced with images of satin sheets and tangled bodies. She jumped into her car and floored the accelerator. Tomorrow … she would make him pay.

****

"What the hell was that crash?"

Derrick turned in his seat at the kitchen bar to face his brother as David rushed into the kitchen. He held a handkerchief to his bleeding forehead and shrugged when David looked from the shattered kitchen cabinet back to him.

"Hard night?"

"You wouldn't believe me if I told you."

"Try me." David struggled out of his skin-tight leather jacket, threw it on the back of a chair and settled down beside his sulking, slightly concussed brother. His expression changed from concern to amusement as Derrick imparted his tale of deception.

"You dog."

"I know, I know. You couldn't make me feel any worse than I already do."

"Then why did you do it? I thought you wanted to keep your distance from the little firecracker?"

"So did I, but when I arrived at the gym and saw her name on the massage list … I couldn't help myself." He raked his fingers through his hair and shook his head. "I needed to be close to her, to touch her. I've never wanted something so bad in my life."

"Well, spill. Was it worth it?"

A sly grin curled the corners of Derrick's mouth as he nodded and blew out a long breath. "Yes. Yes … it was worth it."

"So, what happens next?"

"I don't have any idea? I can't be with her … but I can't be without her. She's addictive, seductive. I've tasted a little, now I crave more."

"I really don't see the problem." David told him. "She obviously wants to be with you, so just have at it and take her to your bed."

"We both know that it isn't that simple."

Derrick was no virgin. He had enough experience in the bedroom to realize that he could not control his vampire tendencies in the throes of passion. He would be forced to bite her and after tasting her blood again, he wasn't sure if he would be able to stop. "If we make love, I might lose control."

"If it comes to that, at least you could turn her. There is no downside. Either way, you get what you want."

"What I want is for Anna to experience something that we never had, what Isabelle never had. A life with children of her own and sunshine and—"

"And rainbows and puppy dogs." David shook his head. "You always were the romantic Derrick. When are you going to realize that life doesn't always go to plan."

"I guess that will be around the same time that you stop being cynical and start caring about someone other than yourself."

David's smile disappeared. His eyes lowered to the floor.

Derrick realized he had crossed the line. "I didn't—"

"No. Don't apologize for the truth. I haven't always been there for you and I definitely wasn't there for Isabelle when you both needed me." He touched his brother's shoulder and asked. "How can I help you now? What do you want me to do?"

Derrick rose from his chair and began to clean up the wreckage from his temper tantrum. "I don't know. I've never felt this way before."

"Are you strong enough to stay away from her?"

"I have to be…" Pausing, he asked, "Will you help me?"

Chapter Eight

"Did he say when he'd be back?" Anna struggled to hide the disappointment in her voice as she addressed the aging butler. She had spent more time than usual applying her "war paint" and had squeezed herself into a tiny dress that she had borrowed from Susie in order to tease Derrick, only to be told he had left town.

"I'm sorry, Miss Anna. He didn't say. Would you perhaps like to ask Master David?"

"Is he here?"

"Yes, miss." Evan invited Anna in and led the way to door at the bottom of the stairs. "He's downstairs."

Briefly, Anna waited at the door, wondering what to expect. Maybe there was a coffin after all. Perhaps a coven of vampires waited in ambush? Her heart beat faster, harder, as she slowly eased onto the first step. When Evan called out behind her, "Mr. David. I am sending Miss Anna down to speak with you," she almost lost her footing, stumbling down the next two steps. She was still shaking when she reached the bottom. Too her relief, she noticed there wasn't any sign of a coffin. David was standing behind a large easel, his paintbrush moving furiously over the canvas. Not a sign of a single vampire or for that matter—a window. *Strange*. The workshop was flooded with artificial light. Completely sealed from the sun's glare. Fueling her suspicions.

"Sorry about that," David muttered, without looking up from his canvas. "He forgets that the rest of us *aren't* deaf." He finished the stroke before wiping his brush on a piece of rag he kept on the easel.

"I've interrupted your work."

"Not really. It's just something I'm playing around with."

"May I see?"

"Sorry." He stepped in her way before she had a chance to glimpse the painting. "Not till the unveiling. Temperamental artist thing."

"Can't I have just a little peek?" Anna's stuck out her bottom lip in a pout and did her best eyelash flutter.

"That won't work on me pet." He lifted Anna's chin and ran his paint covered finger down her nose, leaving a smear of blue oil color. "Although I *can* see why you have such an effect on my brother." He tossed her a clean piece of cloth.

It was a struggle to remove the paint. Anna scrubbed until David passed her some turpentine. She was tempted to complain about how the turpentine would spoil her makeup and possibly damage her skin but instead asked, "Where *is* Derrick?"

"Away on business."

"I'm his business partner." She reminded him as she passed back the rag and bottle. "He should have told me where he was going and when he'll return. What if there is a problem at the gym?"

"Then you may call on me, chérie."

"Are you a Martial Artist as well?" she asked, noticing that David's build was similar to Derrick, she assumed that he probably worked out too.

"I'm a lover not a fighter." His penetrating eyes gave Anna the impression he was not lying but she sensed he had also had his fair share of brawls. "My brother is the physical one in the family."

"That's why I'm here."

"To get physical with Derrick?" David teased.

She felt the color rush to her face at his innuendo and the cheeky grin that followed.

"No. Of course not." *Not yet anyway.* "I want to take martial arts lessons."

"Derrick left one of his Sempai as a replacement."

"I don't want a replacement, I want Derrick." As soon as the words left her mouth, she inwardly cringed. David would surely use them against her.

Surprisingly, he ignored the opportunity to take advantage of her faux pas. His smile faded and his expression changed. He looked serious, almost sad. "I'm afraid that sometimes we can't have what we want."

Anna's cheeks burned. Was she really so bad for Derrick? Fighting back the tears, she drew on all her strength to find a way to leave with dignity. "I believe that if you want something bad enough and you work hard enough, you'll get what you deserve." She turned her back on the handsome artist and bolted up the stairs as David muttered under his breath.

"Let's hope so, *chérie*. Let's hope so."

****

As she approached the main gate, a familiar car made its way up the drive. She pulled over and waited for the driver to wind down his window.

"What are you doing here, Patrick?"

"I could ask you the same thing."

"I was here to see Derrick."

"Same."

"Well he's not here."

"Where is he?"

"I don't know, Patrick. I'm not his keeper."

"No. But you're his partner."

"Well, he didn't tell me where he was going or when he'll return so we've both wasted our time, haven't we." She turned over the ignition and put the car in first gear ready to leave.

"Wait, Anna. We can't go on like this. Let's have lunch and smoke a peace pipe. There are a few things you might like to know about your business partner."

Anna thought for a moment. She didn't trust Patrick. He was manipulative, self-indulgent and arrogant but he did have an ear for gossip. If Derrick kept secrets from her, maybe Patrick could shed some light on the subject. She glanced back at the house and noticed the heavy drapes move slightly. If someone in the house was concerned to see her talking with Patrick, maybe there was good reason.

"All right." She relented. "I guess lunch will be okay."

Patrick leaned over and opened the passenger side door.

"Leave your car here. I'll drive you back later."

"Only if you let me pick the restaurant this time."

Patrick hesitated. "Not a hamburger joint."

"We'll see." She jumped into the seat beside him. "Head to the beach."

****

"All right, you promised me some gossip." Anna threw another chip to the seagulls as they watched the tide come in from their position on a sand dune.

"You promised me that you would pick a *restaurant*." Patrick complained as he picked at his fish and potato scallops. "We could have dined at Stefano's again."

"Blahh." Anna made a gagging gesture with her finger in her mouth. "I much prefer eating to *dining*." She accentuated the word. "Give me good old fish and chips any day."

"You'll never change, will you, Anna."

"Probably not." She sighed. "The sooner everyone comes to terms with that the better."

If Patrick had picked up on the reference to *everyone*, he didn't acknowledge it.

"Sometimes a change is good." Patrick took a sip

from his can of Pepsi and snorted. "I've been trying to get Derrick to introduce me to some of his friends. He associates with people who could make me more prominent in society. More influential, more powerful, but he refuses to help me."

"He probably has his reasons." Anna shuddered as she remembered the odd group of people that assembled at Derrick's house the night of their ill-fated dinner.

"Yeah. Reasons like he doesn't want me to be as rich or connected as him." He emptied the can, crushing it before hurling it across the sand at an unsuspecting gull.

"Hey." Anna complained as she jumped up to retrieve the can. She could feel Patrick's eyes on her bottom and tugged at the hem of her skirt, realizing that the skin-tight mini-dress was completely inappropriate attire for the beach. She tossed the can into a rubbish bin and sat back down beside him.

"Still protecting the world I see."

Although she knew Patrick's comment was meant to be an insult Anna took it as a compliment. "And you're still trying to rule it."

"I just want to make my mark. I want to be someone people look up to, respect and admire."

"You could be all those things without being rich and powerful, Patrick. Treating others with respect is a good way to start."

"No. You don't understand. You're happy with your simple life."

Tempting as it was to argue, Anna felt sorry for Patrick. He wouldn't be happy until he had all those things but she doubted he would ever find true happiness. He would always want more. Need more.

"I could try and reason with Derrick if you like. Not about you working at the gym, he's made it perfectly clear he doesn't want you there but I don't see why he wouldn't introduce you to a couple of his friends."

"Forget it." Patrick shook his head. "I don't need him anymore. That's what I was on my way to tell him. I've found another sponsor."

"Good for you." *What a relief.* She seriously doubted Derrick would be swayed by her opinion on anything. "Who is it?"

"No one you know. He's from out of town. He moved away a few years back and has returned to take back control of his company. He's promised me wealth and power, Anna."

Anna gasped. Not in reaction to what Patrick had said. In truth she hadn't heard his answer to her question. She had been absently staring out to sea when, to her horror, a dark shadow crept over the landscape spreading a crimson hue in its wake. The color of the water and sky had slowly deepened, before turning completely red. The waves carried the sickening stench of blood as pink foam crashed against the golden sand, scattering the gulls that fossicked for scraps along the shore.

"Patrick…" she said, her voice barely above a whisper as she tried to make sense of what she was seeing. It was a though she wore rose-colored glasses but rather than make the world look rosier, they prophesized destruction and death. Blood oozed from every grain of sand, every drop of water. She could feel the gooey substance between her toes, soaking through her clothes. She could taste the copper in her mouth.

"What is it?"

"Can't you see? Look at the water…" she struggled to her feet, her legs trembled as she pointed to the surf.

"See what?" Patrick turned his head left to right. "Anna. I don't know what you're talking about."

"I … I want to go home." Her voice trembled as she realized that no-one else on the beach reacted to the horrifying scene. Children were playing in the pink froth, waving joyfully to their parents who seemed blissfully unaware of any danger. She alone experienced the horror. What did it mean? Was there some apocalyptic event about to happen or was her life about to end in a bloody tempest? She turned to her companion. "Please, Patrick. Take me home."

Chapter Nine

Anna couldn't understand what had happened at the beach. Why had the sky and ocean turned blood-red? Why had she been the only person to notice? She blamed Derrick. If he hadn't left so suddenly, she wouldn't have accepted Patrick's invitation to lunch and, maybe, she wouldn't have experienced the vision. No. It wasn't fair to blame Derrick. Somehow she had always known that her empathy would evolve into something more but she had also dreaded the day. Normality was an unobtainable dream and it was time that she accepted that. But accepting wasn't enough. If this was to be her life, she had to learn how to control her visions and decipher them.

Torke was real. Evil was real. Anna's thoughts drifted back to the last time she saw her mother. Her mother had warned her that her ability would attract evil. Had her mother known about Torke? *What else had she known?* Her mother had died before she could impart any useful information but, maybe there were clues contained in the numerous boxes that her father kept locked away in his room. She opened the door and steeled herself for what she might find.

As she busied herself with the task at hand, Anna felt compelled to find one particular treasure that had belonged to her mother. At least she thought it must have been a treasure. The way in which her mother guarded the object made it seem particularly interesting to a small child even though outwardly it looked quite unremarkable. *Where did she keep it?* She had put off packing away her father's belongings, hesitant to dredge up painful memories but now seemed like the perfect time to sort through his stuff. Besides, she needed the distraction. After working for hours, Anna had managed to pack away a set of barely used golf clubs, a worn-out sewing machine, some rusty handheld weights, numerous war novels, and an old guitar. The last of her father's things were labelled and carried out to the garage to await donation to the Salvation Army but she still hadn't found what she sought, the old wooden chest that had belonged to her mother. Finally, as she climbed to the top rung of the step ladder and balanced on her toes to reach the top shelf, she spotted the chest. It was far to the back of the wardrobe, covered in a fine layer of dust. No bigger than a bread box, the wooden chest was surprisingly heavy. Anna struggled to balance it over her head as she steadily made her way down the rungs.

For the longest time, she sat cross-legged on the carpeted floor of her parent's room, staring at the object of her mother's reverence. The box had been important to, not only Elena but all the females in her family. Anna remembered her mother telling her the story of how this box was passed down from mother to daughter for centuries. The handing over of the box was a rite of passage and an eagerly awaited ritual for every daughter, a ritual that died with Elena.

"I guess you would have wanted me to have this, Mama," she whispered to the box as she carefully opened the lid and peeled back the purple velvet cloth. An unsuspecting thief would have been disappointed with his find but to Anna, the contents represented the women of her family and she considered each artefact a treasure. One by one, she lovingly removed the items and placed them on the floor beside her. The largest item in the box was a crystal ball made of, what Anna somehow knew to be black obsidian, with an intricately carved wooden stand. She found a deck of tarot cards, a forked stick, a bracelet made of the same stone as her necklace, a small tear-shaped quartz crystal on a chain, and a folded piece of paper. Anna's hands began to shake as she delicately unfolded the worn and faded paper and read the note.

Blessed be, child of light. You have been gifted with a power as with all our family's women. Your gift can provide protection for your loved ones and an insight into the future. Beware of the dark forces that would use you in order to increase their power. Hide your gift from those with the evil eye by wearing the bracelet passed onto you by your mother and develop your powers so you will defeat your enemy. The bracelet has been energized with the power of centuries of our women and will protect you. Use the items in this box to enhance your abilities and heed the advice of your mother who will teach you in the ways of Wicca. May the goddess protect and guide you. Blessed be.

So, mum was a witch. Anna sighed. Her mother never had the opportunity to teach her anything about the craft and her only experience with magic was the blinding visions that were more of a curse than a blessing. She reread a line from the letter. "Use the items in this box to enhance your abilities." *That would be great if I had any idea what these things are.* Anna picked up the forked stick and turned it around in her hand. She poked at the air. *Take that you demon scum. Nah, must be used for something else.* She placed it back in the box before turning her attention to the tarot cards. The edges were worn and curled as if they had been used often. The pictures were beautifully hand-painted but their significance lost on Anna who had no idea what they meant. She shuffled the pack and drew a card from the top of the deck. Death. Having no understanding of the card's meaning, she could only assume the worst. Taking a deep breath, she turned over the second card ... lovers, and decided that it was time to pack the cards away. She wasn't in the mood for thinking about death or lovers. Both had turned her life upside-down.

She packed up the deck and returned them to their place in the box. Next, she examined the bracelet. The moment she placed it in her hand, a warm sensation followed by an uneasiness prickled her skin. She shivered as a sensation of being watched overwhelmed her. Rushing to the window, she studied the dark clouds that had started rolling in and was suddenly reminded of Derrick. As much as she wanted to punish him for his indiscretion, her skin still yearned for his touch. For the short period of time he had been in her life, he dominated her thoughts, plagued her dreams. She wanted him, more than she ever thought she could imagine. If only he hadn't run away.

"Damn!" she said aloud when it suddenly dawned on her that she had left her car at his house. In her rush to leave the beach, she had asked Patrick to drive her straight home. If she hadn't promised to meet Susie in town first thing in the morning, she would have been content to leave it there overnight but she had no intention of getting up any earlier than necessary on a Saturday morning. As she dialed for a cab, she held the cordless receiver in one hand while she packed away most of the heirlooms with her free hand, placing the box in her bedroom on the nightstand. After ordering the cab, she replaced the receiver, fastened the tiny clasp of the bracelet around her right wrist, and waited for the cab.

****

By the time the taxi pulled up outside Derrick's property, the sun had set. Anna stood outside the gates, shivering from the cold and wondering how she would get in. The heavy gates were locked. The usually welcoming estate looked harsh and cold under the shadows of the threatening storm clouds. She spotted an intercom and pressed the buzzer. After a few minutes, a weary male voice answered.

"Hello?"

"Hello, Evan. It's me Anna Derwent."

"Oh, Miss Anna. What are you doing here in this weather? Didn't I mention Master Derrick is away?"

"Yes, you did, Evan." He obviously hadn't noticed her car parked inside when he locked the gates. "I'm here for my car. I left it earlier."

There was a pause and movement at the curtain. A few more moments passed.

"So you did, Miss Anna. So you did."

"Well?"

"Well what?"

"Do you think you could open the gates so I can get it?"

"Oh. Yes, of course." Anna heard a click and then the gates began to move apart. "If you give me a few moments, I'll come out and see you to your vehicle."

Anna expected it would be much longer than a few moments for the aging butler to make it down the stairs, let alone all the way down the driveway to her car. Besides, she would reach the car and be on her way long before that. It hardly seemed worth putting him to the bother.

"Thanks, Evan but don't worry about it. See you later."

"But Miss Anna. It isn't safe for you to be unescorted around this property at night. I would call Master David, but he is out tonight." She heard real concern in his voice. *Why was the property unsafe at night?*

"I'm fine, Evan. I'll be quick as a wink, I promise. Have a good night."

She slipped through the opening and headed

towards her car smiling to herself as she thought of Evan
and his offer of protection. How sweet of the old man to
worry for her safety. If only the other men in her life
would show that sort of consideration. As she made her
way to the car, Anna began to regret her decision to
return at night. The closer she got to the car, the greater
the feeling of apprehension. Her intuition urged her to
hurry as clouds crowded the moon, drenching the garden
in darkness. A howl pierced the silence, reminding her of
a bad horror movie, the kind where a werewolf waited to
attack some stupid tourist who had ignored the warnings
and wandered off the path into the moors.

There's no such thing as werewolves. She
dismissed the idea with a laugh. But then again, up until a
couple of days ago, she hadn't believed in vampires
either. Now, she wasn't sure about anything. Gathering
her light cardigan to her chest, she hurried towards the
car but found that she was making little progress. The
wind increased in intensity, pushing her backward and
bringing along with it the smell of rot and decay. Anna
covered her nose and mouth with her hand and fought the
urge to vomit as the sickeningly sweet smell assaulted her
senses. It smelled of death. An overwhelming sensation
of danger hit her like a ton of bricks. She had noticed that
same rotting smell on the night of the ill-fated dinner, the
night that she met Derrick's strange friends. Her heart
beat wildly in her chest. She began to hyperventilate.
Sweat beaded on her forehead despite the cool night air.
A branch cracked beside her and despite fearing what she
would find, she slowly turned her head in the direction of
the sound. Even the wind seemed to hold its breath as she
gazed into what she could only describe as the eyes of
evil. Terror froze her to the spot. She couldn't move
another step although the safety of the car was only feet
away and when she recognized the voice, she knew she

was in real trouble.

"So nice to see you again, Anna my dear."

Unable to move her feet, Anna watched as the vampire moved casually towards her. His movements seemed unreal, like he was floating inches above the ground.

"Thanks. N-nice to see you too." Instinct told her not to aggravate him. *No sudden movements. Keep your cool Anna.*

"I was hoping for the opportunity to see you again. How fortunate for me to find you here … alone."

"I-I'm not alone. Derrick has just popped into the house for a moment. He'll back soon."

"Tisk, tisk. Anna." Torke waived his gnarled finger in the air, the yellowing nail pointed threateningly as he pursed his lips into a pout and shook his head. "We both know that is not the truth."

"What do you want from me?" Anna somehow forced her feet to move, backing slowly towards her car as Torke shortened the gap between them. His movements were painfully slow, as if he was savoring every moment it took to reach her, enjoying the fear in her expression.

"As I said, little one. I want to *talk* with you … only to talk."

"Well, talk." Anna felt her back connect with the car door. Torke moved close enough that Anna could smell his foul breath. She turned her head to the side and winced. "You're standing too close. Please respect my personal space. Step back."

"I'm sorry my dear." His chuckle was almost as hideous as his grin. "I'm sure Derrick must have told you that you have an intoxicating fragrance." He sniffed the air around her face. "Excuse my bad manners. I was under your enchantment."

Anna doubted the pretty words. She had felt the hate emanating from him on the night that they first met. He knew Derrick was away. She was his intended victim. But why? What could she possibly have done to piss him off? She called his bluff.

"We both know you're lying. Whatever I have done to offend you ... I'm sorry."

"Do you doubt your attraction, Anna? Didn't your mother tell you how special you are?"

Now he had her attention. Big time. "What do you know about my mother?"

"Your mother and I had a long-term relationship." Once again an evil grin twisted the corners of his mouth. "It was such a pity that she had to die. A real waste of a beautiful and talented young woman. She betrayed me, Anna, and in doing so, she sealed your fate."

Any lingering fear subsided, pushed down by anger. Anna's words spat out with venom.

"My mother would never have had anything to do with you. She was a beautiful, faithful wife and mother. She had a perfect life. Why would she risk that for someone as loathsome as you?"

"Oh, dear. You do not believe me to be an attractive man. You have hurt my feelings."

It amazed Anna how fast Torke's expression turned malevolent although his words remained calm and deliberate. His brow furrowed and his eyes glowed ... *red?*

"You should be very careful what you say to me child. I have been known to be a very unforgiving man."

"You don't frighten me." Anna hid her shaking hands behind her back. Pain pierced her temples. "Tell me how you knew my mother. Tell me the truth."

"You *are* your mother's daughter." Torke told her with a chuckle as he paced in front of Anna. While he spoke, he clicked his nails together menacingly. The sound assaulted her ears, turned her stomach.

The pain in her head increased. Pain that began when she first sensed Torke's presence. Flashes of color burst through the darkness, threatening to envelop her. She knew that she was on the verge of passing out.

"I can feel the power humming in you like electricity. Can't you feel it, Anna? Don't you know why I am here? Ah, judging by your confused expression, I assume she did not tell you about me."

"My mother died when I was a child."

"Everyone dies at some point." He shrugged his shoulders. There wasn't an ounce of remorse in his expression. "But Elena, she brought her death on herself. It didn't have to be that way."

"What way?" Anna could feel the cold metal of the car at her back, the handle was within her reach, her fingers brushed the door, searching, but she couldn't risk taking her eyes of Torke. His shoulders hunched forward, his body coiled in anticipation. A snake, ready to strike her down at the sign of any movement.

"She forced my hand. I had no choice but to kill her. She could have chosen to be with me." He leaned towards her. "I'm feeling generous tonight, Anna. I've decided to give you a choice. You are either for me or against me."

"If being for you is what I think you are insinuating … you can count me out."

"It would be wise if you didn't *try* to offend me little one. I have no tolerance for disobedience and you are beginning to try my patience."

"Well then, I'll just leave you alone."

Anna spun around and made a grab for the handle. Torke seized her wrist. Immediately, he withdrew his hand. His skin smoking, his palm scorched. Indentations from the crystal bracelet marked his skin and tiny sparks of fire danced on his arm. He winced in pain, extinguishing the flames with his other hand, giving Anna the opportunity to jump into the driver's seat and lock the door behind her.

Torke leaned forward, resting his rotting forehead on the glass of the driver's side window. Anna imagined a protective shield around the car and forced herself to look away from his hypnotic eyes as her trembling hands struggled to fit the key into the ignition. She turned the engine and thrust the gear stick into first, gunning the accelerator. The car screamed to life. She sped through the open gates of the property, the sound of grinding metal assaulted her ears as he lunged for the car with his talons but she ignored the excruciating sound, concentrating on getting as far away as possible in the shortest amount of time. Only when Torke disappeared in a cloud of dust, did she feel safe to ease off the gas. She glanced up at the rearview mirror and gasped, her right foot hit the brake petal and she skidded to a halt.

In the mirror, she could see her mother running to a car parked near a burning building. Her mother was crying as she drove away. Anna could sense the fear and desperation that her mother was experiencing as she drove at breakneck speed down the mountain towards their home. Something followed her, something in the darkness that caused her to turn her head at regular intervals and look back towards the burning building. Anna could see a darkness reaching out and surrounding the car. She could hear her mother scream as she lost control of the car and it careered over the cliff, flipping and bouncing before finally landing on its roof. Then she heard a sound that would haunt her dreams. The sinister laugh of the man who materialized beside the car. He looked inside at the woman who was lying motionless and trapped upside down by her seatbelt, and smiled with satisfaction before disappearing into thin air. Anna's blood ran cold when she recognized the man. Torke. The vision ended in a flash of light but the fear remained. Tears streamed down Anna's cheeks as she realized that her mother had been forced off the road. She had been murdered by this ... this monster.

Composing herself enough to drive, she headed home but as she neared town, the car radio suddenly switched on, crackled, and to her horror, a familiar voice interrupted the news broadcast. "You have made your choice Anna. Unfortunately, you won't live to regret it."

****

Anna wondered how she had managed to make it home in one piece. Several times she had almost run off the road as she stared at the rearview mirror, looking for signs to indicate Torke followed. She wished she had a cross or holy water or whatever the hell someone would use against a vampire. Because, there was no doubt in her mind ... Torke was a vampire. A blood sucking nightmare that had not only killed her mother, but, for some reason, wanted her dead too.

After locking all the doors and bolting the windows, Anna strung garlic around the door frames and—just in case—poured salt on the floor. She had seen that done in a movie once.

Was that for vampires or demons? It didn't matter ... it was worth a try. During the long wait for dawn, Anna contemplated Torke's reason for knowing her mother, his need to talk with her about their relationship. The thought of her sweet, beautiful Mama having that hideous monster as a lover made her skin crawl. *Oh, God!* She couldn't be his daughter could she? No. It wasn't possible! There was no way her Mama would betray her father. Elena doted on her husband and child.

Their open display of affection for each other was a constant in Anna's life. *No, it must be something else.*

When the first rays of sunlight beamed through the curtains, Anna felt it was safe to pour herself a drink. Many times during the night, she had been desperate to grab the scotch bottle but worried she would be intoxicated and easily overpowered if attacked. Now, the malt liquid's call was too strong and even though she should be getting ready for her meeting with Susie, an Irish coffee for her breakfast seemed like an excellent idea.

Chapter Ten

Anna joined Susie at her table in the café and shrugged when her friend observed, "You look like something the cat dragged in."

"Thanks. I didn't get much sleep last night." She motioned to the waitress for a coffee and as she took off her dark sunglasses she noticed Susie sniff the air.

"I don't mean to stick my nose in your business Anna, but isn't it a little early in the day to be drinking?"

Anna covered her mouth with her hand. "Is it that obvious?"

Susie nodded. "Rough night?" she offered a breath mint which Anna gratefully accepted.

"You don't know the half of it."

"Go on. Spill. Who's the guy?"

"A disgusting, leathery, hideously scarred man."

Susie's eyebrows raised in horror. Her mouth dropped open into an O shape.

"No, no, no. Nothing like that." Anna couldn't help but laugh at her friend's expression. An expression that soon changed when she added, "He was a stalker."

"Oh, Anna, how awful! Did you call the police?"

Anna shook her head and sighed. "I have a feeling they couldn't help me." *How could she explain her situation to the police? Even Susie would think her insane if she mentioned that her stalker was an ancient vampire.*

"Of course they could help. Call them, Anna, or I will."

Anna reached forward and touched her friend's hand. "I appreciate your concern Susie but really … they couldn't help. I don't know where he lives or even his last name."

"Where did you see him?"

"I met him at Derrick's house a few days ago and again last night." She shivered at the very thought of him.

"Did you tell Derrick?"

She shook her head. "He's away on business."

"No." Susie took a sip of her coffee. "He's back. Frank told me this morning."

"When did he get in?"

"Around three in the morning. Frank said he looked agitated. Said he'd never seen him look so angry. I bet he'll kick that guy's arse if you tell him what happened."

The waitress brought Anna's coffee and set in down on the table. Anna waited for her to leave before asking.

"Why?"

"Why would he kick his arse?"

"No, you dork. Why was he so angry?"

"He didn't say. Mind you, you know Frank ... a man of few words. How was your massage by the way? Great hands huh?"

Anna almost chocked on her mouthful of coffee, spitting some in Susie's direction and dribbling more down her chin. Heat rose to her cheeks and, as she coughed, she noticed Susie's inquisitive expression.

"What is it you're not telling me?"

"I ... I never ended up getting that massage from Frank."

"How disappointing."

"Oh, it was anything but disappointing." Anna rolled her eyes and tried unsuccessfully to stop the grin that crept across her face as curiosity furrowed Susie's brows. "And I did get a massage, just not from Frank."

Susie leaned forward, biting her bottom lip and almost bouncing off her seat with enthusiasm. "Tell me, tell me."

"Let's just say … Derrick has hidden talents."

"Oh my god Anna … did you—"

"No." Anna shook her head vehemently.

"Did you *want* to?"

Anna's blush was answer enough to answer Susie's question.

"Then why the hell not?" She slapped Anna's hand.

"He ran away."

"Oh. That's a bummer." Susie sat back in her seat. "What are you going to do about it?"

"What can I do? He obviously isn't attracted to me."

"Let me tell you something…" Susie glanced around the room and leaned closer. "In all the years I've worked here, I've never seen Derrick even date. You are the first woman he's shown any interest in."

"That doesn't mean anything."

"Anna." She smacked the back of Anna's hand again, harder this time. "If you want the man, go get him. I'm telling you, he's yours for the taking."

"He ran away, Susie."

"So … run after him. Sometimes a man needs a little push. Big babies, every one of them."

"Really? Do you really think I should make a play for him?"

"It depends."

"On what?"

"How good was that massage?"

Anna lowered her head and bit her bottom lip. Lifting her chin, she smiled sheepishly. "Oh, it was spectacular."

Susie raised her mug. "Then you'd better make a move before someone else grabs him."

****

Derrick's punch hit David's chin with an intensity that would have knocked out a human but David only stumbled back a few feet. He rubbed his jaw and shook his head as he pointed out, "That one's for free, the next will cost you."

"Why didn't you do something?"

"I would have, had I been here Derrick."

Derrick paced the lounge room floor, clenching and unclenching his fists. "I asked you to look out for her while I was away. How could you let this happen?"

"I didn't expect her to come here. Not after being told you were away."

Derrick felt physically ill for the first time in centuries. "He could have killed her, David!"

"I know, Derrick, and I'm sorry I wasn't here, but nothing happened."

"Aaah!" Derrick screamed in frustration before he picked up a kitchen stool and hurled it at the glass cabinet smashing two glass panels and damaging the wooden doors.

"Lucky I put the cabinet maker on retainer." David shook his head, but his joke went over like a lead balloon. Derrick spun around to accuse his brother.

"We let her down, just like we did with Isabelle."

"Enough, Derrick!" David barked in retaliation.

Derrick's head snapped up in surprise as David finished. "Isabelle was a grown woman with a mind of her own."

"But we could have told her what we knew about Nigel and maybe—"

"I did tell her."

"I don't understand?"

David sighed and took a deep breath before confessing, "Before the wedding, I caught Nigel coming out of a brothel with a prostitute. He was stinking drunk and made no attempt to conceal himself from me. I felt it my duty to tell Isabelle. She was understandingly upset and wanted to go to him and confront him so I went with her and waited outside the room in case things got ugly. When she came out, she was convinced that it was all a misunderstanding and that marriage would change him for the better. There was nothing I could say to convince her otherwise. You know how strong minded she was."

Derrick nodded his agreement. There were many similarities between Isabelle and Anna. He made his way to the couch where he sat silently as David continued his story.

"So, the marriage went ahead but I continued to follow Nigel and monitor his squandering of our family's money. I was forced to halve Isabelle's allowance so Nigel wouldn't spend it at the tavern and, instead of paying the money into their account—which I knew was in Nigel's name—I paid for the upkeep of the estate and grocery bills. I had hoped that this would force Nigel to find a job and start supporting his family but it only infuriated him. He began to associate with undesirables … gamblers, criminals and other low-lives who taught him how to scam and steal. He developed a fast temper and got into bar fights, usually coming home drunk and taking his frustration out on Isabelle."

"You knew about the beatings?" Derrick couldn't believe his brother could allow this to happen. "How could you not—"

David shook his head. "The first time it happened, I was already in Paris. The letter from Isabelle arrived not long after I arrived in France. She said that he had only hit her once, but he had apologized immediately and she hoped it wouldn't happen again but I didn't believe it. I wrote and told her to leave him."

Derrick shook his head. "I can't believe she didn't

tell me. Why didn't I notice the bruises?"

"The second letter informed me that he usually hit her in the stomach so there was no visible evidence. You wouldn't have seen anything."

"How long did this go on?"

"The second letter arrived for me around a month later. She told me that the beatings were becoming a daily occurrence and that she no longer loved him. She planned on leaving him. I told her to wait for me to return so we could confront him together and I booked my passage back the same day."

"So why did it take you so long to get back?"

David frowned. "If you remember, dear brother. I had an encounter with a lady whose company proved to be the *death* of me. My sire was on that very ship and it took a few days after landing for me to control my new *condition* enough to be of any assistance to you, Isabelle, or even myself for that matter. Her wham, bam, thank you ma'am approach left me completely out of control and a danger to everyone."

"Why haven't you told me all of this before?"

"Gee, I don't know, Derrick? Maybe because when I found you beside the body of our sister, beaten half to death and with three thugs and an arse-hole of a brother-in-law wailing on you, I had better things to do."

"You could have told me later."

"Yes, I guess I could have. Except, after I turned you, you told me that you hated me for not allowing you to die with Isabelle and took off for decades. You weren't an easy person to find in those days. My sources told me that when you weren't honing your fighting skills in Japan, you were out on the streets of London looking for thugs to beat up. By the way, I have always wondered … did you have anything to do with Jack's demise? I thought it was a coincidence that the ripper disappeared the day after you arrived."

Derrick shrugged but the corner of his mouth curled into a grin. David poured them both a drink, handed one to Derrick and pulled up a chair beside his brother. He flopped into it with a sigh.

"You have always been hot-tempered and passionate. Stop worrying about the things that have happened in the past or what could happen in the future. Get on with your life. Grab that little firecracker of yours and screw her brains out. God knows you both look like you could use the release. You're both so wound up, being around you is like waiting for a bomb to go off."

"You should write for Hallmark," Derrick told his brother, "your Valentine's Day cards would run off the shelves." He shook his head. "Grab her and screw her brains out. Lovely ... very romantic."

"At least I took your mind off your worries for a moment." David laughed.

"Okay, I realize that I have been a glass half-empty guy for a while, but we still have a serious problem to deal with. What was Torke doing here anyway? His beef is with me, not Anna."

"He wasn't invited if that's what you were thinking."

"Do you think it has anything to do with the scouts he sent to stir up trouble? The three vamps I took out behind Jake's gym?"

"That was years ago Derrick and I doubt that they meant anything to Torke anyway. But ... there have been a recent spate of disappearances in town. He may be recruiting for a hostile takeover. Remember what he insinuated the other night? He is using your reluctance to accept joint leadership to cause a rift in the coven."

Derrick opened his mouth to argue but was interrupted by his brother.

"I know that you were reluctant to rule with me but I think we have overcome our differences. It's time you forgave yourself, and me, and moved on. You have found Zen grasshopper."

"Oh bugger off!" Derrick cursed, but he couldn't restrain his smile.

"Well you know what they say ... united we stand—"

"Okay, okay. You have a point. From now on we work as a team and I am making an executive decision. Torke is going down."

"Good." David sipped his beverage, licking away the thick red liquid that clung to his lips. "I second that motion and in regards to what I said earlier, have you made any decisions about your little firecracker?"

Derrick ran both his hands through his thick black hair, his fingers digging into his scalp. "How could I? I was barely away for a night when Evan called me back. Those twenty-four hours were torture for me. I can't breathe without her."

"Technically you can't breathe at all little brother. At the risk of repeating myself. Why not just have her? Make mad passionate love to her if that's what it will take to make you happy. I really can't see the problem."

"I told you. I can't—"

"Run the risk of biting her, yes, I know that." He took another sip. "And I know you made a promise to yourself that you would never risk hurting her but some promises are meant to be broken."

"Not this one. Not if I can help it."

"So you plan on staying celibate?"

"It shouldn't be a problem." Derrick bit his bottom lip, his elongated teeth tearing into the flesh as he remembered the massage and its effect on both their bodies. "As long as I make sure she never gets me alone."

Chapter Eleven

Derrick locked the gym door behind the last of his Karate students. The class had run longer than usual with a few of the students lingering to ask questions about the Japanese origins of his techniques. Rushing into his dark office he began to strip off his Gi jacket choosing not to waste time showering. There was no need of a light switch; his eyesight was good in the dark. Besides, he was anxious to track down Torke and let him know how swiftly he would come down on him if he ever approached Anna again. Throwing his jacket across the room, he noticed a movement in the corner of the room. He tensed—all his senses on high alert, ready for an impending confrontation.

"Who's there?" He asked, although he already knew who was waiting in ambush and sensed that this encounter may be his undoing.

A shuffling noise. The shadow moved again, this time towards the door. As he heard the click of the lock, he noticed the silhouette glide past the door, the familiar scent already assaulting his senses.

"What are you doing here?"

Slowly she glided towards him. She took her time, each step seductive and sensual. He backed away, knowing all too well what she had on her mind. Her intentions clear. Her pheromones overwhelmed his senses. He was too close to the edge, couldn't take any more temptations, couldn't resist.

He repeated his question. "Anna. What are you doing here?"

She smiled and seductively traced her fingers down the front of the jacket she was wearing. The very same jacket he had discarded moments earlier. Her clothes were stacked neatly on the chair beside the door where she had obviously removed them earlier. He studied her body in the dimly lit room. Beneath the oversized jacket, her legs were bare. He swallowed. Hard. A bead of sweat trickled down his chest. To his amazement, Anna leaned forward and licked the salty trail. Slowly, sensually. He rolled his eyes and reached for her shoulders, holding her at arm's length.

"What are you doing?"

"Can't you tell?" She feigned a pout. "I mustn't be doing it right."

Grasping the neck of the jacket, she slowly—very slowly—eased it open. Derrick gasped as she lifted the jacket off her bare shoulders, lowering it to reveal a strapless red bra, a flat stomach and finally almost transparent lacy red panties. She stood almost naked before him, the jacket once again retired to the office floor.

"If this is about the other night, I'm sorry about the deception." *Be strong. Think of something to say. Anything.* Anything that would draw his attention away from her tantalizing body.

"I'm not sorry." Anna played with the draw string that tied his pants. "If anything, I owe you."

"You don't owe me anything." Of course he knew what she meant. His body shook with anticipation as she tugged the knot loose and his pants dropped to the floor, pooling at his ankles.

Anna smiled and licked her lips. "Ah. I see that along with the Karate, you also like *Commando*?"

Derrick silently cursed his body for betraying him. Even if he had bothered to wear underwear, his erection would have been hard to disguise. No matter what feeble excuses he formed, he knew his attraction betrayed him. His rock hard erection throbbed in anticipation of her touch. Still he tried to reason.

"We can't do this, Anna."

Even as he said the words, his hands reacted on their own accord. Reaching for her, brushing the silky skin on her arms as he unfastened the clasps on her bra, dropping it unceremoniously to the floor. He kissed her neck, lingering for a few moments before his mouth traced down to her shoulders. He lowered his hands to her panties, tearing the silk from her body like tissue paper. When he slipped his hand between her thighs, she forced him back into a chair to straddle his lap. Hovering over him, she dipped slightly, allowing a nipple to brush his face, caress his lips, enticing him to suckle. He drew the firm little peak into his mouth, wrapping his arms around her torso as she sighed and weaved her fingers through his hair.

His erection grew harder as she hovered directly above him, her own arousal moistening the tip of his shaft as she maneuvered herself into position. When he opened his mouth to protest, she silenced him with a kiss. Her warm, sweet mouth silencing his doubts, drawing him into her web of seduction. Unconsciously, his hands moved upwards to caress and cup her breasts. He had often dreamt of their weight and texture in his hands, against his chest, brushing his face and reality did not leave him disappointed. Her kisses became more intense, more desperate as she wiggled in response to his touch. Her soft moans encouraged him on. He could deny her nothing. He knew he was lost and doomed to break his promise because—the moment she drew his tongue into her mouth—she lowered herself down.

Past the point of no return. She had come to the office in order to tease Derrick, offer him pleasure and leave him as unsatisfied as he had left her the night of the massage. Her plan had been flawless until—until he brushed the skin between her thighs and sent a shock of heat through her already sensitized body. Her body cried out for more. More touching, more kissing, and more Derrick. She needed him more than she could ever have imagined. There was no turning back now. She wouldn't allow herself to forgo the experience of making love with this man. Even if it cost her everything: her pride, her reputation, her self-respect. Instead of hovering mercilessly above him until her withdrawal drove him insane, she gave in to her own wants, her own needs. She lowered herself down, gently at first, allowing her body to adjust to the size him, and then she gradually eased lower until she finally impaled herself on the full length of him.

****

Derrick struggled to retain control of his senses. He had already lost control of his body to Anna. Her muscles gripped him, searing his skin with velvet heat while his tongue shared the experience in her mouth. Her groans of pleasure reverberated in his mouth. She held his tongue between her lips while she rode him, stroked him, pleasured the both of them until he could stand no more. Supporting himself on the arms of the chair, Derrick shuddered with release. No way to hold back. She had unleashed his demon and it demanded satisfaction. His head shot back and he growled his orgasm, baring his fangs, feeling the incisors lengthen. With a final thrust of his body he seized her, sinking his fangs deep into her throat, tasting her, drowning in her sweet life force. She struggled uselessly against his vice-like grip. He fed, until her body went limp in his embrace.

When his fangs withdrew, Derrick realized he had gone too far. Anna's head slumped to the side. Her eyes closed and her cheeks stained with tears. Tears that had gone unnoticed during his quest for pleasure.

"Anna?" *How could he have done this?* She had been in pain, crying and he hadn't noticed, hadn't given a thought to how she felt. "Anna, please wake up."

She stirred in his arms, her eyes fluttered open. Her complexion ashen, her freckles stood out like polka dots on her pale cheeks, spotting her nose. Dark circles outlined her pale blue eyes. Her lips parted but it took a few excruciating moments before she spoke.

"What … happened?"

"I'm sorry." He clutched her to his chest, rocking her anxiously on his lap, their bodies still intimately joined. "I should never have allowed this to happen."

****

Anna could hardly move. Her body a dead weight, too heavy, too tired. She leaned into his chest, unable to lift her head as she fought the urge to sleep.

"Vampire," she mumbled, against his broad chest. "You lied to me. You really are a vampire."

"I didn't mean to lie. I just thought it was better you didn't know."

"Better for who?"

"I—I don't know. Better for both of us?"

"Oh, god. Does this mean I'm going to be like you?"

"A vampire? No. No, you can only be turned if I give you my blood."

"Good. That's good." *Sleep, just let me sleep.* "I don't want to change. I don't like change. I just want to be normal." She somehow managed to lift her chin. "Derrick?"

"Yes, Anna."

"I want to go home."

Chapter Twelve

"What's that infernal noise?" Anna struggled to open her eyes while the ringing continued. By the time she recognized the noise as the landline, the caller had given up. Either that, or the call was picked up by the answering machine. It didn't matter either way, she couldn't move. Her body felt weighed down with fatigue. She closed her eyes. Why was she so tired? Did she have a late night? When did she get home? Nothing made sense. She remembered going to the gym but she couldn't remember coming home. *What happened in between?* It was as though the whole of her evening had been erased from memory.

Shaking off the compulsion to remain in bed for the day, Anna slipped out from beneath the sheets and wondered why she was wearing her lacy nightgown when she usually preferred cotton pajamas. Not that it mattered, there was never anyone there to impress anyway. She made the conscious decision to cut back on her alcohol intake, despite its medicinal qualities. Whiskey blocked out the visions and red wine numbed her senses enough to ignore the empathic exchanges between her and whoever crossed her path. Still, if drinking had caused this stupor, she would learn to live without it.

She padded down the hall to make a mug of coffee, passing the flashing red light on the answering machine. For a moment, she considered checking the message but decided the coffee was a better proposition. Returning to the lounge room with a mug in hand, she depressed the button to retrieve her message. A hang up. Whoever called was too impatient to leave a message and Anna could not have cared less. Exhausted, her mind clouded as if and it were stuffed with cotton, she tried to make sense of the situation. *Had she been drinking last night?* She couldn't remember drinking, but then again, the whole night had become a blur.

Finishing her coffee, she strolled into the bathroom to take a quick shower before her jog with Susie. It seemed rather redundant having a shower *before* a workout but Anna felt she needed the hot water to wake her up. The fog in her head clouded her judgement, made it nearly impossible to form a clear thought. She hoped the shower would be the pick-me-up she needed. Susie would tease her mercilessly if she didn't keep up the pace. She reached into the recess and turned on the taps before returning to collect her clothes from the bedroom.

After stripping off her nightgown, she eased her weary body under the steady stream of water and sighed with relief as her tired muscles relaxed slightly with the heat. The shower foam felt luxurious against her bare skin and she felt sensitized, her body tingling as she touched the wash cloth to her breasts, her nipples peaking in response as though remembering a secret lover. Anna mentally shook off the thought and dismissed the idea as a fantasy. She had been having many of those lately. Fantasies of making love with Derrick on the table of the massage room … in the ocean … and one especially vivid dream of seducing him in their office. She turned the temperature of the water down to as cool as she could stand it, then she shampooed and conditioned her hair before wrapping her copper locks in a small towel. Stepping from the cubicle, she rubbed her body dry using a larger towel and noticed her throat stung when she wiped her neck. On inspection, the white terry cloth appeared to be spotted with blood.

That's weird. She didn't remember cutting herself. The nick from her recent mugging had already healed so it shouldn't be bleeding. Wiping away the condensation from the mirror with the edge of her towel, she stepped back in terror, her hand shooting up to cover her open mouth. The mirrored surface acted as movie screen, showing her—blow by blow—the missing parts of the previous night. Not only did the mirror explain the puncture wounds on her throat, it played the whole scene as if she were watching a late night horror movie. There in brilliant technicolor sat Derrick, gloriously naked, his body covered by hers as she straddled him in an erotic lap dance. Their love making continued, thrusting and gyrating to climax. *Oh, my god.* This was no fantasy. She remembered every sensation, every touch, every kiss. Someone had taken her memory of the event and conveniently erased it from her mind. *But why?* Anna stood transfixed as the mirror showed Derrick's lips receding, his teeth elongating. She watched in horror as he threw back his head in ecstasy, moments before sinking the fangs into her exposed throat. Her doppelganger in the mirror squirmed. Its head lolled to one side, its eyes fluttered and finally closed. She heard herself ask to be taken home before losing consciousness. Derrick rose, lifting her in his arms as he whispered a compulsion into her ear. *Nothing happened tonight, Anna. You will not remember any of this.*

The scene in the mirror blurred then disappeared altogether; leaving Anna staring at her own bemused reflection. "Bastard!" She screamed at the top of her lungs. "You selfish bastard!"

****

Evan answered the front door after the tenth knock. By the time he arrived, Anna raged.

"Where is he?"

"Oh, Miss Anna. How nice of you to—"

Anna forced her way past the elderly employee, stepping into the foyer.

"Derrick! Get out here this minute or I swear I'll stake you."

"Master Derrick is sleeping at the moment, Miss Anna." Evan hobbled over to the staircase and stood protectively at the base. "I'll tell him you called."

Anna pushed past him. "I'll tell him myself." She bounded the staircase, two steps at a time leaving Evan confused and mumbling protests, in her wake. She stormed from doorway to doorway opening and slamming doors as she searched for the right room. Finally, at the end of the hall, she discovered a room that seemed to fit the bill. Although she struggled to see in the darkened room, she could smell him. His musky, Armani enhanced scent permeated the room and, for a moment, she had to remind herself of her anger. Reaching her outstretched arms in front of her face in the dark, she touched something cold and hard.

"Derrick?"

"Anna? What are you doing here?"

Anna balled up her fist and took a swing at where she guessed his face would be. It hit something solid. Her wrist crumpled and pain shot up her arm. She screamed more from the frustration than the pain.

"You broke my wrist you bastard!"

"I'm sorry." He caught her hand and fondled the swelling joint. "I don't think it's broken, just sprained."

"Damn wall." She felt around the ink black room for somewhere to sit and found what appeared to be the foot of a large bed. "I was aiming at your face."

"Well, you were on target. You hit me on the chin."

She mumbled an expletive under her breath as she cradled her wrist in her other hand.

"If it makes you feel any better, it will probably bruise."

"Good." Anna mumbled as she rocked on the edge of the bed supporting her throbbing right hand. "I wish I'd knocked your stupid head off."

She sensed Derrick's movements as he approached her. He appeared to have no difficulty navigating a darkened room. *Of course he wouldn't.* She now understood how he was able to do it. When he touched her arm, she pushed him away.

"What is the matter, my little Firecracker?"

"I'm not *your* little anything." She pulled away from his contact. As angry as she was, his touch melted her bones but she was determined to remain annoyed. He had violated her trust and she wanted him to know it wasn't okay. She rose and felt her way around the walls of the room. It seemed massive.

"Where's the damn light switch?"

A surge of white flashed before Anna's eyes and she blinked until her eyes adjusted to the light of the crystal chandelier that Derrick had switched on. Its radiance so bright she fully expected Derrick to burst into flames.

"Better?"

She scanned the room and discovered that other than being completely closed off and sealed from the sunlight, it was a rather spectacular bedroom. Her whole house would fit inside it with room to spare. Well, not quite but damned close. Anna did a quick mental inventory of the décor but her focus was drawn to the larger than life king-size bed. Her fingers itched to glide over the black silk sheets that lay crumpled on the edge but she controlled the urge, determined to stay angry. When she turned back to Derrick, a lump caught in her throat. He stood at the foot of the bed, completely naked and obviously pleased to see her—very pleased indeed.

"Will you stop pointing that thing at me?"

Derrick reached for her. She held him at arm's length with the heel of her hand and sat on the edge of the bed.

"Shouldn't you be in a coffin sleeping until dusk?"

"The bed's more comfortable. Care to join me?"

Anna swallowed another lump. Since the earlier vision, her memory of the previous night had returned in full. All the x-rated segments accentuated by vivid and very physical reactions. It was as though her skin was marked by his touch. It remembered every stroke of his fingers, every lap of his tongue and especially the parts of his body that she found hard to ignore while he stood naked before her. Even now, her nipples strained against the lace of her bra as she tried not to think about how well they fit together. She imagined how soft those sheets would feel against her bare skin as he— *No*. She couldn't allow her hormones to control the situation. She shook her head to dislodge the images. *He bit you damn it. Focus on that.*

"How could you do that to me … and don't try and make excuses this time. You bit me and then you tried to erase my memories. Why would you do that?"

Derrick's jovial expression turned solemn. His eyes lowered to the floor as he offered his excuse.

"I was only trying to help you."

"How? By turning me into a vampire or by taking away my free will?"

"I would never try and turn you, Anna." He sat beside her on the bed but kept his hands to himself although it was a struggle. He desperately wanted her, now more than ever. The sight of her on his bed made him harder than he imagined possible.

"But you took away my memories. Did you intend on making me some type of sex slave? Use me then make me forget after every interlude?"

Derrick stifled a laugh. He knew this was a serious matter but Anna's colorful imagination never ceased to amaze and delight him.

"If you remember *mon amour*, you seduced me. I am, first and foremost a male. As you women like to point out, sometimes our brains go south of the border. It's hard to stay focused sometimes, especially when a beautiful, naked woman straddles me in my office."

Color spread across Anna's face and chest and she lowered her eyes as he continued. "I'm a vampire, Anna. There, are you happy now, I've admitted it. You can't seduce a vampire and not get bitten. You literally *screwed* the demon out of me."

"What do we do now?" She flopped back on the bed and stared up at the ceiling.

"I don't know my love." He gave in to his compulsion and wrapped her in his arms. This time she snuggled against his bare chest, her fingers curled around the sprinkling of chest hairs. "I tried to take away your memories so I could spare you the pain but obviously that didn't work."

"The pain?" Anna looked up into his eyes. "I don't remember any pain but I remember pleasure. Lots and lots of it."

He was glad that her memories included enjoyment of the experience. It was a night that he would never forget. But, could he risk repeating the experience? There had to be a way to control his demon. A way to take comfort in her without risking her mortal soul. He would talk to David. Consult ancients. Find a way to make it work. He couldn't lose her, not now, not ever.

"You were distressed when you realized I'd bitten you. I couldn't bear to see your tears. It was all I could think of to do. I know that sounds selfish."

"You should have given me a choice. That's what you should have done. You could have told me the truth and allowed me to decide if it was worth the risk."

"Where do we go from here?"

"I don't know." Anna shrugged her shoulders and sighed. "My life feels like it's spinning madly out of control. Too many changes. Everything is happening so fast."

"I know there are many complications in your life at the moment, things you aren't prepared to deal with but there's something else we need to talk about."

"Torke?"

"Yes, Anna. Do you know why he is so interested in you?"

"I have no idea what he wants with me but I believe he killed my mother." She swallowed before continuing. He heard the pain in her voice as she told him, "And … I know he plans on killing me."

Derrick grabbed her by the shoulders. His arms shaking as he held her tightly. "He told you that?"

"He made it very clear, Derrick. He said that I had made my choice and that he was sorry I wasn't going to be able to live with it. Correct me if I'm wrong but that sounds like a death threat to me."

"I want you to stay away from him."

"Fine by me, but I think he has other ideas."

"I was afraid of that." Derrick rose from the bed and began pacing the room.

****

To her horror, Anna found herself staring longingly at his lean, naked body as he walked back and forth past the bed. He suddenly stopped directly in front of her. "I'm not usually out of bed at this time of day. If I'd known you were coming, I would have dressed."

"Don't bother on my account."

Derrick dragged her up into his arms. "The way I see it we have two choices…" He kissed a path from her shoulders to her throat.

"Uh-huh."

"I either get dressed so I can focus on you telling me more about your confrontation with Torke or…"

"Mmmmm"

"You take off your clothes and join me in bed."

"Can't you tell me about Torke *while* you take me to your bed?"

"I have a sneaking suspicion what I have to say will be a buzz kill."

"Spoil sport." She pushed him away with both hands. "Get dressed and say what you have to say." Although there was more than enough room for many people in the king size bed, she didn't want to be thinking about Torke while making love with Derrick. It could permanently damage the relationship, if there was one to begin with.

To Anna's disappointment, Derrick dressed quickly into a t-shirt and jeans and sat beside her on the edge of the bed.

"Have you met Torke before that night in the garden?"

"No never." Anna shook her head vehemently. "But he insists he knows me. Said he knew my mother."

Derrick's eyebrows joined in consternation. "Did your mother ever speak of him?"

"Not that I remember, but then again … I was only a child when my mother died. I've only recently learned she cast some sort of memory spell on me so she may have blocked that out too."

"Memory spell? Your mother was a witch?"

"I guess so." Anna agreed with a shrug of her shoulders. "I found a letter in a box that belonged to her.

It seems that the practice of Wicca may have been common on her side of the family."

Derrick thought for a moment. "There used to be a coven of witches who practiced in this area. Possibly your mother was one of them."

"I guess so." Anna shrugged. "But there is no one to confirm that. Dad never spoke about witches and now that he's gone, I have no-one to ask."

"There may be someone we could question. One of the witches from that coven is still alive." Derrick informed her. "She was left for dead with the others but somehow managed to survive, despite being very young at the time."

"What do you mean, left for dead? How many people besides my mother did Torke kill?"

"Six." He informed her. "They tell me that thirteen was the number traditionally said to make up a coven but I have since learned that the number may vary from two to two thousand. This coven was relatively small."

"How did they die?" A chill ran down her spine. Would she suffer the same fate?

"By fire. At least five of them anyway. The other died—"

"By car accident." Anna realized the implication. Her mother was the sixth.

"How did you know?"

"Because the sixth witch was my mother." It all made sense now.

"How long have you known this? Jake never mentioned that his wife had been a witch or that she died in a car accident."

"I only found out recently." Anna looked into his eyes and waited for the reaction that usually came after she admitted her secret. "I was told in a vision."

"Your mother … was she psychic?"

"I guess. She told me once—while we were playing a game—that she had worked as a palm reader. I thought it was part of the game."

"And you inherited these abilities?"

Anna nodded. "Not the palm reading but, since I was a child, I've had visions about the future and sometimes the past, although most of the time I try to block them out."

"Why would you want to block them out?"

"Maybe you had a great childhood, Derrick, but mine was miserable." She rose from the bed and paced the length of the room, wringing her hands as memories of her childhood flooded back. "I could barely cope with the empath thing without experiencing visions of the future. All I have ever wanted was to be normal but it's hard when you can't determine whether the feelings you are experiencing are your own or those of the people around you."

"I guess that is why you were reluctant to share the office?"

Anna nodded. "That, and the fact that every time I came near you, my head felt as though it might split in two. I don't suppose that you had anything to do with that?"

Derrick shrugged. "Sorry about that. I could feel you trying to read my thoughts and I couldn't allow it."

"But, Derrick, I can't read thoughts, only emotions."

"I hate to break this to you love but you were definitely trying to read my mind, whether you knew it or not."

"Damn." She dropped down beside him on the bed and let her head rest in her hands. "It feels like the universe is trying to punish me." She turned to Derrick, her eyes filling with tears. "What have I done to deserve this? What does the universe have against me just blending in?"

"You, my darling, would always stand out in a crowd whether you had powers or not. Your kindness and compassion for others is a beacon. People will always be drawn to you."

He hugged her to his chest as he continued. "Some people would kill to be able to do what you do."

Bursting into tears, Anna announced, "They can have it, I've had enough." Her tears dampened his fresh t-shirt and she scrubbed at it with a tissue as she told him, "I'm tired of blocking the visions but I can't bear to have them. Is there any way you can take them away? Can you use your vampire powers to help me?"

Derrick shook his head. "If you remember, I couldn't even prevent you from remembering our rendezvous in the office."

"In a way, I'm glad that you didn't take *that* memory away from me." She informed him, her smile curling in one corner of her mouth. "One last pleasant memory to take to my grave when Torke kills me."

Derrick grasped her chin, forcing her to face him. "I will never let that happen. Think Anna. Do you remember anything strange happening in your life recently? Something that might relate to Torke?"

"Strange? My whole freaking life has been strange!"

"Such as…"

"Such as having a compulsion to clean or count whenever I feel things are beyond my control. Such as having premonitions about murders before they happen or photocopiers about to catch fire and knowing people are going to call before they do. Sensing danger."

"That power could come in handy," Derrick told

her. "But what I don't get is why Torke suddenly decided to come for you? Why hasn't he attacked you before?"

"I guess I should be grateful for small mercies," Anna confessed. "But I don't understand why either."

"And Jake? He never told you anything about your mother's death or about Torke?"

She shook her head. "Never mentioned it. As a matter of fact, whenever I tried to broach the subject, he seemed to go vague, like he didn't understand what I was talking about."

"Sounds like a compulsion or spell," Derrick informed her. "She must have performed something on your father similar to what she did to you."

"I guess I can understand her concern." Anna conceded although she wished she understood more about her mother's reasoning. "But she kind of left us unprotected by blocking our memories. We were powerless against Torke because we didn't know how to defend ourselves."

"I'm sure she did what she thought was best." She felt his chin resting on the top of her head. "Sometimes our actions hurt those who we love, despite our good intentions."

"That sounds like an apology."

"It is in a way. I have made my share of mistakes and I live with the regret but if I ever hurt you again or thought I would never see your face again; I would go willingly into the light."

"Nice answer." Anna murmured against the granite muscles of his chest. "So … I'll ask you again, where do we go to from here?"

Derrick flopped back onto the bed dragging Anna down with him. He rolled her onto her back and positioned himself between her legs leaving her in no doubt of his intentions, especially when he began to unzip his jeans. His fingers began to open her blouse, one agonizing button at a time.

"Not so fast, buster." She pushed against his shoulders, barely forcing a slight gap between their bodies. I am more than willing to participate in the sex but I need you to promise me that you won't bite me. I don't think I could bear any more changes in my life."

"I'm not sure if I can keep that promise. Not yet anyway."

Derrick climbed off, leaving Anna feeling slightly rejected and somewhat angry with herself.

"I have no control over my hormones or my physical urges, especially when I'm with you. I have no right to ask you to risk your life this way." He continued, "I should never have allowed you to seduce me. We should have waited until I learned how to control my demon."

"I … seduced … you?" Anna raised herself onto her elbows. "I seem to remember a massage that got way out of control … a law suit in the making in fact. Human resources would have your guts for garters."

"My behavior was inexcusable."

"You're damn right it was!"

"I've said I'm sorry, Anna." His voice trembled. "And if you remember, it wasn't *me* who paraded around naked and gave *you* a lap dance."

"That was payback."

"So, turnabout is fair play?"

"In this case … yes." Anna sat up on the bed and wiggled over to the edge. When her toes touched the floor, she rose to her feet. "I wanted you to know how it felt to be driven to the brink of sexual frustration and left wanting—"

Before she could finish her sentence he had closed the distance between them. His cool breath kissed her cheek.

"You think I don't feel that every day?" he leaned in closer, his cheek nuzzled her neck. "Every fiber of my being wants you … all of you. I want to drown in the warmth of you, drink my fill of you and bring you more pleasure than you could ever imagine possible."

Anna's breath caught in her throat and her heart beat double time. Her knees began to buckle under the weight of her trembling legs. His words reverberated in her head "bring you more pleasure than you could ever imagine possible." She wanted him as much as he wanted her but would she be willing to pay the price for his love?

"As much as it pains me to say this," she told him, "I think we should back pedal, at least until we work out Torke's agenda."

Derrick mouth slowly curved into a grin. "You are as wise as you are beautiful."

She lowered her chin to hide the color she felt rush to her cheeks. He lifted her chin with his index finger. "It's about time we started working together instead of butting heads."

Anna agreed. "It would make a pleasant change from arguing and, to be completely honest, I don't think I can face Torke on my own."

"Okay then. Tonight I'll take you to visit the surviving witch. She's a family friend and runs a store in town. I'm sure she'll be willing to help."

"Tonight? Why not now?"

Derrick lowered his chin and looked up at her through his long eyelashes. "It's way past my bedtime, if you catch my drift."

"Oh," her hand shot to her mouth as she realized the implications. She had barged into his sanctuary mid-morning. The sun was directly overhead. "I guess I'd better let you get back to bed." She turned but a tug at her wrist forced her to turn around.

"I know we promised to take things slower so I won't ask you to join me in bed, but, would a goodnight kiss be out of the question?"

She allowed him to draw her into his arms, where she stayed, for most of the afternoon.

Chapter Thirteen

Anna sat at her desk, contemplating her next step when there was a quiet knock at the door.

"Come in."

The instant she spoke the words, she wondered if she had lost her mind. Anyone could be waiting outside that door and "anyone" could have sharp fangs and claws. She was now well aware of the things that go bump in the night. When she recognized the blonde head, she relaxed back in her chair.

"Hey, Susie. What's up?"

"Thought you might like to go shopping with me. I have a blind date tonight and I want to look drop dead gorgeous just in case he turns out to be *Mr. Right*."

Anna shuddered at the words. *Drop dead gorgeous*. How would it feel to be forever young and beautiful?

"Sure. I need to get a bit of fresh air anyway."

"It's blowing a gale outside … is that fresh enough for you?"

Anna strolled over to the coat rack and retrieved her woolen jacket. "Let's go shopping."

****

The dress Susie chose for her blind date was stunning and she looked totally hot in it. They were on their way home when Anna spotted a tiny store wedged between a café and a butcher shop. Soft lights burned enticingly from the window and the faint smell of incense lured her over to inspect the shop front.

"Heavenly aspects," she read aloud.

"Yeah, one of those New Age places." Anna winced as Susie elbowed her rib. "Let's go in and have a sticky beak, just for laughs."

"I'm game if you are."

"You never know what we might find in there and I have an hour to kill before I need to get ready. Maybe I could buy a love spell?"

"I wonder if they would give us a discount if we buy two?" Anna added half-heartedly. "Fine. Let's get it over with." She grabbed Susie's arm and dragged her inside.

A little bell hanging over the door frame heralded their entrance and a small voice called out in greeting.

"I'll be right with you."

Anna glanced around in wonder. From the outside, the store appeared tiny but inside … it seemed much larger. There was something familiar about the fragrance burning in a long wooden incense holder. Something Anna couldn't quite put her finger on, but she recognized the scent.

A middle-aged woman appeared between beaded curtains that divided a small room from the main store. "Good evening, young ladies. Please browse. If you would like anything explained, I'll be more than happy to help you."

"How about everything?" Susie giggled. "I wouldn't know where to start with most of this stuff." She held up a pink tear-drop shape crystal dangling from a silver chain.

"That's a rose quartz pendulum. You use it for scrying," Anna told her without thinking.

"How did you know that Anna?"

"I have no idea." Anna shrugged her shoulders. "It just popped into my head. I must have read it somewhere."

"You are correct." The shopkeeper informed her as she made her way over to show Susie some more stones, her white cane brushing the bottom of the counter. "We have many crystals. Some clear quartz crystal or …

this lovely obsidian pendulum." She held out the crystal for Anna and Susie to inspect. They stared at each other in amazement. Scars ran across both the woman's eyelids. Her eyes were clouded and lifeless and yet, she knew exactly what she held. Anna's heart skipped a beat. Was this her mother's friend?

"That's really pretty, Anna." Susie told her although Anna could tell from Susie's tone that she wasn't really interested in anything in the shop. She was barely pausing as she circumnavigated the store.

Anna took the pendulum from the middle-aged woman, her fingers casually brushing the woman's palm.

The woman recoiled at her touch.

"Take it, you will need it."

"Okay."

Anna pulled a face at Susie who had covered her mouth with her hand and was trying not to laugh.

"How much?"

"Nothing. It's a gift."

"Oh, no. Thank you but I couldn't accept. Let me buy it."

"My name is Sofie, I knew your mother," she whispered. "We were part of the same coven." Sofie's face paled, her whole body trembled.

"Are you all right?" Anna located a chair and helped the woman sit. "Can I get you anything?"

"No, thank you dear. I'll be fine in moment." She smiled but when she patted Anna's hand, her own hand was trembling. Her lifeless eyes seemed to gaze into Anna's, unnerving her. Suddenly Sofie whispered, "He's back, isn't he?"

"Who?" Anna asked although she already knew the answer that Sofie wanted.

"I am only blind in this world child. My eyes see many things in my dreams and on the astral planes."

"Yes," Anna admitted. "Torke is back."

Turning Anna's hand, Sofie began to trace the inside of the palm with her finger.

"I remember your mother … her gift was strong. I was so envious of her talent. Torke recognized her talent too and was enamored by her beauty." She touched Anna's face. "You look like her." Anna turned to Susie who shrugged and pulled a face.

"I may not have sight, but I have insight. You are the spitting image of your mother, Anna. Torke will be drawn to your beauty … and your talents."

A ripple of fear thread its way through Anna's body. It was a though Torke was reaching into her soul, touching her with his gnarled fingers.

"Yes. He is repulsive." Sofie nodded. "But he wasn't always that way. He was a handsome man once."

"I'll take your word for it." Anna turned to make sure that Susie was out of earshot. "Why hasn't he attempted to contact me before now?"

"I sense a spell. Something blocking him." She stilled for a moment. "You blocked him Anna. You have been trying to hide your powers but, recently, you have let your guard down and…"

"And what?"

"Ah, I see we have a mutual friend. How *is* Derrick?" Sofie smiled and somehow Anna knew that the blind woman had seen the meeting at Derrick's house.

Anna looked at her watch. "By now, Derrick should be out looking for Torke. Let's hope he finds him soon. As a matter of fact, we had planned on visiting you tonight."

"Fate brought you here today, Anna. You must stay on guard at all times and prepare yourself for psychic attacks on you *and* your friends." Sofie reached out for Anna's arm and pulled her close to whisper, "Your friend

Susie is in danger." She reached into her pocket and took out a small crystal before grasping the arms of her chair and easing herself up. She made her way over to Susie who was browsing through New Age books on a nearby shelf and placed a crystal in her hand, closing her fingers around it.

"Keep this with you always. It will keep you safe."

"Thanks, but I'm not really into that sort of stuff." Susie told her before placing the crystal on the counter and heading for the door, tilting her head to motion for Anna to follow her out. "It's getting late, Anna. Maybe we should head home?"

"Sure, we must get you ready for this date." She needed more time with Sofie but Susie was already halfway out the door. She turned back to Sofie and asked, "Would it be all right if I came back some other time?"

The woman nodded, reached out and held tight to Anna's hand. There was urgency in her voice when she warned Anna. "He will try to influence you by hurting your friends." Her head inclined towards Susie. "Don't let her meet with this man tonight."

"Anna. Could we please leave?" Susie voice sounded agitated as she called from the door. "It's started raining and I have to get ready for my date."

"No date … not tonight," Sofie pleaded as she released Anna's hand.

"I'll watch out for her," Anna promised although she had no idea how she was going to stop Susie from keeping her appointment. She said her goodbyes and left the shop. Susie was waiting anxiously outside.

"Was that creepy or what?" She pulled a face and shivered. "Do you believe what she said to you … that stuff about your Mum I mean?"

"She seemed to know quite a bit about me." Anna

reasoned. "Something else, Susie."

"What is it?"

"The man she spoke of. The evil man who she says killed my Mum…"

"Go on."

"He is the guy who has been stalking me. You know … the creepy guy who attacked me the other night."

Susie's face visibly paled as she grabbed Anna's hands.

"You have to tell Derrick."

"I've told Derrick."

"And?"

"It's complicated."

"Anna. What are you going to do? I'm frightened for you."

"I'll be all right." Suddenly a clap of thunder rattled the windows beside them. Rain poured down, drenching them as they ran for the car. "That's if we don't catch pneumonia."

****

"Are you sure I can't talk you out of going on this blind date?" Something felt wrong. Anna was beginning to have her own reservations about Susie's blind date. She sat on a bench in the ladies' change room while Susie put the finishing touches on her hair and makeup.

"Are you kidding? I haven't been out in ages and Carol said this guy is gorgeous. Six foot two, eyes of—"

"Let me guess … blue?"

"Ha, ha, very funny. His eyes are green actually or so I've been told." She turned to Anna for approval. "How do I look?"

"Gorgeous. He's going to be bowled over."

"It's been a long time since I've had a date. I really hope he likes me, Anna."

"I really hope *you* like him." She followed Susie to the door. "And don't forget—"

"I know … you've told me ten times already. If I'm feeling anxious or I just want to get away from him, I'll send you a text message to come and rescue me."

"Let's hope it doesn't come to that."

"Fingers crossed."

Both crossed their fingers and giggled. Susie gave Anna a kiss on the cheek and dashed out to her car as the wind and rain threatened to ruin her outfit. Anna watched as her best friend drove down the street. She wished she could feel enthusiastic but the knot in her stomach warned her of impending danger. She closed her eyes and sent up a silent prayer. *Please keep her safe.*

Chapter Fourteen

Anna found sleeping difficult that night. She missed Derrick and wished she could tell him about the conversation with Sofie but he had insisted she remain sequestered at home. Several times she reached for her mobile phone to check for messages from Susie but there were none, so she assumed that all was well, despite her feelings to the contrary. The next morning, she came in to work early, anxious to check in on her friend. Susie had skipped their morning run without even a phone call to cancel. It was uncharacteristic but, not surprising. *She probably slept in after a big night and headed straight to work.* As Anna opened the front door of the gym, she caught the tail end of a conversation between the receptionist and a patron.

"What do you mean Susie didn't come in this morning? We had an appointment at 9 a.m."

"I'm sorry, Mrs. Livingstone. It's not like Susie to not call if she going to be late. We can reschedule if you like, unless you would like to wait for Stephen?" Carol glanced in Anna's direction and rolled her eyes.

"Last time I worked with Stephen he left me aching all over," the obese, middle-aged woman complained. "It took me a week to get over it."

"In that case, we should throw in a complimentary massage and beauty treatment," Anna interrupted. "If that's all right with you, Mrs. Livingstone?"

"Well, all right Anna. Seeing as how I'm already in my workout clothes." She waddled into the cardio room to wait for the substitute trainer.

"Thanks." Carol fake wiped her brow and smiled as she let out a sigh. "She's not our easiest customer."

"No problem. Did I hear you say that Susie hasn't

called in?"

"Yeah and it's not like her. I called her mobile a couple of times and it went straight to voicemail. She's not answering her landline either."

"She blew off our run this morning too." Bile rose in her throat. Something was very wrong with this situation. "I'll call around to her house, just in case she's under the weather."

"Maybe you should take some chicken soup?"

Carol's suggestion was thoughtful but Anna knew in her heart that Susie wasn't ill. Silently she prayed her friend was still alive.

"Good idea. I'll buy some on the way."

****

The drive to Susie's small flat seemed agonizingly slow despite the fact Anna drove over the speed limit for the whole journey. Not surprisingly, there was no answer as she pounded on the door calling out her friend's name. She sat down on the stoop and waited for over an hour before deciding to call Derrick.

"Good morning. Corel residence."

"Evan, its Anna Derwent. I need to speak with Mr. Corel. It's urgent."

"Hello, Miss Derwent. I'll see if he's available."

Anna heard the click off the phone being put down on a table and the scuffling of old slippers on tiled floor. It felt like an eternity before she heard the receiver being lifted.

"Anna?"

"Derrick. Something terrible has happened and I didn't know who else to—"

"It's all right honey. Tell me what's happened."

She started her story but her words dissolved into sobs. *Please god, don't let it be too late.*

"Anna. Take a deep breath and tell me what has

happened. Are you hurt?"

"No. Not me." She took a few cleansing breaths and started again. "My friend Susie, from the gym. She went on a blind date last night and hasn't returned."

"The little blonde fitness instructor?"

"Yes, that's her. I'm afraid she might be dead."

"That's a bit drastic don't you think? Maybe she just got lucky."

"How dare you insinuate such things about a sweet person like Susie."

"I'm sorry, Anna. I didn't mean anything by it. My way of trying to ease the tension."

"Well it's not funny."

"At least it stopped you from going hysterical. Do you think you can tell me now why you are presuming the worst?"

"If you make fun of me I'll—"

"Go on. I promise to behave."

"I spoke with Sofie yesterday and she was able to tell me things about my family that make sense. She warned me to stop Susie from going on the blind date. I wish I had listened."

"You met Sofie? How did you know where to find her?"

"Purely by accident. Susie and I were shopping and we stumbled across her store. Derrick. She knew that Torke was back."

"Okay, now I understand your concern. You have my full attention. What did she say about Torke?"

"She warned me that he would come after me through my friends. She tried to convince Sofie to cancel her date." Anna waited for a response. "Derrick, are you still there?"

"Yes, Anna. Listen to me. Torke is a very dangerous man. Where are you?"

"Sitting on Susie's porch."

"It's getting late and I don't want you to go out after dark. As a matter of fact, go straight home now and lock the doors and windows."

"What about Susie?"

"I will look into the disappearance of your friend. I give you my word."

"Derrick?"

"Yes, Anna."

"Please find her."

****

Derrick shouted down the telephone line at his brother. "It's been two days since Susie's disappearance. Haven't you heard anything?"

"If I had, Derrick, I would have come straight to you with the information. I have ears and eyes everywhere, figuratively speaking of course. As soon as I hear anything, I'll let you know."

"I'm sorry, David. The longer he remains at large, the more I fear for Anna and her friend."

"And Anna? How is she coping?"

"She believes the worst. I must admit. I don't hold out much hope of finding her alive either. If Torke has the girl—"

"No. I still believe he is holding her as bait. She wouldn't be a bargaining tool is she was dead. He's sure to make a move soon."

"As much as I want to head straight to Anna's house, I should check in at the gym. Torke may go after other staff members."

"Let me do that. You need to be with Anna and I'm sure she needs you."

"Really? Thanks, David. I owe you." He hung up the phone and bolted for his Porsche.

Chapter Fifteen

David did a double take when he opened the office door. "What are you doing here? I thought I told you to stay at home?"

Anna sat at the desk. Dark circles ringed her eyes and strands of her hair stood on end as though they hadn't seen a brush for days.

"I was getting cabin fever." Anna shuffled together some of the papers on her desk and carried them to the filing cabinet. "I must have lost track of time. It must be dark if you're here."

"I have no idea what you mean by that?"

"Come on, David. Enough with the jokes. I'm too tired to play this game and Derrick must have told you that I know what you are."

"You mean that we're devilishly handsome, super rich, and generously endowed."

"David!"

"Okay. At least I'm those things. Derrick is moderately attractive, comfortably rich, and adequately endowed."

"Fine, play your games, but could you at least tell me where Derrick is?"

"Probably waiting on your doorstep."

"Damn. I had hoped to be home before he got there." She checked her watch. "He's probably going to be pissed."

A commotion outside the office caught their attention and Anna raced to open the door.

"What is it?" she asked Carol who was sobbing in Stephen's arms.

"They just announced on the radio … it's so awful."

"What's awful?" she shook Carol by her shoulders. "What is it Carol?"

"A body. The police have found the body of a young blonde woman stuffed behind the industrial bins in an alley on Shelly Beach road. They say she's been dead a couple of days. Oh, Anna, do you think it is … oh, god."

"No. It's not her. It can't be." *Surely she would have sensed something?* Anna ran back to her office and grabbed her handbag. She rummaged in it for her car keys as she ran to the car park. David was already there waiting.

"Stay here, Anna. I'll go and see if it's your friend."

"No, David. Get out of my way." She vainly tried to move him away from the driver's side of her car until it was obviously useless. Breaking down in tears she begged him, "Please, David. I must know."

"Derrick is going to kill me for this but … all right. If you must go, let me drive you."

They rushed to David's gray Aston Martin and tore out of the car park, tires squealing.

Using their telepathic connection, David informed Derrick of the situation. *"Stay with her,"* Derrick begged his brother. *"Don't let her out of your sight."*

****

David pulled up to the curb beside a police car instructing Anna to stay in the car until he had spoken with the officer in charge. She watched the expression on the officer's face turn from irritation to compliance as David stared into his eyes while he spoke. She realized he was using a compulsion, much like Derrick had used on her when he erased her memories. David followed the officer into the alley behind the group of stores and disappeared from view. She waited impatiently as minutes passed without a sign. Ten minutes later, two men in dark jumpsuits wheeled a body bag from the alley. It was more than Anna could bear. She jumped from the car and ran towards the stretcher, hitting what felt like a solid wall. "No, Anna. You don't want to see what's in that bag."

"Derrick?" Anna looked up from the silk covered chest that blocked her path and into the violet blue eyes she had missed for twenty-four hours. One day felt like a lifetime.

"If it's Susie, she wouldn't want you to see her that way."

"I have to know for sure." Anna sobbed. "Please, let me go."

"No need to put yourself through the horror of opening that bag, Anna." David announced as he approached. "I've saved you the trouble."

"Is it—?"

"No. It wasn't your friend Susie."

"Are you sure, David?"

"Positive."

Anna's legs crumpled and she fell into Derrick's arms. He scooped her up and held her as David explained.

"It was a young blonde woman but unless Susie suddenly lost around twenty kilos since I saw her last and managed to hide a multitude of track marks, it was not her."

"Any idea who she was?" David carried Anna over to a bench and helped her sit. She clung to him, afraid he would disappear the moment she let go.

"The police believe she was a runaway who was living on the streets. She probably came here to meet a drug dealer and was ambushed by vampires."

"Was it Torke's handiwork?" Anna struggled to

even say his name.

"I doubt it."

"How can you be sure?"

"Because it was a very brutal attack. Torke has a reputation for leaving tidy corpses. His methods are quick and neat. This poor young woman was torn apart. Most likely an entire rogue coven judging by the multiple wounds."

Anna buried her head inside Derrick's jacket and shuddered. *What if Susie had met the same fate?* "Oh god. What if they got Susie too?"

"We're going to find her. I promise you that."

She raised her head in time to see Derrick stare his brother squarely in the face as he made his pledge. David nodded and left.

****

As they walked back to Derrick's Porsche, Anna remembered her conversation with Sofie and she enlightened Derrick about her experience. He admitted that there may be some truth in the woman's story.

"Maybe it's time we paid Sofie another visit."

"Do you think she may know what happened to Susie?"

"Even if she can't help, I don't see any harm in asking."

"It's late night shopping so the store should be open. It's not far from here so we may as well walk."

As they strolled the short distance to the store, Anna glanced at a missing person poster attached to a street light post. She turned her head and saw that all the posts in the street were covered with similar posters. "How many of these people do you think met with the same fate as the young woman in the alley?"

"I don't think you want to know." Derrick stared blankly ahead but gave Anna's hand a squeeze.

"I thought we were past keeping secrets, Derrick. Tell me the truth, no sugar coating."

"All of them."

"You're not serious?" she froze on the spot.

"You said you wanted the truth." He turned to face her. "I believe all the people on those posters are dead."

"Did you—?"

"No. None of them. How could you even think that?"

"I'm no expert but as far as I know you don't drink vegetable juice."

"I'm not a killer, not anymore—not unless I'm forced."

"So you don't kill when you drink human blood?"

"No, I don't. Can we drop this subject? I think we have more pressing matters."

Anna remained silent but David's reluctance to answer worried her. How was she to learn about his way of life if he refused to discuss it? Maybe Sofie had the answers?

Sofie was in the process of hanging the closed sign on the door to the shop when Anna and Derrick approached but opened the door and motioned for them to enter before pulling the shades.

"I was expecting you." She hugged each in turn. "So pleased to see you Derrick."

"Do you know where she is?" Anna felt there was no use beating around the bush. Sofie had been right about the danger; she probably knew what had happened.

"I warned you about Torke. He will stop at nothing to get you and in answer to your question, yes ... he has Susie."

"Is she—?"

Sofie felt her way down Anna's arm to find her

hand. She gave it a squeeze. "She's alive, Anna. At least for now."

"How? How did he get his hands on her?" In the short time that Anna had known Susie, she had come to the conclusion that she had street smarts. There is no way she would go willingly with a man like Torke.

"The blind date." Sofie reminded her. "Torke set up a trap. The man drugged her drink and he took her to Torke."

"This man—is he a vampire?"

"No. Not a vampire, just a bad person." She motioned for them to sit and did the same.

"Why would he want to help Torke?"

"Evil men are attracted to vampires and what they represent. He wants something from Torke. It could be power, fortune, or even eternal life. In this case, I think this man wants all those things and will stop at nothing to get them."

Anna slumped back in her chair. "He *wants* to be made into a vampire?"

"Yes, I believe he has wanted that for a long time."

"I can't believe there are people who would actually choose to become monsters."

"Not all vampires are monsters, Anna. Your man—Derrick, he's a good man. His brother is also a good man. Cheeky, but good."

"How do you know them?"

"Derrick helped me and my daughter when my husband passed away. He is very kind and I sense he loves you very much."

Anna waited until Derrick moved away to examine a statue at the other end of the story. She whispered. "He's a secretive man."

"Secrets are a necessary evil sometimes. Take

your situation for example."

She shook her head. "You're wrong, Sofie. I'm an open book. My parents used to joke that I always wore my heart on my sleeve and my face was always a giveaway when I tried to lie."

"I'm talking about the secrets *involving* you, Anna. Before Torke came to our town, your mother sensed his arrival and knew that he would be attracted to our coven's power. She feared that if we challenged him, he would blackmail us by threatening to hurt our loved ones. She gave us each a spell to place on objects for our families to block Torke from connecting them to us and another to wipe any memory of the family of those who passed away so that Torke couldn't use our memories to track down other families. Your mother tried to hide you from Torke and she did the same with your father. Until the day you walked into my shop and I touched your palm, my memories of you were gone. She did this to protect us all from Torke's probing. She was a wonderful, brave woman."

"I know." Anna nodded, although she was beginning to realize that she didn't really know her mother at all. She turned to Derrick. "Do you think you could wait outside? I have a few things I would like to discuss with Sofie, in private."

He narrowed his eyes and his lips tightened but he left the store without complaint. Anna waited until he was across the street before asking, "What about Derrick and David? How much do you know about them? Do they have anything to do with Torke's history here?"

"One question at a time, Anna. It was David who came to my attention first…" She smiled as if a memory had interrupted her thoughts. "That man is such a tremendous flirt. I don't believe there is a serious bone in his body. He started visiting me when the brothers first arrived from England, just after the fire in the warehouse. I believe it was his duty to find out as much about the incident as he could so he could report back to the Vampire council. In all these years, I have never felt any danger in his presence and I actually feel safer when he is around. To be honest, I've had a little crush on David and more than a few fantasies—"

"That's more that I need to know about David." Anna did not want Sofie to elaborate on her x-rated fantasies.

"Sorry." Sofie cleared her throat. "What I mean to say is that these men are not killers. Although…"

"Although what?"

"David once told me that when he was turned, his first instinct was to kill. The demon inside him was hard to control but he conquered his lust for the hunt. Not all vampires succeed. Some are consumed by the blood lust and never recover. Others only lose control for short periods of time. There is no way of knowing the outcome until after the transformation."

"So, if Torke turns me into a vampire, I may attack humans?" She shuddered at the thought.

"David and Derrick would not allow that to happen. They are strong leaders, sent here as to take over the area after Torke had left. Torke was self-absorbed and didn't bother to train the vampires that he had turned so they became a real problem in the community. It was the Corel brothers' responsibility to clean up the streets, so to speak, and they did a great job."

"What about all the 'missing' posters around town," Anna pointed out. "They couldn't be doing as good a job as you describe."

"All these posters went up the day after you arrived." Sofie told her. "It was the strangest thing, like a plague had hit town."

"So *I* brought death to Azure Waters?" Her hand shot to her throat. *All those people ... dead because of me?*

"No, Anna. I'm saying that *Torke* brought death back here and he will continue to kill as long as he remains on this earth."

"But he came for me?"

"Unfortunately, yes."

Anna wasn't sure how to react. She already knew in her heart that this was the case but hearing it out loud made it seem more real.

She reached out and took Sofie's hand, trying not to be offended when Sofie shuddered at her touch. "Your premonitions seem pretty accurate. Please tell me, am I going to die?"

"He hasn't decided yet," Sofie answered honestly. "He would like to make you an immortal as a payback to your mother, but he harbors so much hate, he may kill you outright." She patted Anna's hand and added, "I'm so sorry to be blunt but you need to know that you are in real danger."

"Well..." Anna sighed. "...I did ask for an honest answer." She thought for a minute and then asked, "What did my mother do to him to piss him off so badly that he tried to kill a whole coven of witches along with my entire family?"

"Vanity is a trait shared by humans and supernatural beings," Sofie informed her.

"As I was saying, Torke was once a handsome man, not as handsome as Derrick and David mind you, but definitely a head turner."

Anna was tempted to ask how Sofie could tell that the brothers were handsome seeing as how she was blind but considering Sofie's talents, she assumed there was a way.

"He used his looks to attract willing victims, humans who would gladly offer some of their blood in order to spend time with him."

"Did he kill them?"

"Not at first. He was satisfied with taking enough blood for a meal and compelling the victims to forget afterwards. But after a while, he became bored and began to take advantage of some of the women, sexually. Our coven confronted him and ordered him to stop."

"I guess he didn't listen?"

Sofie shook her head and continued. "Your mother was our strongest witch and our elected leader. She demanded that he stop or else she would hex him. He laughed in her face and we found out that the next day he had raped and then killed a young woman. Your mother called a meeting at the warehouse. We knew that we weren't strong enough, even as a group, to stop him completely, so Elena decided that we should put a curse on him, making him as ugly on the outside as he was on the inside which would make it difficult for him to attract his victims. She also blocked his ability to compel his victims so he had no way, besides ambush to feed on humans."

"I guess that didn't go over very well."

"Especially because it was clear to all of us that Torke lusted after your mother. He took her rejection hard and the hex very personally."

"So … what happened on the night of the fire?"

"He came seeking vengeance. Your mother was late getting to the meeting, you had a bad cold and she was reluctant to leave you. By the time she arrived, the building was ablaze and all besides me were dead."

"How did you escape?"

"Strangely enough, it was Torke who saved me. I was young and overconfident. I tried to be a heroine by confronting him. He struck me, his claws raking my eyes, and the force of the blow sent me sailing through one of the windows. I was unconscious outside in the gutter when he set fire to the warehouse and by time I regained consciousness, it was all over."

"That must have been awful for you Sofie." Anna leaned across and hugged her. "You must have felt so helpless."

"Feeling unable to help those you love is a terrible burden, Anna," Sofie told her. "It can influence your behavior and it often leads to misunderstandings."

"I'm sure it does," Anna agreed, although she wondered why Sofie shared this information.

"Torke is an evil man but not all vampires are evil." Sofie stood up and walked to one of the counters, holding her cane in front although she seemed to know by instinct and memory where she was going.

Anna rose too and followed, arguing, "But they drink blood."

"Yes, and you eat meat."

"That's not the same."

"In some cultures, eating meat is considered barbaric."

"I don't kill the meat myself and I certainly don't eat the meat while it's alive."

"Not all vampires kill to eat and there are some humans who offer their blood freely."

"Why?"

"It's a pleasurable experience." She winked a knowing smile.

Heat rose to Anna's cheeks. Her experience of being a human beverage *did* come with a certain amount of pleasure.

"I don't want to discuss blood sucking anymore today. I want to find Susie before it's too late. Can you help me?"

"Tonight I will call upon the spirits of my ancestors to help us in our quest. You must do the same. Tomorrow we will meet here, the same time as today. We work this out together."

"That's easier said than done. *How* do I call on my ancestors?"

Sofie rummaged through the contents of a cabinet until she found what she needed. Before handing Anna the white candle, she waved her hand over the wick and said a silent prayer.

"Sit in a darkened room. Light this candle. Close your eyes and meditate. The answer will come to you." Touching Anna's cheek, she added. "Take care, sweet Anna. Until you open the door to your powers, you will be unprepared for any attacks from the grave. Unfortunately, once you embrace your gift, the danger will come tenfold."

"Great. That makes me feel so much better."

Sofie walked to the door and held her hand against the frame. She visibly shuddered and turned towards Anna. "There are many shadows outside tonight. Don't leave Derrick's side. No matter what happens."

"You're scaring me." Anna peered outside but the street was deserted except for Derrick who stood, arms crossed and looking annoyed. "What did you see?"

"Nothing." She pat Anna's arm. "Just be careful."

Anna leaned forward and planted a kiss on Sofie's cheek. "Lock up behind me. Tomorrow we'll get to the bottom of this, once and for all."

Chapter Sixteen

Anna awoke the next morning alone in an unfamiliar bed. She had a vague recollection of sitting on a sofa, being offered a glass of Scotch and downing several while Derrick kept her wrapped in the warmth of his embrace, but no memory of how she ended up in this room.

Sunlight peeked through the lace curtains. This was obviously a guest room. Neither Derrick nor David would have been able to stay in a room that wasn't sealed from the sun.

To her surprise, she also noticed that she was wearing a cotton nightgown. Derrick could have taken advantage of her inebriation and taken her to his bed but he had dressed her in a modest nightgown and given her privacy. The act of a true gentleman. Why then, was she disappointed? The thought of him running his hands over her flesh sent a wave of heat through her. Carnal thoughts stirred. Her skin warmed to the thought of sharing his bed. She remembered the pleasure he had brought her with his magical hands. She slid down under the sheets, closed her eyes and began to fantasize until a knock on the bedroom door shattered her fantasy.

"Miss Anna. I have your breakfast." There was a pause. "May I come in?"

It took Anna a second to remember where she was. "Yes, Evan. Please come in."

Evan shuffled into the room balancing a breakfast tray. He placed it on the bedside table while Anna struggled to sit up.

"Let me help you, Miss Anna." He picked up a cushion from the settee and placed it behind her shoulders, propping her up before he unfolded the legs on the tray and positioned it across her lap.

Anna inhaled the enticing aroma of the English breakfast and sighed. "Evan, you shouldn't have gone to so much trouble." She smiled broadly as she added, "But I'm glad you did. It smells wonderful."

The elderly man returned the smile. "It feels good to have someone to cook for again." He paused, his face showing concern and tried to correct his mistake. "Um, the masters eat out a lot and rarely entertain guests."

"It's all right Evan. I completely understand."

Evan studied her face. "I'm not sure I understand your meaning, Miss Anna."

"Firstly, I would like to think that we could be friends…" She noticed Evan was nodding. "So I would feel more comfortable if you cut out the Miss and just call me Anna, okay?"

"As you wish, Mi—Anna."

"And we both know the real reason why the masters don't eat," she raised her hand and wiggled her index finger to stop Evan from protesting. "But … I'll respect your desire to keep that confidential … as long as you don't try and pull the wool over my eyes."

The old man shrugged and slipped from the room closing the door behind him while Anna attacked her bacon and eggs with enthusiasm. She had missed the home cooked breakfasts that her father always prepared on Sunday mornings. Since living alone, she rarely took the time to eat breakfast let alone cook up a big meal. She dipped a toast soldier into the runny egg and smiled while she savored the flavor and texture of her breakfast but the smile soon faded when her thoughts returned to Derrick. Since her realization that Derrick was a vampire, she had often wondered if she would be able to live his lifestyle … hiding in shadows, having abilities that surpassed her own, but, until now, she hadn't considered the eating part of the equation. Do vampires eat food at all or do they survive on blood alone? Must they take the blood from humans and animals or do they purchase it from some specialist store? Mid chew, she lost her appetite.

Evan tried unsuccessfully to keep Anna from calling a cab and leaving the mansion but she was adamant she wanted to return to her home in case Susie called. On the journey home she watched as the sun rose higher in the sky promising a glorious day. An experience she would never be able to share with Derrick. As her taxi slowed down to a stop outside her house, Anna fought back a sob. How would they be able to make this relationship work?

****

"What do you mean she left?"

"I'm sorry, Master Derrick. I pleaded with her to stay but she wouldn't listen."

Derrick ignored the old man and returned to the living room where his brother was finishing his breakfast IV bag. The sun was still high in the sky and his patience was in short supply.

"Don't you think you're being a bit hard on the old man? It's not like he could physically restrain her, she is a little powder keg."

"I'll apologize later." Derrick downed his own drink and refilled his glass. "But I can't help but worry about her, especially after Sofie's warning."

"What warning?"

"Sofie believes that Torke has found a protégé and this man lured Susie out on her blind date. She wasn't sure if he has been turned yet, but that is his wish."

"We know his kind. Blind, stupid, greedy. She could be describing half the town."

Derrick nodded. "There's more to her premonition. Torke has made up his mind to kill Anna but he's undecided on whether to turn her."

"Then, there's hope." David smile quickly turned to a frown when Derrick snapped.

"No. Neither of those scenarios are acceptable. Either way, I lose her."

"Well, we'd better put our heads together and work out a third option." David drummed his fingers on the kitchen bench. "We know that Torke has gone to ground but I've contacted every member of the coven. We'll find him."

Derrick turned to his brother and sighed. "She's pulling away from me. I can feel it. I know she has feelings for me but I don't believe she could ever accept our way of life. She is so determined to live a normal life, a life that would only become more paranormal with me. We can never truly be together."

"Give her time."

"I'm afraid that time is running out … for her and Susie."

Chapter Seventeen

Anna heard the phone ring but allowed the answering machine to take the call. She needed space to think. Life just wasn't fair. She had finally found the perfect man, a man who treated her like a goddess and made her feel like a woman at the same time, but … being with him would involve the biggest sacrifice she could ever make—her life.

Anna shook her head. As much as she loved him, she wasn't sure if she was ready to give up the sun on her skin or the pleasure of tucking into a cheeseburger or the jogs down to the beach on a beautiful summer's day. Being around him confused her thoughts. When he touched her … she believed that being with him was enough, but, he represented everything she hated about her life. Worse still, if he turned her, she may become a killer.

The answering machine instructed the caller to leave a message. Anna was startled out of her thoughts by a familiar voice.

"Anna? Are you there?"

The voice whimpered, barely above a whisper but Anna recognized it immediately. She ran for the phone and lifted the receiver.

"Susie? Is that you? Don't hang up."

"Anna. Oh thank God you're there." The whimpering evolved into crying and Anna heard the terror in her friend's voice. "I'm sorry to involve you but he said he would kill me if I didn't call you."

"It's all right honey; just tell me where you are?"

"I … I don't know but it's really dark and smells foul."

"Are you hurt?"

The answer came in heavy sobs that tore at

Anna's heart. "He bites me Anna. The monster actually *bites* me and it hurts—"

Anna heard a struggle for the phone and muffled protests before Susie spoke again.

"He says … he says that if you want to see me again—alive—you must come here alone, tonight. If he senses Derrick with you, he will… Oh god, Anna, he says he will kill me."

"Don't worry Susie…" Anna hoped the terror she was feeling wasn't evident in her voice as she tried to comfort her best friend, "I'll be there, just tell me where."

There was a pregnant pause and then Susie's tone changed; her voice became stronger, more direct. "No! Don't come here or he'll kill you. Don't trust him An—"

Anna heard a loud smack and then the sound of something heavy hitting the floor. Her heart raced as she waited for Susie to pick up the receiver. The phone crackled and then another familiar voice, one that sent a chill of ice water through her veins, spoke to her.

"Hello, Anna."

"What have you done with Susie you foul monster?"

"She's having a little nap … but I assure you she is still very much alive … for the time being."

"If you hurt her, Torke, I swear I'll—"

"Kill me?" Torke's laugh turned Anna's stomach, the bile caught in her throat as she tried to remain calm. "It's a little late for that, don't you think?"

"I'll find a way to end you, that's a promise."

"Little Anna. Didn't your mother tell you that it's rude to make promises you can't keep? Oh, that's right. I killed your mother."

Bastard! You'll pay for that. "What do you want, Torke?"

"You know what I want. I want you to pay for

what they did to me."

"You've already had your vengeance. Why can't you leave us alone?"

"Because when I see your face I see your mother. We could have been happy together, Elena and I. She was beautiful and powerful. We would have made an undefeatable couple." He snarled. "Your mother and her coven of bitches changed me from a handsome, desirable man into a repulsive monster. Do you know how it feels to slowly starve to death, Anna? Or see those who once sought out your company, recoil from you? I will not be satisfied until I destroy you and every witch in the country!"

"From what I hear, you were already a repulsive monster," Anna told him. "The witches only made it possible for people to see the real you."

"Your little friend is going to pay for that remark." He warned her. "I'm sure my disciples will have a fine time with her before they actually eat her."

Anna heard fabric tearing and Susie scream.

"No! Stop, Torke!"

Torke shouted a command and the sounds of screaming were replaced by protests from the other vampires as their voices faded.

"You will come to me?"

"Do I have a choice?"

"If you come to me, I will spare your friend."

"I want more than that Torke."

"Ah, you wish to bargain with me. I like a little bit of spunk in my women. Yes, go ahead … ask away."

"If I come to you, you must promise to leave *all* my friends alone. Forever."

"And by all your friends you mean the brothers Grimm." The sarcasm in his voice made Anna angry and she used the anger to drive home her conditions.

"Yes. I mean Derrick and David Corel, plus all my other friends. And, as far as I am concerned … everyone in this town is my friend."

"No. That would be inconvenient. I need to feed, as do my disciples."

"Then you'll have to do that somewhere else."

"I am content here, Anna. I have no wish to leave this place—"

"Then I have no wish to come to you."

"You forget about your little friend."

"No, I have not forgotten about Susie nor would I." Anna silently prayed that her gamble would pay off without costing Susie her life. "But if you want me to come to you, you must be willing to make sacrifices as well."

"Bravo, little Anna. You are quite the little blackmailer."

"Do we have a deal or not?"

"Yes, of course my dear, as long as you come to me tonight, after the sun has set—I have waited long enough to taste you. We both know this is inevitable, Anna. Blame your mother for your fate. Her hex was powerful and I have since learned that it has only one antidote, one way to restore my looks." Anna held her breathe already knowing in her heart that she was part of the solution. She listened in silent horror as he told her. "The answer is in your blood."

Anna shuddered. The thought of that vile creature pressing his body against hers made her physically ill and now she had promised to go to him willingly. She opened her curtains a little and peered out the window, noticing that the sky was turning a warmer shade of pink. It was almost dawn and she knew this would be her last day in the sun.

"Give me the address before I change my mind."

Chapter Eighteen

"Torke has ordered his minions to leave town."

Derrick's elation suddenly turned to horror as he realized the significance of the revelation. "David, he wouldn't leave unless he has what he wanted."

"You think he has Anna?"

Derrick's inner demon struggled to surface as he visualized his beloved Anna in the hands of a monster like Torke. If he killed her, he would no doubt do it in the cruelest way he could imagine but Derrick suspected that he would choose to turn her and use her blossoming powers to take back control of the town. The conversion would be painful not just physically but also emotionally for Anna. She wouldn't want to live as a vampire but Torke wouldn't care about her objections. A ruthless killer, Torke had a reputation for taking what he wanted in the most brutal way possible. Worse still, she would be tied to him through the sire bond.

"Derrick." David shook his brother until he came to his senses. "Are you going to answer my question?"

"What?"

"I asked if you think he has Anna."

"I don't know … it's possible I guess. She hasn't answered my calls."

"Then we had best try and locate her before Torke does."

"Contact the others." Derrick headed towards the front door of his home but swung around when David grabbed his elbow, preventing him from leaving. "What are you doing?"

"Are you so anxious to die brother? Surely you can feel the sun."

"But Torke—"

"Torke will be underground, as will *our* allies. There is nothing we can do until sunset." He slapped Derrick's back. "I will instruct Evan to continue ringing Anna and check on her whereabouts."

Derrick nodded. He would be of no use to Anna if he allowed the sun to burn his skin. The last time he was exposed, it took a few days of healing in the soil before he recovered fully. No, he couldn't take the chance. He would need all his strength in order to defeat Torke. Reluctantly, he followed his brother up the stairs towards their separate sanctuaries.

****

Before the sun had set, Anna had finished packing all her belongings into cardboard boxes and covered the furniture with sheets. There was no time to draw up a legal will so she hoped that the note left on her bedside table would suffice. If Susie lived through her ordeal, she would inherit the house and car. It was the least she could do after putting her friend's life in danger. She closed her eyes. *Stay strong, Susie. I'll be there soon.*

As she peered out the window, she made a decision. She would not waste a single hour of daylight indoors today. Every second of the day would be committed to her memory, something she could look back on fondly in the afterlife, if in fact there was one. She wondered if dying would be a painful experience, especially at the hands of a monster like Torke. She wondered if he would allow his followers to assault her and feed from her as he had mentioned in his threat against Susie. The thought made gag. She barely made it to the bathroom before vomiting. The bile burned her throat and she wondered if human blood tasted as vile. *Good.* She hoped that her blood tasted disgusting and that the vampires would choke on her as she died. Once again, she wretched into the toilet and remained on the bathroom floor until she could push the thoughts of Torke far enough out of her mind to get on with her day. After a thorough cleaning of the house and twice brushing her teeth, Anna headed for the front door. She had barely opened it a crack when the phone rang. This time she rushed to answer it.

"Hello?" She answered, half expecting to hear Susie's voice.

"Anna?"

"Sofie," Anna sighed and instantly hoped her friend didn't hear the disappointment in her voice. "What can I—"

"Don't do it, Anna. It's a trap."

Realizing that there was no point in fabricating a story, Anna sighed and admitted, "I know Sofie, but I can't let him kill her."

"You really believe he will let your Susie go free if you give yourself to him? That monster … he'll kill her anyway or worst, he'll turn you and make *you* kill her. That is his way."

Anna gasped. Torke could probably *compel* her to kill her friend. She covered her mouth with her palm, trying unsuccessfully to suppress a sob. The tears burned behind her eyes and spilled down her cheeks. What could she do?

"You tell Derrick and David. That is what you do."

"No. I can't bring them into this. Torke warned me that if he sensed Derrick or David, Susie would be killed, possibly Derrick and David as well. This is all my fault. I brought evil back to Azure Waters. It's up to me to finish it before anyone else gets killed."

"This is *Torke's* fault. He is a greedy, evil creature who covets you because he couldn't have your mother. He will use you, Anna, your mind *and* your body. Are you prepared for that?"

Anna couldn't suppress the revulsion that sent a tremor through her body. She shook her head vehemently. *No, she would not ... could not, ever submit to him physically.*

"Sofie, you must promise me you won't tell Derrick, or David."

"I promise Anna, but I'm not happy about this."

"I know, and I appreciate your concern Sofie, you've been a good friend." She paused for a moment to consider the consequences of her actions.

"There is something else you must promise me."

"No. I can't do that. I won't do it."

"Please, Sofie. I can't become a monster like Torke," *And I can't guarantee how the change will affect me.* "You must find a way to kill me if I'm turned. I don't want to live like that."

"You have such compassion in you, little Anna, you would never become a monster."

"There is no way of knowing what I would become. I can't take the chance when there is the possibility I could hurt innocent people."

She hung up the phone before Sofie could respond to her statement. There was no point arguing. She had made up her mind. One way or another. *This all ends tonight.*

****

The sun had not yet set but Derrick was already pacing the floor in his darkened bedroom, anxious to find Anna. He had barely slept and needed to feed but his energy was not diminished. The tattered remains of his room were evidence to the fact that he could take on a raging rhinoceros if necessary in order to protect the woman he loved.

His acute hearing told him that Evan was

shuffling up the stairs towards his door and for a second he forgot to worry about Anna, his concern for his old friend and servant claimed his attention. Poor old Evan. How difficult it must be for him now to climb those stairs. He deserved a long rest on a tropical island where he could relax and have someone wait on him for a change. Derrick decided that after they found Anna that is exactly what he would do for his faithful friend.

The soft rap on the door heralded Evan's arrival.

"Master Derrick? Are you awake?" His voice came in breathless gasps, the exertion of the stairs obviously too much for his arthritic body.

"Yes, Evan."

"I'm sorry to disturb you, sir, but I thought I heard you moving around up here and I have a message for you."

"Come in then."

Evan switched the light on. His eyes surveyed the trashed room. Derrick knew that, in his temper, he had made a mess for Evan to clean up but the old man made no mention of it.

"I know that you have had a lot on your mind, Master Derrick. I brought you an early drink." He handed Derrick the tall mug of warm, sticky liquid. "And some news about Miss Anna."

Derrick almost dropped the mug. "What have you heard?"

"Sofie—the lady from the strange shop in town—called a few minutes ago. She said that she had a phone conversation with Miss Anna who told her that she was going to see that detestable creature, Torke."

"Why would she do that? Has she gone mad?"

The mug shook in his hand. Evan took it from Derrick and placed it on the coffee table. "Sofie said that Torke contacted Anna and ordered her to come to him or else he would kill her friend."

"So, Torke *does* have Susie. I suspected as much." His hands clenched and unclenched at his sides as he imagined Anna with Torke. "I'll kill that bastard once and for all … I'll rip his head off and scatter his ashes all over town to let the others know what will happen to them if they hurt Anna."

"Yes … that's sounds delightful, sir, but don't you think we could use some help?"

Derrick studied Evan's expression and almost laughed out loud. The old man had a way of calming him down and had been successful with his technique for as long as Derrick could remember.

"Fine, wake David and get him to assemble some of the others. Evan, what else did Sofie tell you?"

"Not much, Master Derrick, she was sobbing, poor woman. It seems she made a promise to Miss Anna that she wouldn't tell you or Master David, that's why she called me. Although technically she didn't break her promise, she still feels like it was a betrayal. She didn't get an address but she sensed it was in an abandoned building somewhere in the industrial area on the other side of town." He hesitated for a moment before relaying the rest of the information. "Master Derrick … Miss Anna made Sofie promise something else..."

"Well, spit it out."

"If Torke turned her into a vampire, she wanted to be destroyed."

"Thank you for your honesty, Evan. I know that would have been hard for you to tell me. It's all right, I'm a big boy … I can handle the truth. Please go now and tell my brother I will discuss our plan of action with him after I finish my drink."

He picked up his mug and feigned interest in the blood. His only source of nourishment for many, many years, suddenly made him feel sick to his stomach. Anna would rather end her life than spend eternity with him. Whether she lived through this or died a vampire, they would never be together.

Chapter Nineteen

Anna drove to the designated spot earlier than Torke had demanded. She had plans of her own and wanted to be sure Susie was still alive before diving headlong into disaster. She parked her car a block away and walked to the abandoned construction site, conscious that Torke may have protected the area with human guards. Her sneakers assured her of a quiet entrance as she carefully opened a side door and slipped into the abandoned factory. The hard financial climate had forced the owners to abandon their plans mid-way through construction and no one had shown any interest in completing the project. Despite being unused, the interior smelled of decay and rotting food. Anna cringed and wrinkled her nose as she forced herself to venture further into the building. Darkness was creeping across the floor and she suspected that below her, Torke would soon be rising from a shallow grave.

She glanced up at a high window and noticed to her horror that the sun had almost set. She hadn't anticipated taking so long to finalize her plans and now she would be walking into Torke's trap without any real assurance that Susie was still alive. Anna shook her head. It didn't really matter if she was sacrificing herself for nothing. Fate brought her to this moment, there was no escaping it. If it was her destiny to die at the hands of Torke, it was better this way, before anyone else that she loved was killed. Of course she realized that she might become a killer like Torke and go after the very people she wished to protect, so she hoped that Sofie would keep her promise to find a way to kill her before she caused any harm.

Funny, really. Her rejection of Derrick had been

based on her aversion to becoming a vampire and now she would die without the benefits of spending eternity with him. Tears burned behind her eyes as she wished she had been able to see Derrick, just once more. She wished that she could confess to him that she loved him with all her heart. Her body longed for his touch, her whole being ached to be with him despite her reservations about his lifestyle.

Muffled voices attracted her attention back to reality. They were coming from behind a door to her left which appeared to lead downstairs. She could distinguish two male voices: one was definitely Torke—she could tell by the way it turned her stomach—the other was too whispered to identify, but decidedly male. A female voice called out in protest to something the males had said.

"No! You can't do that! I'll warn her."

Susie. Anna wasn't sure whether to laugh or cry. Susie was alive but obviously in trouble. Anna pressed her ear against the door as Torke ordered the other male to gag her friend.

"Leave now. Anna will be here presently and …. ah. I do believe my little Anna is early."

Anna took a deep breath and opened the door, realizing that her presence was already known so there was no use putting of the inevitable. Hurried steps crossed the room and a door slammed as someone left the room from the other side of the building. The sight that greeted her eyes filled Anna with a mixture of revulsion and anger. Susie was chained to a wall, her beautiful features beaten and bruised, her hair matted and caked with her own dried blood. Puncture marks in the shape of teeth dotted her arms, legs and neck. The bastard had used her as food.

"You animal!" She rushed to Susie but Torke suddenly materialized in her way, halting her action.

Anna took a step back, not wanting to be close enough for Torke to reach her although she knew there was nothing she could do to stop him if he chose to. "I did as you asked, I'm here alone. Release her now."

"Take off your bracelet Anna."

Anna shook her head defiantly. "Not until you release Susie."

"It appears we have what you call a *Mexican standoff* my dear. I will not release her until you take off your protective amulet."

Anna noticed that behind Torke, Susie was shaking her head vehemently, warning her that trusting Torke was not such a good idea.

"No. How can I trust that you will let her go?"

"I am losing my patience, Anna." Torke's complexion turned grayer than usual. He bared his yellowed fangs threateningly and hissed. "Be warned, I am not a forgiving man."

"You're not *even* a man!" Anna spat back at him. "You're an evil monster. My mother should have killed you." She instantly regretted her insult as Torke backhanded Susie's bruised face. She groaned beneath the gag before her head lolled forward.

"Bastard!" Anna rushed at him but he dematerialized before she reached him, re-emerging behind her as she felt for a pulse on Susie's wrist.

"This is your fault Anna. I have no desire to hurt your friend but as you refuse me, I have no other choice."

"Liar!" Anna fought to control her temper. "Inflicting pain is *all* you desire. You would hurt her anyway, just because you like it."

Torke laughed. His cackle nauseating and filled with menace. "Yes. You are *so* perceptive, Anna. You will be the only one of my subordinates I can trust to always tell me the truth. You are already my favorite and when my looks are restored, you will willingly become my lover."

Anna shook her head. "Not even if you looked like Brad Pitt."

There was a shuffling sound outside the door and Anna turned her head towards the sound, giving Torke the opportunity to move closer. Her hand shot up to protect her nose from his foul breath that was inches from her face. He grabbed her by the shoulders, preventing her from backing away although, by the way he grimaced, it was obvious the action caused him pain.

"You see, Anna, I am still able to touch you. Years of enduring torture at the hands of my enemies have given me a high pain threshold so, as you refuse to take off the talisman, I will do it for you." He released one shoulder and using a razor sharp fingernail, hooked a link in the bracelet and broke it, scratching the delicate skin inside her wrist in the process. Blood trickled down to her fingers, the sight of it inciting Torke into a feeding frenzy. He lunged for her wrist, sinking his teeth deep into the veins. Anna cried out in pain as she fought with her free hand to beat him off.

There was a loud crash. Torke momentarily lifted his head from the blood. A trickle of the thick liquid dribbled down his chin as he bellowed towards the door. "I told you! Wait until I have turned her, *then* you can do what you want with the other woman."

Anna was horrified, but not really surprised that Torke had lied. She was ashamed to have been foolish enough to hope that he would keep his promise and even more regretful that her stupidity was about to get her friend killed. If only she had gone to Derrick, at least she might have saved Susie.

She tried to pull away but Torke grabbed her again, this time going in for the carotid artery, his fangs aimed at her throat, his vice-like grip holding her helpless against his assault. She reached into her jacket, her fingers fumbling through the pocket until they touched wood. Fisting the wooden stake, she raised her hand behind Torke's shoulders and drove it into his neck.

"I'll consider that foreplay," he told her through clenched teeth before resuming his attack.

Just as she felt the pain of his fangs penetrating her skin, Anna heard the crack of splintering wood. The door came off its hinges and sailed across the room. Torke lifted his head, eyes blazing as he prepared to punish someone for the intrusion. His expression changed from anger to shock before he was propelled back against the wall by some unseen force. Anna gasped. Torke's appearance was changing before her eyes. His dried skin was softening and plumping. He looked more youthful. Even his hair thickened and became blonder and she could see the yellow of his teeth whiten. He had told her the truth when he said that the antidote was in her blood. His looks were improving. He was almost handsome. Almost.

"Get out of here, Anna." Derrick suddenly appeared at her side. His clothes disheveled and spattered with blood.

"No. I won't leave without Susie." Anna hurried to her friend's side to untie the gag that dug into the sides of her mouth.

Torke rushed at Derrick with extended arms. His claws curled, his lips pulled tautly back revealing his newly whitened fangs, his eyes blazed with hate. Derrick side-stepped and used Torke's momentum against him, directing him into the wall on the other side of the room with such force, that the bricks split in two, leaving a crater.

"Go!" Derrick ordered Anna again. "Leave here

now."

"No!" Anna shouted back at him despite her shock. In truth, she didn't know if she had the energy to *stand* let alone run and besides, she would not leave her friend behind.

Torke seized on the opportunity to attack, sinking his fangs into the back of Derrick's neck. Anna screamed but Derrick calmly twisted around, driving his elbow into Torke's forehead with enough pressure to crack his skull. Torke pulled back in agony, holding his head and shrieking in a pitch so high, it hurt Anna's ears. She held her hands over her ears and she too began to scream. It all seemed so surreal—the sounds, the violence, and the blood.

****

After slamming Torke onto the floor and wrapping his fingers around the vampire's throat, Derrick took a second to check on Anna. Somehow, she had overcome her fear and untied Susie. The women were making their way towards the broken door, albeit very slowly. His heart felt full to bursting with pride. Her courage and compassion astounded him.

"Do you think you can make it to the hospital?" he called to her as he tightened his grip on Torke's throat.

"Don't worry about us," she told him. "Just make sure you kill the bastard."

Derrick used his telepathic link to contact his brother. *Anna's on her way out, make sure she has a clear path to her car.*

On it. David answered. *I've already delivered them to the car. There are at least three vamps I have to deal with.*

"The woman belongs to me, Corel!" Torke could barely manage more than a whisper, Derrick's grip on his throat crushing his larynx. "You are as incapable of protecting her as you are of leading the coven."

"Anna is mine!" Derrick increased his grip and felt his nails cut into the flesh of Torke's neck, blood began to run beneath his thumbs followed by the sound of bones crunching. "You will never touch her again."

A twisted smile curled the corner of Torke's mouth allowing a steady stream of blood to trickle down his chin but—defiant to the end—he pushed Derrick's patience further. "I will do a lot more than touch her, young friend."

Derrick lost control. His grip on Torke's neck tightened as his fangs lengthened in preparation for the kill. He thought of Nigel and Isabelle and how he had not been able to defeat the men who beat him almost to death. This time he would protect the woman he loved, even if it cost him his own life. He concentrated his anger on Torke's throat as the ancient clawed at his skin. He was consumed with hatred. Hatred of all men who abused women. Using his rage to fuel his strength, he barely noticed as his fingers tore completely through Torke's neck, severing his head from his body. The evil skull hit the floor of the basement and rolled towards the door, its mouth still trying to form words. It took Derrick a few moments to realize it was over.

He dropped the twitching, headless body and walked, trancelike, to the head which was now face down on the ground. Unceremoniously, he kicked it towards its body and began searching for kindling. When the funeral pyre was fully stoked, he lit the old newspapers that he had placed under the body and waited until the rogue vampire had been fully consumed by the flames and reduced to a stinking pile of ash before he left the building.

Chapter Twenty

"You should go home and rest."

Anna opened her eyes and realized that she had fallen asleep, her head resting on the hospital bed beside Susie's legs. She stretched and turned to the night nurse who was checking Susie's vital signs.

"I'm sorry, what did you say?"

"I think you should go home. Your friend is in good hands here. Her condition is stable and there is nothing more you can do for her tonight. Get some sleep and come back in the morning."

Something wasn't right. Anna had been assured that the danger had passed but … no, something was amiss. A loose end. But what?

"I can't go until she wakes up. What if she needs me?"

"She's heavily sedated. I doubt that she'll wake up until mid-morning. Come back then."

Anna checked her watch. One a.m. Derrick would probably be wondering where she was. She rose from her chair, gently kissed Susie's battered cheek and after a quick nod to the nurse, left the room. As she walked down the corridor towards the elevator, her phone rang. She checked the caller I.D.

"Derrick. Are you all right?"

"It's over Anna. Torke's body has been destroyed. His coven wiped out. How is Susie?"

"Stable, but she looks dreadful. She lost a lot of blood."

"She's strong. We'll be there to help her through this, you and I. Are you still at the hospital?"

"Leaving now. Would it be all right if I came to your place? I don't want to be alone tonight." It didn't make sense. Why did she still feel the presence of evil?

"Stay there and I'll come get you."

"No. Don't be silly. I have my car here. I'll be there in twenty minutes."

"You really are a stubborn little fire cracker. Fine, have it your way. I'll be waiting, rather impatiently I might add."

"Good. Absence makes the heart grow fonder," she teased. A smile curled her lips.

"Not possible." He told her as he hung up the phone.

The elevator doors opened and before Anna had stepped completely in, a hand reached out and covered her mouth, pulling her inside. She struggled, but the more she did, the harder her attacker forced the gag across her mouth and nose. The sickly sweet, almost chemical odor overpowered her. Her head swam and the last thing she remembered before losing consciousness was a familiar voice.

"Sweet dreams, Angel."

****

The fog in her head was beginning to lift. Anna opened her eyes and took a moment to allow them to adjust to the darkness of the room. This wasn't the hospital. Where was she? Struggling to think, she remembered being carried from the elevator and placed in the back seat of a car but after that … nothing. Whatever had been on the gag had given her a migraine and the sound of someone approaching sent bolts of pain to her temples. The door flung open.

"It's about time you woke up."

"Patrick? Why did take me from the hospital?"

"Relax, babe. Here, drink this coffee." He placed the cup on the bedside table. "You had a fainting spell in the elevator. I brought you here to recover."

Fainting spell? Could she have imagined the attack?

"I thought it would be the safest place. No one would expect to find you here."

"Why would someone be looking for me?" Anna knew Torke was dead and there was no way Patrick would have known about him. Her head throbbed as though it would split in two. She cupped her forehead in her palm and winced.

Patrick kept his head turned from her as he said, "I was told that you and Susie were attacked. I was worried that whoever did it would come after you."

"Thanks for the concern but the danger is over." Bile rose in her throat and with it, the taste of the chloroform. *Someone drugged me.* She had not imagined the attack.

"What do you mean, babe? Has he been arrested?"

"No, but he won't be bothering me again, or Susie for that matter." Anna sipped the coffee, hoping to dilute the sickly taste in her mouth. Her throat felt dry from the medication and she needed the caffeine to kick start her brain. Everything seemed weird ... hazy, dangerous.

"Oh." Patrick gave the impression of being surprised but more than that ... disappointed. "I guess that changes things."

"Yes." Anna agreed finishing her coffee and swinging her feet over the side of the bed. Her instincts warned her to get as far away from Patrick as possible. "Although I appreciate your concern, there's no need to worry about me anymore. I'll just call a taxi and—"

He reached out and grabbed her wrist. "There's no hurry. I want to know more about what happened." He edged Anna back into the bed and sat down close beside her, his grip on her wrist tightening.

Pain scorched the back of her eyes and she instinctively closed them. "Derrick's waiting for me. He'll come looking for me."

She held her free palm to her forehead and winced. The pain was getting stronger by the moment making it harder to think. She wanted to run but couldn't understand the compulsion. Her legs began to shake violently, she wondered if she would even be able to stand. A voice in her head told her it was time to leave, run, and get away as fast as she could but she was paralyzed with pain.

"Let him wait." The tone in his voice frightened her. *So much anger*.

"I heard that the vampire who took Susie wanted to lure you to him so he could drain your blood or force you to become part of his coven."

Auras flashed behind Anna's eyes. A rainbow of colors exploded in her head, the blasts of light blinded her, mesmerized her, turned her stomach.

"Who told you that?" Anna knew that Derrick would never speak with Patrick unless it was to order him away. *How did Patrick know?*

"It must have been Susie. Yes—I think … no I'm sure. Susie told me. Patrick's eyes glanced up at the ceiling, a habit that had formed back in their relationship when he was trying to lie.

"How did you know Susie was attacked?"

"What is this, fifty questions?" He released her hand and walked over to his desk. "I don't remember how I knew but I just knew … okay?"

Anna rubbed her wrist. It had already begun to bruise and swell. "How did you know she was in danger? As a matter of fact, how do you know Susie at all?"

"We met on a blind date last week. She seemed like a nice girl so—"

Anna edged along the bed and away from Patrick, steadying herself to bolt for the door the moment she had the opportunity.

"*You* were Susie's blind date?" Susie had told her that all she knew about her blind date was that he had green eyes. Patrick had green eyes. She raised her head to face him and gasped. Her vision had not been impaired by blood-shot eyes. His eyes had actually *turned* red. Suddenly everything was beginning to make sense.

Patrick smiled, baring his newly acquired fangs. "Are you jealous?" He closed the distance between them. Anna noticed that he was wearing a cravat to cover his neck. "There is no need to be jealous," he told her. "I only have eyes for you, babe."

He leaned closer. Anna sprung to her feet. He pushed her down, leaning heavily on her shoulders, preventing her from moving despite her desperate attempt to fight. She was no match for his supernatural strength.

"What do you want from me Patrick? You know that I can't sell you my share of the business without Derrick's approval."

"Things have changed, Angel. I don't want the business anymore, actually I never did."

"I don't understand. You said that Derrick wouldn't help you, you wanted in."

"I wanted him to turn me. Make me an immortal! I wanted all the money, the lifestyle, the women, and especially the power that Derrick and his brother have. But that bastard boyfriend of yours wouldn't do it. He's always been jealous of my looks and talent. It must have really pissed him off to know that I screwed you before he did."

Anna felt her blood run cold. To think that she had allowed this man to take her virginity, her happiness and now, more than likely, he would also take her life.

She shook her head. As if Derrick would envy Patrick for anything. Derrick was more handsome, had more class, more composure, more … everything. No matter what she may have once felt for Patrick, Anna's love for Derrick was epic by comparison.

"Let me go, Patrick." She struggled against his grip but he didn't budge. "You have what you wanted. You don't need me anymore."

"But I do need you, Anna. Together we could build a great coven of vampires. With your powers and my knowhow, we could rule this town."

"No Patrick. I can't be with you… I don't love you, and besides, I have no interest in becoming a vampire."

"Why do you still hate me?"

"I don't hate you Patrick. I never did." If Patrick *was* the man who lured Susie to Torke, she doubted if she could ever find it in her heart to forgive him, but … she did pity him for his stupidity. "I just don't understand why you would choose such a life. Never to walk in the sun again. Feeding off humans. Why would you want that?"

"Grow up Anna. Power is everything. I want it all. The money, the women, and the lifestyle."

Anna shook her head. Derrick had been right to refuse Patrick's demands, but someone had not been so wise.

"Who turned you?"

"Our mutual friend, Torke."

"Torke! That doesn't make sense. He could just kill you and take your blood anyway. How did you convince him?"

"I offered him you." Patrick's triumphant smile turned Anna's stomach. This was the man she had once loved … had intended to marry. "I told him I could draw you to him."

"Well you don't owe him anything now he's dead. You can let me go. I will keep your secret if you leave town without hurting anyone."

"It isn't that simple, love." Patrick shook his head, his lips thinned as he stared into her eyes. "You see, I want the power that Torke saw in you. Whatever it is, it should be mine. *You*—should be mine."

"Torke had a vendetta against my family. The antidote was draining my blood. He didn't want me for any powers, Patrick, he just wanted me dead."

Patrick shook his head. "I don't believe that for a minute. You have Derrick and his whole coven of vampires doting on you and now you tell me you also have powerful blood? You belong to me. I claim first dibs."

Tears brimmed Anna's eyes. "If I mean anything to you at all, Patrick. Please ... let me go."

"Can't do that, Angel. Don't get me wrong ... you don't mean *that* much to me, not that the idea of screwing you hasn't crossed my mind since Derrick Corel started showing an interest..." He leaned down and licked a trail from her chin to her forehead. "It's just that while I have you, and by that I mean in every sense of the meaning, I hold the power. You will be tied to me by a sire bond. Linked to me forever on a telepathic level. With your powers, I can rule the whole town, maybe even the country."

Anna pulled away and wiped the saliva from her face with the back of her hand, squirming in disgust. "I won't do anything to help you, sire bond or not and you can't force me. I don't even understand what it is I am supposed to be able to do."

"You won't be able to fight it, Angel. Once I turn you, I will always be able to locate you. I will be your sire and you will be my magical concubine. We'll make a powerful couple."

"Never!" *This can't be happeni*ng. This was the second time she had been made to feel as if she was a prize to be won. First Torke saying they would make a beautiful couple, and now Patrick. If she had no choice in becoming a vampire, why couldn't she have been bound to Derrick? Now it appeared as though she would be calling on Sofie's magic after all. She would need Sofie to help her die.

She pushed herself off the bed, and her sudden movement caught Patrick unaware as she raced towards the door. Patrick passed her in a blur of speed, blocking her exit. He lunged. She ducked and drove her fist into his groin before diving for the bathroom door.

"You'll pay for that love." He hissed, the points of his razor sharp fangs glistening with saliva. He closed the distance easily and grabbed her hair, pulling her towards the bed as she kicked out and swung at him with her fists.

Patrick spun her around and grabbed her wrists, clutching both hands tightly together over her head as he pushing her down onto her back, forcing his body between her legs as she lay, pinned under him on the bed. "This will only hurt for a minute, Angel."

Defiant to the end, she baited him. "You don't have to tell me that I'll only feel a little prick because we've had sex before."

Patrick leaned down, his cold cheek resting against hers as he whispered into her ear, "You'll pay for that one, Anna … over, and over, and over."

****

"Where are you?" Derrick screamed at the speaker of his hands-free mobile phone as he raced his car down the main street of town.

"I'm with Sofie at her shop. She hasn't heard from Anna either," David told him.

"I've checked everywhere. Her car's still in the hospital carpark but no-one here has seen her." *Where would she have gone?*

"Derrick what do ... hold on a minute— Derrick listened to the muffled voices of David and Sofie as he drove erratically through the streets with no particular direction in mind. *Come on, come on.* He was about to hang up the phone when David's voice broke the silence.

"Sofie just had a vision of Anna. Miller has her and it doesn't look good."

Derrick swung the car into a 90 degree turn. *If he has done anything to harm her—.*

****

"Stop struggling and it will hurt less," Patrick ordered as he positioned his fangs over Anna's carotid artery. She continued in her attempt to push Patrick away, even after she felt the sting of his fangs puncturing her skin, even though she knew in her heart it was already too late. As the blood—and with it, her life force—drained away, Anna lost the strength to fight. Soon she had resigned herself to her fate. Today she would join her parents. Today she was going to die.

Suddenly, the front door flew off its hinges landing in the kitchen. In a blur of speed, Derrick grabbed Patrick by his collar and threw him against a wall. Anna tried to sit up but could barely open her eyes. She managed to turn her head slightly towards the commotion in the adjoining room and willed herself to focus. Derrick held Patrick off the ground, his fingers pressing into the rogue vampire's throat. Patrick fought back, jabbing a fist into Derrick's solar plexus, giving him the opportunity to squirm free and bolt towards Anna. Derrick dove through the air, grabbing Patrick's legs and tackling him to the ground where he began pounding on his face. Raining punches down on Patrick's face.

"You … will … pay … for … what … you … have … done … to … Anna."

"You mean … because I beat you to her?" Patrick goaded as he blocked the next strike with his forearm. He looked in Anna's direction and laughed. "Ah, well. Looks like no one gets her."

****

Derrick turned his attention to Anna whose face was grayish-white, her lips turning blue. Her pale blue eyes stared lifelessly at him and his powerful hearing could only detect a faint heartbeat. She was dying.

Patrick took the opportunity to escape out of front door, leaving Derrick with the decision to either follow or go to Anna. It was an easy choice.

"Stop him," Anna whispered as Derrick lifted her into his arms. "He'll kill someone."

"David will find him," Derrick had no doubt that his brother would destroy the new vampire "I'm not leaving you."

"Derrick?"

"Yes my love."

"I'm dying … aren't I? Please don't lie"

"Yes, my little firecracker, you are."

Anna blinked, releasing a single tear which trickled down her cheek. Derrick kissed it away.

"It's kinda peaceful really. Doesn't hurt much anymore, only the leaving part." Anna's voice was weaker.

Derrick's blood-tinged tears trickled down on her face as he pleaded with the love of his life. "Anna, you still have a choice. I can save you."

"You know how I feel about that. I couldn't live like you."

Anna was close to death, there wasn't time to argue but, he had to try.

"So you would rather die than be with me?

"Of course not. I love you, you know I do."

"Then if you really love me, I hope you will eventually find it in your heart to forgive me."

"Forgive you? Forgive you for—"

Derrick fangs stole the question from her throat bringing her as close to the brink of death as he felt safe. Pulling away, he tore into his wrist with his teeth and forced his blood into Anna's mouth.

****

Unable to find the strength to resist, she lay helplessly as the coppery-tasting liquid ran down her throat. The sensation was a mixture of pleasure and pain. The blood burned and yet tantalized her taste buds. She could feel her energy returning within moments of receiving the transfusion then, almost as suddenly, the pain hit her with a force that took her breath away. Convulsing on the bed, she barely noticed David arrive. He looked from her to Derrick and she heard Derrick protest.

"I had no choice. I arrived too late … she was already dying."

They turned to her and she heard David say. "I'm sure she'll understand."

****

Derrick noticed the fire in Anna's eyes. His hope for forgiveness fading as he watched her fight the transformation.

She turned her face from him. Obviously embarrassed as she made her one-word request for assistance.

"Bathroom."

He swept her up into his arms and carried her into

the en-suite. Once inside, she forced him to put her down and motioned for him to leave, locking the door behind him. Both he and David were forced to wait helplessly outside while Anna suffered through the last painful throes of her humanity alone.

Chapter Twenty-One

"She's been in there for an hour."

"You *know* these things can't be hurried, Derrick."

"But David … an hour? What if she's…?"

David walked over to the bathroom door and softly rapped on the wood. "Anna, *cherie*? Are you okay?"

When his question went unanswered, Derrick pushed his brother aside and pounded on the door. "Anna!" He struggled with the locked door, breaking the handle before he gave up and kicked the door in. Anna was gone. He turned to his brother.

"How?"

David pointed to the open window.

"David, what if she's still in the process of changing? She could get hurt."

"In case you have forgotten brother, we're five stories up. The only way she could have made that jump was if she has *fully* turned. I think we should be more worried about humans getting hurt … she is likely to be starving and confused."

"Where do you think she would go?"

"No idea, but I know someone who might."

****

The actual leap from the window was surprisingly easy. Convincing herself to jump in the first place proved the most difficult part. Sure, she felt invincible, but did that necessarily mean that she was now immortal? Was she merely fueled by anger? Would her mistake result in a bone-crunching fall? Eventually she had decided to take the risk. She had nothing to lose but her life and if she was correct, she'd already paid that price.

The street was empty but somehow Anna could sense the people moving around in their apartments and homes. Their blood called to her and the temptation to feed was stronger than she could ever have imagined. She licked her lips. The lingering taste of Derrick's blood sent a shiver of pleasure down her spine, her incisors lengthened. She could almost hear the blood pumping through the veins of the individuals who lived in the homes she passed as she made her way back to the hospital. She had to be sure Susie was all right. Patrick had escaped. He may head straight for Susie.

After entering the hospital grounds, Anna realized she had made a huge mistake. Assaulted by the scent of blood from every direction, she somehow managed to find the strength to pass the man slumped in a waiting room chair, a large gash on his head bleeding profusely while the triage nurse assessed his wounds. She ran down the corridor trying to ignore the call of blood as it cried out from a multitude of potential victims. When she finally reached Susie's room, she found her friend asleep, a catheter feeding her a transfusion to make up for the blood loss caused by her attack. Anna stared at the bag of red fluid and was horrified to realize she was salivating at the sight.

"Anna? Oh, Anna! Thank God you're okay." Susie reached out and grabbed Anna's wrist. "The nurse said you'd gone home."

Anna tried to answer but her attention was focused on the bright blue vein throbbing in Susie's wrist.

She shook her head. "I have to go, Susie. I just came to say goodbye."

"Goodbye? I don't understand. Where are you going?"

"I … I don't know yet. I'll call you when I'm settled somewhere, I promise." It hurt to lie to her friend but Anna knew that Susie would try and stop her if she knew Anna's true intentions.

"No. Don't leave, Anna. I need you to help me through this. I'm still confused about what actually happened. Sometimes I feel as though it was all a bad dream until I wake up and realize it was all true. Please don't leave me."

"If I stay, I'd only make things worse for you." Anna stared at her feet, fearful that Susie would see the monster she was becoming and recognize the danger "I'm not the same person, Susie."

"Neither am I. What happened to me has changed me but I know we can get through this together. Derrick was here earlier. He said he will help—"

"Derrick is no longer a part of my life." Anna slowly raised her head.

Susie's hands flew to her mouth, too slow to mute the gasp of horror. "Anna … your eyes." Her hands trembled, her fingers flittering in front of her face as she squealed her accusation. "You're one of *them*."

Anna sucked in a sob and bit down on her bottom lip. The taste of her own blood, exciting her. Reminding her of what she had become. A monster. The pain and terror in Susie's expression ripped a giant hole in her heart. A hole that could never heal. She would never forget the fear in her friend's eyes. "Now you know why I must leave. Goodbye, Susie … I'm sorry."

As Anna ran from the room, she expected to hear Susie call for security. Instead she heard her friend's mournful sobs. She carried the pain of the Susie's accusation with her as she sprinted down the hall and into the car park.

****

I've calmed her down," David informed Derrick when they met outside Susie's room. "She won't remember Anna's visit now, so there shouldn't be any problem later."

"Did she know where Anna was headed?"

"No. Only that she was leaving. She believes Anna will contact her once she is settled in a new town."

"We both know that's not true." Derrick's heart ached as he realized her plans. His sire connection with Anna had not fully formed, but her intentions were clear. "She will try to find a way to end herself."

"You may be wrong," David reasoned with him. "She might decide to give our life a try."

"You didn't hear her, David." Derrick's voice trembled with emotional pain. "When she lay dying, I asked her to allow me to change her and she refused. She'd rather be dead than like us. No matter what happens now—if she survives as a vampire or perishes at her own hand—she's still lost to me. She'll never forgive me for what I have done to her."

"*You* forgave *me*," David reminded him.

Derrick nodded. He recalled the day that his brother had returned from Paris and found him dying. He too had insisted on being allowed to die but, fortunately, David ignored his plea and turned him. It took a while, a long while, but eventually he came to accept his fate and forgave his brother for taking away his right to choose.

"Anna's much tougher and smarter than you're giving her credit for, you can't give up on her now."

"I'm not giving up on *her*, she's giving up on *me*."

David threw his hands in the air. "Oh suck it up you stupid son of a bitch. She needs you to man up."

Derrick grabbed his brother by the collar and forced him against the wall. "At least I'm man enough to go after the woman I love."

"What do you mean by that?" David, in turn,

grabbed Derrick and rammed him into the wall on the opposite side of the room.

"I've seen the paintings you have been doing for years ... all of the same beautiful blonde. You stare at them for hours after you've finished and then immediately start sketching another. You're obsessed with her. If you love this woman ... why haven't I ever seen her? Aren't *you* man enough to go after the woman you want?"

"Mind your own business. You should be concentrating on finding Anna and saving what's left of your love life. Leave me out of the equation." He released his grip and straightened his collar. "Go see Sofie. She may know where Anna is headed next."

"I will." Derrick nodded and headed for the door. Mid step, he turned to his brother. "David, I'm—"

"Yes, I know. Me too, sort of." David grinned back.

"You really should approach the woman ... the blonde. Tell her how you feel."

"Okay. I promise you that when I see her I will do just that."

As Derrick hurried away, he made an attempt to telepathically connect with his brother and caught him mid-thought. What he heard surprised him. *Tell her how you feel?* David sighed *That's easy for you to say, brother. If I could, I would walk over broken glass to tell the woman from my visions how much she means to me. There is only one problem... I just haven't met her yet.*

Chapter Twenty-Two

Anna wasn't surprised when the doorknob turned easily. She knew that Sofie would have anticipated her arrival. She found her friend pretending to dust a display of crystals in the back room.

"Oh, Anna … what a nice surprise."

"You can't fool me, Sofie. I know you were expecting me and you know why I'm here."

Sofie sighed. "Yes. I had a vision of what happened. I'm sorry child. It's not fair."

"What's done is done." Anna shrugged despite knowing that Sofie would not have seen the telling movement of her shoulders. "You are the only one who can help me now. I'm here to ask you to fulfil your promise."

"I am sorry, Anna, but what you ask is murder."

Anna grabbed the woman by her shoulders and looked into her sightless eyes. "You can't murder someone who is already dead."

"No. Not dead Anna, *undead*. There is a difference. Derrick and David will teach you how to live as a vampire. You must try and accept this way of life."

"Dead, undead, I don't care what you want to call it … I'm not human."

Anna slammed her fist into a wall, leaving a gaping hole, and instantly regretted her action when Sofie jumped, startled by the noise. "If you could only see me, Sofie. I wouldn't need to explain how different I am. I'm a monster."

"I *can* see you child. Maybe not in the conventional sense but I can see your soul. You are a beautiful woman, both inside *and* out. Now you will always be beautiful. You will never age, not like me. You will never become weak and helpless. You are strong now and getting stronger every day. Derrick can teach you how better to protect yourself and I will train you in the ways of Wicca. It will be all right, you'll see."

"Nothing has changed Sofie. I still don't want this type of life. I could hardly control myself when I visited Susie at the hospital. Do you even realize how much danger you are in at this very moment?"

She was grateful that Sofie couldn't see her face. "You don't understand this hunger for blood. It's driving me insane." She wondered how Derrick had been able to control his thirst on each of their encounters. He never gave her cause to believe she was in any danger yet he must have used incredible willpower in order to keep his hunger at bay. The call of the blood was strong … possibly more than she could bear.

"You are wrong Anna." Sofie told her, her voice surprising calm considering her present situation. "I *do* realize the danger and I *do* feel your need to take my blood, but … I also feel you *fighting* that urge with every cell in your body. You *can* survive this ordeal. I have faith in you."

"Faith?" Anna laughed. "I had faith in Derrick. I trusted him not to turn me into a vampire and yet … here I am."

"He had no choice."

"No!" Anna's protest reverberated around the small shop, shaking the glass in the window. "He should have let me die."

"How *could* he let you die, Anna?" Sofie found a chair and gingerly sat down. "Derrick loves you."

Anna knew there was truth in Sofie's words. She felt his love now more than ever. Since turning, she could feel the mental connection or sire bond that she had heard about. His mind was in turmoil. He needed her as much as she needed him. Despite this, she still argued her point.

"If he loves me so much, why did he turn me into a killer?"

"You do not have to *kill* to eat. I have given David blood on occasions when he was caught in town and in need of nourishment and I'm clearly still here to tell the tale. Come Anna … take some of my blood." She held out her wrist. "There is no need to compel me or kill me. I have no fear of you."

For what seemed to her like an eternity, Anna stared at the wrinkled skin of Sofie's wrist. Blue veins throbbed beneath the paper-thin, pale skin, promising rich sustenance to quench her terrible thirst. Her gums burned, her fangs elongated in anticipation. She tried to cover her mouth with the back of her hand but, try as she might, she couldn't tear her eyes away from the sight of the blood as it pulsed through Sofie's veins.

Unconsciously, she took the offered wrist and raised it to her lips before coming to her senses. "No!" she protested as she pushed the woman away. "I can't do this … I *won't*."

Before Sofie could argue, Anna bolted from the store, slamming the door hard enough to break the glass in the front window. Shards of glass flew into the shop shattering over the floor at Sofie's feet. A few stray splinters hit the woman's legs piercing tiny holes in her skin which immediately dotted with spots of blood. Although already meters away, Anna could smell the blood calling to her. She screamed in protest, picking up speed in an attempt to escape the pull of the precious red fluid. Within moments, she had managed to cover a distance of a few kilometers, a feat that both shocked and delighted her. The distraction helped lessen the call of Sofie's blood. How fast could she run? Her mouth twisted into a smile when she decided … *why not find out?*

Anna reached the town boundary without breaking a sweat. For a few moments, she held her fingers to her throat trying to check her pulse and almost laughed at her own naiveté when she realized *why* she couldn't find it. The realization brought home the reason why she was running in the first place. She had been tempted by the call of blood. Willing to take a chance with the life of someone she cared about for a meal. What if she had killed Sofie? How could she even contemplate doing something so gross? Drinking blood from someone's wrist or neck would be disgusting, *wouldn't it?* Anna remembered how tempting the blood had looked as it coursed through Sofie's wrist. Even the plasma bag attached to Susie's arm had looked appetizing. She recalled the hospital visit and was disgusted with herself for salivating at the thought of making a meal from the contents of the bag.

Once again, she began to run, this time towards town with no particular direction in mind. She needed to clear her head and the thrill of passing cars as if they were stationary was becoming addictive. She soon realized that her speed was undetectable to the human eye. Despite herself, Anna found she was enjoying the new power as she darted around the town, timing her movements. Delighting in beating her own best time again and again. The game was distracting, amusing, until she suddenly stopped cold in her tracks.
Something's wrong.

Something in the glass of a store window attracted her attention. Like the vision in her bathroom mirror, the glass showed her a scene, but this time it was different. This time she knew it was not a memory but a premonition. Sofie was sweeping up the glass from the broken door and placing it in a small bin. A small shard cut her hand and she covered the blood with a handkerchief before heading out to the kitchenette to make a pot of tea. Anna could almost smell the blood seeping through the hanky. She licked her lips and swallowed the lump in her throat as she watched Sofie settle down in her chair to enjoy her herbal beverage. A gust of wind blew the door open. Anna gasped in surprise when her vision became audible.

"Nice place."

"Thank you." Sofie felt for the table and slowly placed her cup back on its saucer. "I'm sorry but the store is closed, sir. If you come back tomorrow morning, I'll be happy to help you."

"I think we both know I can't do that," Patrick said as he picked up a quartz crystal and feigned interest. "*Really* ... nice shop. You have a lot of interesting things here."

"Thank you but I must insist that you leave."

Patrick ignored her request. "Lots of witchy looking things." He picked up a pack of Tarot cards and looked at the instructions on the box. "Are you a witch?"

"If you're not going to leave..." Sofie rose from her chair and headed toward the counter feeling for the silent alarm. "...maybe you could tell me what it is you are interested in?"

"Nothing in particular, everything in general." Patrick informed her. "I actually came into town for a quick bite but now I've come to the conclusion that I was drawn here for a reason." Patrick continued his exploration of the shop, examining and replacing items as he teased his prey.

"I don't understand. Why would you be drawn to my humble store? Are you interested in crystal healing?"

"One of the interesting aspects of being a vampire—oh, don't pretend you don't know what I am—

" he warned "is that we can sense each other." Sniffing the air, he smiled. "Anna has been here … and recently, which means that Derrick turned her." The smile quickly dissolved and Sofie stumbled back in shock when Patrick suddenly flipped a heavy table with ease, shattering porcelain ornaments and scattering knick-knacks everywhere.

"She was mine! Do you understand? *Mine* to sire and Corel had no right to take that away from me!"

"Corel? I'm sorry but I—"

"Don't lie to me, woman."

In a blur of speed, Patrick grabbed Sofie by her throat, lifting the blind woman off her feet so her face was only inches away from his fangs. "Derrick and his brother have been in this store many times. Their stench fouls up the place."

"I don't want any trouble. Just leave. I'll tell Derrick you want talk to him, okay?"

Patrick smiled and shook his head. "I didn't come to ask you to talk to Derrick on my behalf. I'm hungry and you're the only place open tonight. I would have preferred to eat a young chick but I'm hungry enough to settle for an old bird like you. The smell of your blood drew me in. You may be getting on in years but I bet you're still tasty."

"I hope you choke on me, you dirty demon." She spat at his face, a drop of spittle hitting his cheek.

"Well, I was going to kill you fast but…" He wiped the spit away with the sleeve of his shirt, "now I think I'll make it hurt."

He twisted his grip so her neck, exposing the wrinkled throat. She flailed helplessly. The breath stolen from her lungs.

"Enough talk, I'm hungry."

Before his fangs were able to break the skin, Sofie

dropped to the ground and Patrick slammed through the wall at the opposite end of the store. Plaster cracked as the wall shattered. A cloud of powdery mist filled the store.

"*Interesting*. I didn't realize how much fun that would be." Anna turned to Sofie and asked "Are you all right, Sofie?"

Sofie nodded. "I was hoping you would get my message."

Anna lifted the woman to her feet. "I'm sorry I'm late. It took a few minutes to work out what I was seeing."

"Well, well, well." Patrick laughed as he brushed the debris away from his suit. "So you allowed him to turn you after all."

"Rather him than *you*." Anna could not allow Patrick the satisfaction of knowing how upset she was with the transformation.

Patrick looked past her towards the door and shrugged. "So, where is he then? Dumped you already?"

"More like I dumped him."

"Nice to know you finally came to your senses, Angel. We can rule this town together." He reached for Anna but she disappeared in a blur of speed, re-appearing with Sofie at the other end of the store where she ushered the woman towards the back door.

"If you leave now, I may allow you to live," she warned him, surprised at how confident she sounded. She hardly recognized her own voice. It sounded richer, almost sensual.

"Oh, I'm not going anywhere, Angel." Patrick was at her side in seconds, his arms wrapped around her as he kissed the puncture marks on her neck. "You look sooo hot babe. Let's kill the witch together and screw until the sun comes up."

"You repulse me." She pushed him away, sending him sailing over a glass cabinet, surprised to realize what little effort it took to accomplish the feat.

In less than a heartbeat, he came upon her, fangs bared, his nails biting into the flesh on her arms. "Make your choice, Anna. Rule with me or die with Corel."

"I'm already dead you idiot…" She drove her palm up under his chin, a maneuver that could have killed a mortal but barely knocked Patrick back a few feet, "thanks to you."

"I only brought you to the brink of death. It was Corel who pushed you over the edge."

"You gave him no choice." Even as she said the words, Anna realized the difficult situation Derrick must have found himself in. She would have done the same for him had the roles been reversed. He loved her. Watching her die would have been more than he could bear.

"He would have turned you eventually. Face it, Anna, if you develop those premonition thingies that you do, we could have an unstoppable vampire coven. We could use your talents to be rich and powerful—"

"Talents? So *now* you call what I have a talent? I remember when you treated my visions as some sort of handicap. You made me feel like I was a lunatic."

"That's all in the past love. Our future is going to be spectacular."

Anna shook her head. "No, Patrick. There is no future for us, not together or even separately."

"Well, Angel. I guess it's time I left."

Before Anna had time to react, Patrick had shot past her and out the back door, grabbing Sofie who had been standing in the alley, afraid to go any further alone. With Sofie tucked under his arm, he disappeared into the night.

It took Anna only a few seconds to catch up with

them at the beach, over a kilometer away from the shop. Patrick had Sofie pinned down on the sand, he had begun to feed. Anna lost control. She grabbed his shirt collar from behind and hurled him into the water. Before he had a chance to react, she was on him, pummeling him, the speed of her punches a blur to the human eye. His jaw cracked and caved but she was consumed by rage, driven by anger. Out of control. She continued her attack, breaking his ribs, his arm. Blood pumped from his arteries, tainting the water. His body and face no longer resembled the man who she had once considered handsome. It hardly even looked like a face. His cheekbones caved, his eye sockets shattered and his teeth resembled a picket fence but she continued to pound the flesh that clung precariously to his bones.

"Stop!"

Anna recognized the voice but the rage inside her was stronger than she could control. Strong arms wrapped around her and she found herself being dragged back onto the beach.

"Let me go!" she screamed at Derrick as he pulled her down onto the sand. "He killed Sofie. He'll kill again!"

Derrick shook his head and allowed Anna enough leeway to sit up although he held her tightly to his chest. She could see David and another man—who she recognized as the "*Lurch*" impersonator from the ill-fated romantic evening—tearing up Patrick's body and hurling it into the ocean, far from shore. A series of splashes and the blur of fins reminded Anna that vampires were not the only predators in the water this night. But there was something else … something familiar. Dark clouds clustered above her and threatened to storm and she realized that the water was red with Patrick's blood. Breaking waves churned into pink foam as they reached the sand. It was exactly as she had seen in her vision the day she and Patrick had eaten lunch on the sand. Only her vision had not enlightened her as to whose blood would be staining the pristine ocean nor how she would be viewing the scene as a vampire. Anna watched as David and Lurch stepped from the surf and wondered how often they had performed this task. *How many vampires had they killed?*

David stopped to face her, his expression uncharacteristically formal. "Now that you are part of this coven, you must follow the rules. There is a chain of command which must be obeyed. It is the responsibility of the *elders* to execute unscrupulous vampires and no deviation to this rule will be tolerated. The penalty for breaking this rule is true death."

"But he—"

"We cannot kill in retribution, Anna. Self-defense is one thing, but vengeance and anger is quite another." He turned to Derrick. "As co-leader, and Anna's sire, she is your responsibility now, brother. Make sure she learns that—as her sire—you are also accountable for her behavior."

As he walked away, David looked over his shoulder and added, "But whatever he tells you, remember, *cherie*. He is only the boss *outside* the bedroom." With a wink, he was gone.

"Is anyone there?"

"I'm coming, Sofie!" Anna called, delighted her friend was alive. *How strange.* How could see her friend clearly, despite it being the middle of the night? How was that even possible?

"Anna. Is that you? Where are you? I'm frightened."

Anna and Derrick made their way to Sofie at a human pace, careful not to frighten her more than necessary. As she looked at Derrick, she realized that she could see him clearly. She could see the colors in their clothes as clear as day yet it was a dark and a moonless night.

"I have night vision?"

"Among other things." Derrick informed her as he reached down and picked up Sofie, cradling the terrified woman in his arms. He touched the woman's wound and the bleeding ceased. "We can talk about this later Anna. I think we should get Sofie to a hospital, she has lost a lot of blood."

"Did you bring your car?"

Derrick rewarded Anna with a cheeky grin. "Why don't we just go for a little jog?" He took off into the night, with Sofie in his arms and Anna close at his heels. She found it difficult to concentrate on the task at hand. The transformation had been sudden and she had revolted against the change, until now. Now, the world seemed to be brighter, sharper than she had ever imagined. They blazed past the shops and traffic lights, the colors ribboned in their wake, as if it the world, and not her, traveled at inhuman speed.

When they reached the emergency ward of the hospital, Derrick spoke with the triage nurse while Anna studied the people waiting to be seen by the doctor. It seemed to be a quiet night and there were only a few people waiting. Within seconds, she had already deduced their ailments, none of which were life-threatening. The three-year-old who was crying in his mother's lap had stuffed a bead up his nostril which was making it difficult for him to breathe and gave off an awful odor. The doctor would be able to see and remove it easily. A middle-aged man was rushed past them on a gurney, pale faced, sweat beading on his brow and holding his chest. Anna smiled. It was not the man's heart that was causing the pain but the Szechuan chicken he had eaten for dinner, a simple case of indigestion.

"Anna."

She turned her attention back to Derrick. "Oh, sorry."

"Sofie is being admitted and she is only allowed to have one person stay with her. Would you stay with her while I go to collect her daughter? She'll be concerned when she arrives to pick up Sofie and finds the shop in disarray and her mother missing."

"Of course." She agreed, absently. "You do what you have to do."

"Promise you won't leave."

She nodded and shooed him away. He frowned his concern. "Fine. I *promise* I will be here when you get back." She emphasized the vow by drawing the sign of a cross on her chest.

Derrick hesitated, turned to walk away and then turned back. He took her into his arms and kissed her with such passion she thought her bones would liquefy. Her senses exploded like a wave of fireworks shooting through her every fiber, every pore. She wanted him now. Right there in the middle of the waiting room if necessary.

You don't know how much I want you too. Derrick told her telepathically, their sire bond initiated. *But we have a responsibility to Sofie.*

Go. She answered, thrilled with her new power. *But hurry back.*

He walked to the door at a human speed. Once again he paused to communicate to Anna but this time he called out loud in a volume clear enough for everyone in the room to hear.

"I love you, Anna Derwent."

While waiting for Derrick's return, Anna learned

that she had another power. Frustrated with answering questions as to Sofie's blood loss, she compelled the doctor and nurse into believing that the blind woman was simply anemic due to a poor diet and even *suggested* that despite her low income, she should be given a private room. The doctor ordered a transfusion and gave Sofie strict instructions on eating better, advising her that Meals on Wheels could deliver nourishing meals for a small fee. The witch scoffed at the idea of having someone else prepare her meals and shooed the doctor away. Anna was pleased to see that Sofie still had her fighting spirit but the new flush of color to the old woman's cheeks reminded Anna of her hunger. She couldn't stay a moment longer.

You can handle this. Derrick's voice echoed in her head and she wondered if it was her imagination until he spoke again. *I am nearly there, Anna. Hold on.*

Sofie must have sensed Anna's discomfort, adding her own words of encouragement. "I trust you."

"You probably shouldn't." Anna began to wring her hands in her typical OCD fashion as she tried not to stare at the blood dripping down from the tube attached to Sofie's arm. For the first time in her life, she was tempted to steal. She wanted to snatch the blood and make it her own special "happy meal." It was as if her corpuscles were screaming at her … begging for nourishment. She needed it as much as Sofie, maybe more.

"I'm sorry," she told the woman as she dreamily traced her finger down Sofie's forearm, stopping at the pulsating vein in her wrist, "but I must go."

"Mum!"

The young woman—who looked a few years younger than herself—appeared in the doorway just as Anna attempted to make her escape. It took everything in her power to stop before she knocked her to the ground.

Unaware of her near-death experience, the woman hurried to her mother's side, showering her face and hands with kisses. Outside the room, Anna found herself suddenly in Derrick's arms. He pulled her into his embrace and held her tight as she began to shake violently from the effects of hunger and shock. Shock from the realization that she almost slammed into Sofie's daughter with a force that may have killed her ... a fine way to repay the woman for her kindness.

"We must get you some blood," Derrick whispered to her in a tone that sounded more like an order than an observation.

"No." she argued, although the thought of it now made her salivate. "I don't want to hurt anyone and if you suggest I eat a rat, I'm going to throw up on those expensive looking shoes."

"I'd rather you didn't." He laughed. "These are my favorite." He scooped her into his arms and carried her to the hospital parking station.

Her body began to shake and she feared that she was about to die ... permanently this time. As she began to lose consciousness, she heard his voice in her head pleading. *Hold on, Anna. Hold on.*

Chapter Twenty-Three

Although it felt like only a moment had passed since she had closed her eyes, Anna found herself waking up naked in Derrick's huge bed and this time she was not alone.

"Before you blast me for taking advantage, I assure you, nothing happened."

"Then why am I naked?"

"I was using my body heat to warm you. Your skin was as freezing as marble."

Anna found the excuse hard to believe. "Look who's talking, Mr. Cold as ice."

As she reached out and touched his skin, she was shocked at the warmth radiating from him. She touched her own chest and shuddered at the difference in temperature. Her expression telegraphed her shock even before Derrick read her thoughts.

"Not what you were expecting?"

"Why are you so warm?" she asked. "You usually feel like an icicle."

"While you were sleeping, I fed. The blood warms our bodies," he told her, and before she had time to ask the question aloud, he added, "and no, I didn't kill anyone to do it. There are many ways to get blood Anna. Some of us have human volunteers. David for example, has no shortage of humans offering themselves for a snack—"

"I can just imagine the skanky women lining up to have him suck on their necks."

"What makes you think that the volunteers are all female?" He teased. A wicked grin twisted the corner of his mouth.

"You mean he's…?"

"No, no, no..." Derrick said emphatically. "He's definitely heterosexual, although ... I must remember to tell him what you said later."

She slapped his chest and frowned. "Don't you dare. Now, explain the blood thing."

"There are employees at the blood bank who are more than happy to sell us bags and we even have a choice in the blood type. It's a bit like going to the liquor store."

"What about rats? I have seen movies where vampires eat rats." Anna cringed at the thought and made a gagging gesture.

"A thing of the past. These days blood is easier to come by."

"I still don't think I can do it, Derrick. Drinking from someone, it seems so ... intimate."

"It *can* be a very intimate and sexual experience." Derrick admitted, leaning in close enough for Anna to feel the heat from his skin. "That's why I want you to feed from me."

"I can do that?" The idea had never occurred to her. "How does that work? Wouldn't I be draining you?"

"It would just mean that we would have to do it twice a night instead of once."

Anna raised her eyebrows. "Do it?"

"Feed. But if feeding you twice a day leads to other things ... I have no objections."

When he kissed her, Anna melted in his arms, momentarily forgetting the hunger that gnawed away at her insides. His lips were warm and soft and ... yummy? She thrust her tongue inside his mouth, lapping up the coppery taste and savoring the flavor until it was gone. Desperate for more, she pulled him on top of her, sucking his bottom lip as she searched for another hit of whatever substance he had been consuming. She ignored the sting as her incisors lengthened and split her gums. She barely heard the groan of pleasure from Derrick as her new fangs broke the skin of his lip and the blood trickled into her mouth, but she could not ignore the sensation of Derrick's blood as it filtered into her own blood stream. It amazed her how only a few drops could make her feel so alive, so aroused.

She wrapped her legs around him and deftly wrestled him onto his back where she straddled his hips. She leaned over him, her breasts hanging close to his mouth. He kissed each breast, and then drew one nipple into his mouth, sucking hard, causing her to gasp. She lowered herself back until she felt the tip of his sex licking at the entrance of hers and slowly eased down, only slightly, before drawing *almost* off again. Derrick groaned as Anna continued to slide up and down the tip of his erection with deliberate, slow movements. He held her breasts, rolling her nipples between his thumbs and index fingers. She could feel the sire bond. He was telepathically pleading with her. Trying to compel her to fully impale herself, but his caressing triggered a different reaction.

She closed her eyes and threw back her head as her incisors grew to full length. When she opened her eyes, she stared down at his carotid artery, mesmerized. She pinned Derrick down by his shoulders, sinking her fangs into his neck, drawing the coppery fluid into her mouth simultaneously impaling herself on the length of him. The blood excited her, sensitized her. She rode him faster and harder, experiencing sensations she had only ever read about. A slave to her desire for blood, for flesh. Every inch of her skin cried out for him and he obliged. She grabbed his hands and moved them over her body, placing them where she felt the most need but continually moving them when another part of her called out for pleasure of his touch. He groaned her name as he shuddered inside her and she felt her own body climax in glorious synchronicity. But she wanted more. More touching, more Derrick, more blood.

"Anna." he wrapped her in his arms as he rolled her onto her back, her fangs still firmly attached to his neck. "You are going to be the death of me if you don't stop now."

Anna broke contact. She lapped the few drops of blood that oozed from the puncture wounds in his skin and watched in wonder as her saliva healed the holes.

"Wow," she gasped. "I can't believe I just did that."

"Well, I for one am certainly glad you did." Derrick sighed as he raised his arms above his head. "And not just for your sake."

"That was the most satisfying meal I have ever eaten." She rolled off him and onto her side. As she traced her fingers over Derrick's chest, twisting the fine chest hairs around her fingers, she asked, "Will it always be like that?"

"Why do you think I only want you to feed from me?" he wrapped one arm around her and she snuggled against him.

"And who will be feeding *you*?" a pang of jealousy suddenly hit Anna as she imagined Derrick taking sustenance from a human female. Experiencing the same physical response that left her body tingling.

"You have my word. The blood bank will be my sole supermarket," he promised, planting a third eye kiss on her forehead. "But I may need to make a large withdrawal if your first feed was any indication. You haven't even come into your full strength yet."

"If it wasn't for giving up the beach, I could grow to become perfectly satisfied with this lifestyle," Anna confessed, adding, "Especially the feeding part."

"There's nothing stopping you going to the beach, my love. The only difference is you'll be swimming after dusk."

"What about sharks?" Anna sat up; horrified that Derrick would suggest swimming at one of the most dangerous times of the day.

Derrick laughed. "We are the most dangerous creatures out at night. The sharks fear us."

Anna shrugged. "I'll still miss the sun."

"As do we all, but you'll find beauty in the moonlight. Think of it as trading up."

Anna swung her legs onto the floor and sat looking towards the window. The heavy drapes blocked any light but she somehow knew that the sun's rays warmed the panes of glass. With her back towards Derrick, she asked, "How long before dusk?"

"Are you anxious to go to the beach already?"

"No. I wanted to visit Susie and Sofie at the hospital and take them some flowers or something. It's my fault they were both drawn into this mess."

"Let's get something straight," Derrick sat up and turned Anna around to face him. "None of this is your fault. Both Patrick and Torke were power-hungry madmen who wanted to exploit you for their own advantage. It's regrettable that your friends were hurt in the process but I doubt either one would hold you responsible."

"I'd still like to take them something."

"*We* have already sent them each a dozen red roses." He smiled at her shocked expression. "I arranged it this morning with my florist. We can pick up something nice for them from the jewelers on the way if you like. David assures me that diamonds have a way of making a woman's day."

"I wouldn't know." She laughed. "I only ever had one and I sold that to help my Dad with the cost of my non-wedding to Patrick."

"I had a feeling you would say that." Derrick reached under his pillow and produced a small blue box. "I know this may be a bit soon and you literally have an eternity to make up your mind but—"

Anna opened the box and stared at the ring. The oval cut diamond was as big as a pebble and even the golden band was encrusted with tiny stones. She drew her free hand to her mouth, looked from the ring to Derrick and started to cry.

"If it's too soon—"

"No." She shook her head. "I'm crying because I never would have believed I could be so happy, especially now that I am dead."

"Undead."

"Whatever." She faked a frown and continued. "I only wish that my dad could have been alive to see us together."

"I'm not sure he would have approved."

"You may have been his partner but you didn't know him as well as I did. I'm his only child, he would have been happy to see me happy."

"You don't know how relieved I am to hear that." Derrick pulled her into his arms and kissed her. "So, does that mean the answer is yes?"

She nodded.

"I need you to say, I love you, Derrick Corel, and I want to spend eternity as your wife. Yes! I *will* marry you.'"

Anna crinkled her nose. "Is that some type of vampire custom, like needing to be invited before you can enter human homes?"

"No." Derrick laughed so hard he fell back on the

bed, dragging Anna down with him. "I just *want* to hear you say it."

Anna slapped his chest and tried to look annoyed until Derrick added.

"I've been dreaming of this day since I first met you. I've envisioned proposing to you and hearing you say the words that mean you love me as much as I love you." His expression was that of complete honesty and Anna felt the ice that Patrick had shot into her heart melt away. She knew now, that she belonged to Derrick and he belonged to her.

She held his face in the palms of her hands as gently as she held his heart when she spoke the words she knew he had longed to hear.

"I love you, Derrick Corel and I want to spend eternity as your wife. Yes. I will marry you."

The End

www.annieharlandcreek.com

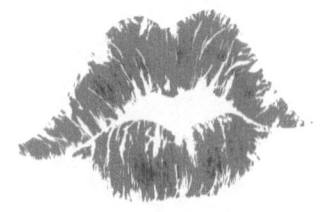

EVERNIGHT PUBLISHING ®

www.evernightpublishing.com